A magical kiss . . .

Gazing at Gareth, Susanna's heart thumped so loudly that she feared it might burst.

She'd never kissed a man before. Oh, she'd *been* kissed, but never had she initiated it. But when Gareth had kissed her, then pulled away, apprehension heavy in his eyes, she'd only thought to reassure him.

A shiver ran through her at the remembrance of how wonderful it had felt to be held—even for an instant—in his arms. She knew she must have this man.

"Cold?" Gareth's eyes were full of concern. "We should start back to the castle."

Susanna wanted to say "no," that she had no desire to leave this place. That he was quite wrong and that there *was* something magical about the ruined stone circle and she wanted them both to stay within its confines forever. To forget about everything else but each other . . .

D0837136

Coming next month

A LADY OF LETTERS
by Andrea Pickens

The Earl of Sheffield respects the political commentator known as "Firebrand," but has little patience for Lady Augusta Hadleyr. But how would he react if he discovered they were one and the same?

"A classy new addition to the ranks of top Regency authors." —*Romantic Times*

0-451-20170-1/$4.99

ONCE UPON A CHRISTMAS
by Diane Farr

After a tragic loss, Celia Delacourt accepts an unexpected holiday invitation—which is, in fact, a thinly veiled matchmaking attempt. For the lonely Celia and a reluctant young man, it turns out to be a Christmas they'll never forget....

"Ms. Farr beguiles...." —*Romantic Times*

0-451-20162-0/$4.99

MISTLETOE MISCHIEF
by Sandra Heath

Sir Greville Seton cannot abide women who work as companions. But when he meets his cousin's companion, the lovely Megan Mortimer, the Christmas spirit allows him to embrace the greatest gift of all....

0-451-20147-7/$4.99

To order call: 1-800-788-6262

Miss Chadwick's Champion

Melinda McRae

A SIGNET BOOK

SIGNET
Published by New American Library, a division of
Penguin Putnam Inc., 375 Hudson Street,
New York, New York 10014, U.S.A.
Penguin Books Ltd, 27 Wrights Lane,
London W8 5TZ, England
Penguin Books Australia Ltd, Ringwood,
Victoria, Australia
Penguin Books Canada Ltd, 10 Alcorn Avenue,
Toronto, Ontario, Canada M4V 3B2
Penguin Books (N.Z.) Ltd, 182–190 Wairau Road,
Auckland 10, New Zealand

Penguin Books Ltd. Registered Offices:
Harmondsworth, Middlesex, England

First published by Signet, an imprint of New American Library,
a division of Penguin Putnam Inc.

First Printing, September 2000
10 9 8 7 6 5 4 3 2 1

To all my new friends
at NSCC.
And to Jen—for keeping
me sane during a very tough year.

Chapter 1

Come ye to seek a champion's aid,
on palfrey white, with harper hoar,
Like errant damosel of yore?
          —Sir Walter Scott
          Lady of the Lake

Susanna Chadwick stared with growing horror at her cousin's unconscious form sprawled on the floor and dropped the heavy porcelain pitcher she'd used to hit him.

What had she done?

A thin trickle of blood ran down his temple, staining the well-worn carpet of the shabby room in the tiny Yorkshire inn.

Was he dead? Had she killed him?

She knelt by Jonathan Wilding's side and gingerly laid her hand on his chest. The gentle rise and fall of his breath told her that the worst had not happened. She snatched her hand away and scrambled to her feet.

Now, before he regained consciousness, she had to get away. As far away as possible. Susanna grabbed for his greatcoat, slung across the end of the bed, and rummaged in his pockets until she found his purse.

Jonathan groaned loudly.

She jumped. Hastily, she stuffed the money into her reticule, snatched up her cloak, and dashed out the door.

The faint sound of laughter echoed from the taproom below, and the odor of stale beer and tobacco smoke permeated the corridor. She hurried down the narrow hallway to the stairs leading to the stable yard.

Susanna never would have imagined that she'd find herself in such a place when she'd left her uncle's house yesterday afternoon with her cousin for what was to have been a simple drive in the park.

Jonathan wanted to get his hands on her inheritance, and after her continued refusal to marry him, he'd decided to take matters into his own hands and carry her off to Scotland. Which is why she found herself in this out-of-the-way Yorkshire inn, with her cousin unconscious upstairs and miles and miles of road between her and the safety of her own home in Suffolk.

She peered nervously out the door, but on seeing no one lingering about, she stepped into the inn yard and hastened toward the stable, praying that her cousin's shillings would silence any awkward questions from the stable hands. She had to leave quickly.

It seemed to take forever for the ostler to hitch up the team and she nervously fidgeted from foot to foot, fearing Jonathan would catch her before she could get away. But finally, she jumped into the tilbury and guided the horses through the gate. Once she reached the Great North Road, she would turn south toward York and . . .

Susanna realized that route offered no clear escape. Of course Jonathan would head south the moment he discovered her flight. A lone woman in a carriage would be easily remembered and he'd be able to track her with no effort. On a swift horse, it would not be long before he caught up with her.

But what else could she do? She had to get home.

She must throw him off the track. If he expected her to travel south, she would confound him by traveling north, instead. It would take her longer to reach home by a circuitous route, but by the time she arrived, he would no longer be looking for her there.

Why had she ever accepted Uncle's invitation to join him and Jonathan in London? She should have suspected they were hatching some nefarious plot. Now, she had to rely on her own wits to save herself.

Being an heiress was hell.

* * *

Susanna quickly discovered that fleeing north was not the best idea, either. There were far too many travelers heading south, people whom Jonathan could question. She needed to get off on one of the side roads, and look for a small village inn where she could rest and plan her flight.

At the next crossroad, she turned west and soon found herself in a rolling countryside of green hills, crisscrossed with stone fences and an occasional farmhouse. She might have appreciated the rustic beauty of the scene if she was not in such a desperate situation. She had to put as many miles as she could between herself and her odious cousin before dark.

The first "village" she reached was no more than a cluster of cottages, so she pressed on. The next village had an inn of sorts attached to the tavern, but it did not look to be the kind of place for a lone woman to stay. Perhaps she should return to the main road; at least at the posting houses she'd be assured of some semblance of comfort—and safety.

If she turned north, and then east, she would be back at the road again. It was silly to think that Jonathan would ever look for her in the north; he was not that clever. He'd head south the moment his head cleared.

The sun, which had been dodging in and out of the clouds for the last hour, finally disappeared behind a blanket of gray and a chill crept into the air. Susanna shivered and urged the horses forward. She needed to find shelter. Shouldn't she have reached the main road by now?

A light rain began falling and Susanna realized she could no longer afford to be too fastidious. She resolved to take a room in whatever inn was available at the next village, which, according to the last signpost, was only a scant three miles away.

Yet no village miraculously appeared through the increasing rain, which threatened to become a full-blown storm. The horses tossed their heads restlessly as she halted at the next crossroads. She looked forlornly at the signpost, but the paint was too weathered for her to read from this distance. Muttering invectives anew at her cousin, she climbed down from the coach and went over to examine the sign more closely.

A loud clap of thunder boomed overhead and the frightened horses bolted.

"Stop!" Susanna shrieked, running after them for several fruitless steps until she realized there was no hope of catching the frightened animals. She halted and stared disconsolately at the rapidly vanishing carriage.

Now what was she going to do?

The rain was coming down harder than ever and a bright flash of lightning flared across the sky, She winced as the thunder sounded again. The poor horses probably wouldn't stop running until they were halfway to London.

If London even lay in that direction. The dark clouds hid any hint of the sun and Susanna did not know if she was facing east, north, west, or south. All she knew was that she was cold, wet, and on foot somewhere in the midst of the Yorkshire hills.

Surely, there must be a house nearby. By this time, Susanna was willing to settle for a bed in a modest farm cottage. Anything would do, as long as it was dry and warm. She looked again at the worn and faded signpost, but could only make out a few letters on each arm. None gave a clue as to what awaited her in any direction.

Sighing, Susanna decided that she would continue on in the direction the horses had run. There was always the chance that she might find them again.

The continuing downpour quickly turned the road into a sea of squishy, squelching mud. Her satin shoes were horridly ill-suited to trudging thorough the mire. Had she known she would find herself in this fix, Susanna would have brought her sturdy half boots, but when she'd left the house yesterday she had not anticipated ending up on foot in the wilds of Yorkshire in a driving rain.

The sky grew ever darker as twilight approached and Susanna felt the first twinges of fear. She had been walking for nearly an hour, she guessed, and had seen no signs of habitation anywhere. Yet stone fences bordered the road; someone must be farming this land. Where was their house?

If she hadn't stumbled over a rut in the road she might have missed it. But as Susanna glanced to her right, she saw a narrow gap in the unending wall of stone, leading off into the darkness. Just the sort of lane that would lead to a farmhouse.

She hesitated. Dare she risk leaving the road? What if there was a village ahead, around the next curve? But she had been using that argument to force herself to keep walking for the last hour, and no habitation had miraculously appeared. This lane had to lead somewhere. By now, Susannah would settle for an abandoned farmhouse, or even a barn—anything that would get her out of the rain.

Susanna hiked up her skirts and started down the rutted track.

Gareth Stavely, the Sixteenth Baron Lindale, sat in a faded Queen Anne chair in the drawing room of Belden Castle and eyed his younger brother with growing suspicion.

"You've been home three days now with nary a word. How bad is it this time?"

"Bad?" Gawaine Stavely, perched restlessly on the edge of a chair, raked a hand through his dark, curly hair. "What do you mean, bad?"

"You would never come home at this time of year unless you were desperate," Gareth said. "Is it money again?"

Without meeting his eyes, Gawaine nodded glumly.

Gareth shook his head. When would his brother learn that he could not afford to keep company with his wealthier companions? Gareth knew he should shoulder some of the blame. As the elder brother, he had sheltered both Gawaine and the even younger Gaheris as best he could through the family's continual financial crises. But perhaps that had been a mistake. Scrimping and borrowing to send Gawaine to Oxford had only given him a fondness for high living and expensive pursuits that he could ill afford.

A handsome face and a glib manner were no substitute for cold hard cash in the London world.

"Don't look at me like that," Gawaine protested.

"How do you want me to look?" Gareth asked. "Pleased that you gambled your allowance away again?"

"But I was winning," Gawaine argued.

"Then why didn't you stop when you were ahead?" Gareth said sourly.

Gawaine shrugged. "How was I to know my luck was going to turn?"

"Because your luck always turns," Gareth retorted. "The moment you sit down at the gaming table, you are doomed. Haven't you realized that yet?"

"It's only a few hundred pounds," Gawaine said. "And I would have had it all back the next day if Jackman's horse hadn't come up lame at Newmarket."

"Well, I don't have a few hundred pounds—or even a few pounds—to lend you this time," Gareth said. "You'll have to find the money on your own—or wait until the next quarter."

"All I need is a bit of stake—something to get me started. I know I'll win this time. There's a horse running at Doncaster next week and with that I know—"

"No." Gareth cut him off. "Absolutely not. Not a single penny for one of your insane wagers."

"But what am I going to do?" Gawaine asked. "I have to pay Jackman."

"The first hay cutting is near," Gareth said. "I can always use an extra hand."

"Work? For wages?" His brother stared at him, aghast. "You must be joking."

"I'll pay you a working man's wage for a working man's job," Gareth said.

"It would take a lifetime of hay cutting to pay off the debt."

"Then I suggest you try to find a more highly paid position," Gareth said.

"I don't see why you don't sell this moldy pile of stone and be done with it." Gawaine directed his scowl toward the window that looked over the cobbled courtyard. "Trying to get money out of this holding is like getting blood out of a turnip."

"Sell the castle?" an irate voice demanded.

Gaheris, "Harry," the youngest Stavely, who'd been hunched over his papers in the far corner by the window, looked up from his work and stared at his brothers. "You have to be joking. You can't sell Belden."

"Never fear, youngling," Gareth responded dryly. "There is not much of a demand for falling-down castles."

"The stone must be worth something," Gawaine insisted. "A damn site more than a few acres of hay and some sheep."

"Are you suggesting we dismantle the only home we have?" Gareth asked. "To live where? In a gypsy caravan?"

"There has to be some way to get money out of this estate." Gawaine grabbed the poker and stabbed at the smoldering coals. "What good is a decaying pile of rock? If you weren't spending every cent you had on upkeep, there might be something for the rest of us."

Gareth arched a brow. "So you can lose it at the gaming tables in a single night?"

Flushing, Gareth fidgeted with the poker. "I know I shouldn't have been playing with Eversdale and his cronies. But what did you want me to do? Tell them I can't afford their company? London would be dull indeed if I only associated with those as poor as I."

"I don't see why you want to go to London in the first place," Harry said. "'Tis much more pleasant here."

"You can bury yourself in your boring books and papers, but don't expect me to do the same," Gawaine said. "I like London."

Harry shot him an angry glance. "I think Gareth is right. You should find a job."

Gawaine snorted derisively.

"Well, your only other option is to marry an heiress," Harry observed.

Gawaine's scowl deepened and he walked toward the sideboard to pour himself a glass of brandy. "And what are the chances of an heiress showing up in this godforsaken place?"

Gareth shook his head. It always ended like this. Gawaine did not understand what the castle's history meant to his younger brother—to all of them, really. It was a symbol of what they were, what the family had been through the generations. Stavelys had dominated the dale before the Conqueror, and Gareth had no intention of being the last baron to occupy the castle. He would move heaven and earth to make sure they stayed here.

Harry was right, as usual. Marrying an heiress was the fastest way to restore the family's fortunes. But as Gawaine had so sarcastically noted, heiresses were a rare commodity in the dales of Yorkshire.

Susanna trudged down the muddied, rutted track, wishing she'd never left the other road. If this small lane had once led to some farmhouse, it must be long gone, for she had not seen a single sign of any man-made structure, tumbledown or otherwise. She felt faint from cold, hunger, and despair.

The light was fading fast and she feared facing a night in the open, without any shelter at all. Her stomach rumbled with hunger; her fingers were numb with the cold.

Despair washed over her and she realized that if she perished during the night, no one would even know. Her body would lie here undiscovered for months—even years, her disappearance an unanswered mystery. Only Uncle and Jonathan cared what happened to her—and once her birthday passed, and the fortune slipped from her hands, their minimal interest would quickly fade.

Marriage to Jonathan did not seem such a miserable prospect after all.

Then suddenly, out of the gloom, a dark shape loomed ahead. A building! Eagerly, she started to race forward on her numb feet, stumbled, and found herself rolling head over heels down a grassy slope. When she finally stopped, she lay there for a moment, gasping for breath. A dark stone wall towered over her. *What sort of person would put a ditch next to their house?*

Slowly, she struggled back up the slope, her feet slipping and sliding on the wet grass, her head aching. She saw now that the lane took a sharp turn at the edge of the ditch and she followed the path that paralleled the high wall, searching for an opening.

The wall angled left and she saw a wooden bridge ahead, spanning the wide ditch.

Not a ditch, she realized with a start. It was a moat. And the tall stone walls . . . She'd stumbled on an abandoned castle. No doubt the only inhabitants were pigeons and field mice and there probably wasn't a roof standing in the whole place. But somewhere, somehow, she just might find a tiny corner that offered some shelter from the rain.

She took a cautious step onto the bridge but it felt surprisingly sturdy underfoot. With more confidence, she walked forward, through the arched gateway into the stone courtyard beyond.

And stopped and stared, rubbing her eyes in disbelief. She'd expected to find the crumbled remains of an ancient keep, choked with weeds and brush. Instead, she saw lights streaming from high, diamond-paned windows in the very sturdy house on the far side of the yard.

She staggered across the cobbles, toward the front door. Her numbed fingers touched the wood with disbelief, then she began pounding her fists against the heavy oak, crying out for help.

The door opened inward and Susanna collapsed into the arms of the astonished, motherly, looking woman standing there.

Chapter 2

Susanna blinked sleepily, then closed her eyes to the morning brightness and snuggled deeper under the warm blankets. It was such a relief to be back in her own room, in her own comfortable bed—

Her eyes snapped open and she stared in dismay at the faded brocade canopy that stretched overhead.

This wasn't her room, or her bed. Was she back at that horrid inn with Jonathan? Then memory came flooding back and she offered up a prayer of thanks for her newfound sanctuary. She was safe, for now, from her odious cousin.

She had only vague memories of being brought to this room last night: a man's voice, the kind woman who'd tucked her into bed. Susanna sat up, staring about her with eager curiosity. The room was small and sparsely furnished, with only the bed, a chair, and a small table. Dark, carved beams crossed the low ceiling, and the room would have been gloomy if not for the diamond-paned windows that ran the length of one wall. It all looked very old, but decidedly uncastle-like.

At least she hadn't been relegated to the dungeons. She burrowed back into the covers, a contented smile on her face. Jonathan would never find her here.

She had barely pulled the blanket back up to her chin when the door on the far wall opened and the gray-haired woman who'd met her at the door last night entered, carrying a bundle in her arms.

"Oh, you are awake!" she exclaimed. "You poor lamb. Are you feeling well? You have not taken a chill?"

"I feel fine." Susanna sat up again. "Please, tell me where I am."

"Why, you're in Belden Castle, miss."

The name meant nothing to Susanna. "Are we near York?"

"York? That's leagues away from here. Is that where you were going?"

"I—not actually," Susanna replied, suddenly cautious. "I was searching for—I hoped to find an inn nearby."

The woman smiled warmly. "There's no decent inn within miles of here. But don't fret yourself—the baron will insist that you stay. Why, the very idea of a young lady like you wandering around the countryside alone . . ." She shook her head in dismay.

"I thought this place was abandoned," Susanna confessed. "When I saw the light in the window, I thought I was imagining things."

"Belden may not be much to look like on the outside, but it's been in the family for eight hundred years," the woman announced proudly. Then her expression turned curious. "What were you doing out on such a dreadful night?"

Once again, Susanna felt a stab of uncertainty. Dare she trust this woman—and the others who lived here? If Jonathan or her uncle learned she was here, they would come for her in a trice.

She pressed her fingers to her temples. "I . . . I don't know. I can't think . . ."

"Oh, you poor dear!" the woman exclaimed. "That bump on your head must have affected your memory."

Susanna gingerly ran her fingers over her skull, wincing at the sore spot she found. Yes, there was a lump at the back. She must have hit her head when she'd tumbled down into the dry moat.

"Now, don't you worry." The woman patted her hand. "It's common enough to be a bit befuddled after such an ordeal. No doubt you'll remember everything in a few days."

She thinks I've lost my memory, Susanna realized and suddenly saw a solution to her predicament. She could remain here in anonymity for several days until she decided what to do, and where she would go.

"I do feel a bit . . . confused," she admitted. Which was not a falsehood.

"Do you know your name?" The woman's eyes were filled with kindly concern.

Susanna wrinkled her brow. "I . . . I can't remember."

The woman patted her hand again. "Now, don't you worry about a thing, miss. I'll take the very best care of you."

Susanna sank back against the pillows. She did not like the idea of deceiving this kindly woman, but it would only be for a day or two. Until she decided her next step.

"Do tell me your name," Susanna said.

"I'm Mrs. Jenkins."

"Have you been at the castle long?"

Long?" Mrs. Jenkins laughed. "Why, I remember when the baron was a young lad in leading strings."

"How many people live here?" Susanna asked.

"Just the baron and his brothers. And right concerned they was, when you collapsed like that on the doorstep. Insisted I take you to the best chamber and pop you into bed."

"I am very grateful," Susanna said.

"Oh, it's a treat to have a young lady to pamper and protect. We don't get many visitors."

"Is the baron a recluse?" Susanna asked with growing hope. That would make it even easier for her to remain here undetected.

The woman gave an audible sniff of disapproval. "He tries to be, slaving away at the home farm during the day and burying himself in the estate books at night. Why, if it weren't for the fact that master Gawaine is at home, we probably all would have been abed and never heard you knocking."

"Gawaine?"

"His lordship's brother." Mrs. Jenkins looked exasperated. "He spends most of his time in the south but he's back now— no doubt he ran out of money and is cooling his heels here until quarter day."

"You said there is a third brother?" Susanna asked.

"That'll be Gaheris—Harry, the baby. 'Course, he's not a baby anymore—turns twenty in the fall, he does, but I still think of him as the baby."

Gaheris? Gawaine? Susanna fought back a giggle and wondered if she'd hit her head harder than she thought and this was all a dream. It only needed the presence of Sir Lancelot— or even Arthur himself—to make the fantasy complete.

"Dare I ask the baron's Christian name?" she inquired, half-fearing to learn it was Lancelot or Arthur.

"Gareth."

Gareth, Gawaine, Gaheris. Obviously, their parents had been enamored of the Arthurian legends. Although it seemed appropriate for a family that still lived in a castle.

A castle that was in an out-of-the-way corner of Yorkshire, with a baron who never entertained and no inn within miles. Jonathan could comb the countryside for weeks and never find her. This might prove to be the perfect hideaway. She only needed it for a little while, just until her birthday.

"Are you ready to have some breakfast?" the woman asked, but before Susanna answered, two men peered through the doorway. Susanna's eyes widened at the sight of their handsome faces.

Obviously, two of the brothers. There was no doubt of their relationship. While one was taller, and the other's hair blonder, there was no mistaking the family resemblance. They each had the same crystal-blue eyes, the well-shaped nose, the strong chin.

"Is she awake?" the blond-haired lad asked.

"Can we see her?" demanded the other.

Without waiting for an answer, they stepped into the room.

"Off with you," Mrs. Jenkins said, shooing them with her hands.

"We won't stay long," the tall man reassured her. "We only want to greet her."

"And find out who she is," the other added.

"Oh, you two!" Mrs. Jenkins glared at them. "Give the

poor girl a chance to collect her thoughts before you start badgering her with questions."

"I do not mind," Susanna said.

The blond man, who looked to be the younger, bowed low. "I am Gaheris, my lady."

Susanna smiled. All he needed was a suit of armor to match his courtly air.

His older brother walked toward the bed and boldly took her hand, bringing it to his lips. "I'm Gawaine," he said. "And I must say you are the loveliest guest we've ever had at the castle."

Susanna laughed lightly, embarrassed at such flummery. "What unusual names. When may I expect Sir Lancelot to visit?"

"Only Gareth's left," Gaheris said. "And he probably won't come up because he's grumbling about Gawaine's debts again and—"

"Be quiet, youngling!" Gawaine hissed at him. He turned back to Susanna with an easy smile. "Don't mind the lad. He is not much in company and does not have full command of his manners."

"At least I don't come around badgering Gareth for money." The younger man shot his brother a sharp look.

Mrs. Jenkins clapped her hands. "The young lady does not care about your petty complaints. Out!"

"As soon as I have learned the lovely lady's name." Gawaine gave Susanna a wide smile.

Goodness, he was handsome. Surely such a gallant knight would take pity on a damsel in distress. But she could not be certain—not yet.

Susanna shook her head. "I am afraid I don't remember."

"Don't remember?" Harry looked puzzled. "But that's—"

"There's a nasty bump on her head that no doubt accounts for her confusion," Mrs. Jenkins said firmly, shooing them toward the door. "Now out, the both of you. You may talk with her later—if she wishes to speak with you again after intruding so rudely."

With reluctant looks, the two men retreated. Gawaine turned and gave her a broad wink as he exited the room.

"I will be back with your breakfast," Mrs. Jenkins said as she followed them out the door.

Instinctively, Susanna knew she was safe—albeit temporarily—with these people.

Alone again, she stretched languidly and sat back with a self-satisfied smile. They did not know her name, or anything about her fortune and yet were willing to help her. And unless the baron was a changeling, she had the added pleasure of sharing the company of three handsome gentlemen.

She was very glad she'd decided to trudge down that overgrown lane last night.

Gareth stared glumly at the column of figures before him. No matter how he added, subtracted, or divided them, the answer was the same—the debts were mounting up quickly. He needed an unusually large corn harvest and a good price to set things right.

Gawaine and Harry burst into the room. Gareth frowned, irritated by the interruption.

"We've seen her," Gawaine announced eagerly. "She's a looker. Long, dark hair; huge, chocolate-brown eyes."

"You have to let her stay," Harry added.

Gareth winced at their naïveté. "She is not a stray dog. Her family will be looking for her."

"But she does not know who she is," Harry announced triumphantly. "No one is going to be coming after her."

"What?" Gareth stared at his brother in disbelief.

"She is a true lady of mystery." Gawaine plopped into one of the frayed upholstered chairs beside the desk and flung a leg over the arm. "From out of the mist. Maybe she's one of the fairy folk."

"It's called amnesia." Harry glared at Gawaine. "It means she can't remember certain things—like her name."

"Too bad *you* don't have the same problem; we might be

rid of you then." Gawaine reached out to ruffle his younger brother's hair, but Harry jerked away.

Gareth regarded the two of them with growing exasperation. "Why were you bothering her in the first place?"

"Mrs. Jenkins was with her," Harry replied. "We only wanted to see what she looked like since you wouldn't let us get a glimpse of her last night."

"For which there was no need," Gareth said, although he admitted he shared his brothers' curiosity about their unexpected guest. All he'd caught sight of last night was a mud-splattered, bedraggled young lady with dark hair before his competent housekeeper whisked her off to a hot bath and bed.

Gawaine leaned forward. "Why do you suppose she was out in the storm in the first place?"

"She might have been wandering about for days, lost and confused," Harry suggested eagerly. "Oughtn't we get the doctor?"

"If she truly cannot remember who she is, I know nothing that a doctor can do to improve matters," Gareth said.

"What are we going to call her?" Harry asked.

"I suggest you let her decide," Gareth replied dryly. "No doubt after a few days' rest she will recall who she is and we can write her family."

"But what if she never remembers?" Gawaine asked.

"Then we will have to find her family for her," Gareth said.

"What if she is running away from a cruel father?" Harry asked. "Or a husband who beats her?"

"You've been reading too many romances," Gawaine accused him.

"Well, I don't think we should force her to go back to a situation like that," Harry said.

"We don't even know what her situation is," Gareth said, tossing up his hands in exasperation. "And until we do, it's silly of you to go on speculating."

"I want to make certain you won't send her away until we know she is safe, wherever she is going," Harry said.

"What do you think I am, a cruel monster?" Gareth demanded. "Of course I'm not going to shove her out the door the moment she is out of bed. But I'm not going to waste my time spinning fantastical theories for why she was wandering out on the dales, either. She will remember eventually and then you will know the truth."

"I think you should go upstairs and talk with her," Harry said. "Reassure her that she can stay here until she is better."

"More likely reassure her that my two brothers are not out of their minds." Gareth tossed down his quill and stood, giving both of them a dark look for having destroyed his concentration. "She's probably demanding her clothes so she can get away from here immediately."

"We were polite," Harry protested.

Gareth snorted with derision as he pushed out the door.

Climbing the stairs, he shook his head. Sometimes he wondered if his brothers were changelings. Harry was so wrapped up in his history and legends he saw everything as a medieval romance. And Gawaine . . . well, Gawaine was thoroughly grounded in the nineteenth century, but still lacked sense.

And it was his job to keep the two of them out of trouble. Which in Gawaine's case, at least, had been a dismal failure.

As he approached the girl's room, Gareth felt a flash of relief in knowing that at least there'd been a habitable room to put her in. Although, once she was out of her room and saw the rest of the castle, she would learn soon enough about the sorry state of his home.

He knocked lightly on the door.

"Come in," a soft, feminine voice called.

Gareth pushed open the door. His guest was sitting in front of the fire, wrapped in what he recognized as one of

Gawaine's foppish brocade dressing gowns, her long, dark hair falling over her shoulders.

He took an involuntary breath. For once, Gawaine had not exaggerated. She *was* beautiful. Far too lovely to be lost and on her own. Surely someone was searching for her. He felt a stab of regret that she would not be here very long.

Her dark eyes studied him intently and he self-consciously straightened his cravat.

"You must be the baron." She smiled as she rose to her feet, and executed a neat curtsy.

Gareth flushed with embarrassment and motioned for her to sit. "Please, we do not stand on ceremony here. I came to inquire about your health, Miss . . . Miss?"

She gave him a wan smile. "I fear I cannot tell you who I am, my lord."

"Is there anything that you do remember?" he asked. "Where you were going, or how you happened to be alone?"

"I am sorry—I remember nothing before I reached the doorway of the castle."

He gave her an encouraging smile. "I am sure that your memory will return once you are rested. Is there anything that you need?"

"Mrs. Jenkins is taking excellent care of me."

He glanced at the dressing gown she wore. "I regret that we are not well-prepared for female guests."

She laughed lightly. "Mrs. Jenkins said my own clothes are quite ruined, so I am grateful to have anything to wear. She is gathering clothing for me."

"You are welcome to join us downstairs in the drawing room when you are ready. We live quite informally here." He tried to look encouraging. "Or, you can remain here if you prefer. We will not bother you."

"I should like to come down when I have something suitable to wear," she said. "I enjoyed your brothers' visit earlier."

"I apologize for their intrusion. I assure you, they are usually more well-mannered."

"Oh, I did not mind." A smile flitted over her face. "They were rather amusing."

"Well then." He could not think of anything else to say. Had it been so long since he'd been in the company of an attractive young lady that he had forgotten all the social niceties? "Luncheon is catch-as-catch-can and we dine early. Country hours. I hope that will not inconvenience you."

She smiled again. "I can hardly say if it will, since I cannot recall what I am accustomed to. Your schedule will suit me perfectly."

"I look forward to seeing you downstairs then," he said, bowing low. "Good day, Miss . . . Miss."

She nodded in farewell.

After meeting the baron, Susanna felt a sharp pang of guilt over the deception she was promoting. He seemed so very nice. She almost wanted to confess all and throw herself on his mercy.

But she could not take the chance that he would immediately notify Uncle of her presence here. No, she must keep her identity a secret for a while longer, until she was assured of her safety.

Gareth was not the handsomest of the three—the genial Gawaine easily took those honors. The baron seemed far more serious, in appearance and mien. Of course, from what Mrs. Jenkins had said, he had a great deal to be concerned about.

Still, it would be a pleasant experience to be in the company of three handsome young men—men who knew nothing about her money. She would not have to be suspicious or skeptical of every word they uttered. If they were pleasant to her, it was because they were well-mannered, not merely trying to ingratiate themselves.

And perhaps, once she had the measure of the brothers, she could tell her story and know that they would keep her safe. Her birthday was not far off, after all. Once that date passed, she would be safe from Jonathan and her uncle's machinations.

Once her birthday came and went without seeing her married, her grandfather's fortune went elsewhere and Susanna would at last be free of that curse.

It would be hard to leave the only place she'd known as home, but the will was firm. She'd be left with only a modest sum from her mother; enough to allow her a small cottage in the country, if she practiced careful economy.

Susanna tried not to think ill of her grandfather for the provisions of his will. He'd been concerned about her future, wanting to make certain she would be properly taken care of. Had he known the torment his terms had caused her, he surely would have done things differently.

She crossed the room and gazed out at the rain-soaked cobbles below. There was no use fretting about that which could not be changed. Genteel poverty was far more appealing than opulent luxury in the company of her cousin—or the dozens of other fortune hunters who'd pursued her. She would live by herself, if she must, rather than marry a man who only wanted her fortune.

Still, Susanna thought wistfully of one day finding someone who would love her, even without her money. But she knew it was unlikely. Once the money was gone, there would be no more trips to London, or new gowns for every occasion, or invitations to attend balls and dinners. She would be branded an eccentric spinster for throwing her grandfather's money away.

Another rap sounded on the door and Mrs. Jenkins came in, a bundle of clothing over her arm.

"Look what I found, dearie! Some of the late baroness's clothing. It's not in the most current style, but it will give you a few things to wear."

She held up a gown of patterned muslin, with long straight sleeves.

"It looks quite suitable," Susanna exclaimed.

"It is a bit too large for you," Mrs. Jenkins said apologetically. "But if you like, I can take in some tucks so you can wear it."

"That would be very kind of you," Susanna said. "I am feeling much better and I should like to go downstairs later today. The baron said I would be welcome."

"Ah, so his lordship came up to visit, did he? I hope he was more polite than those two young rascals."

"Oh, the baron was very correct," Susanna said, then smiled. "Almost too correct. Is he always so reserved?"

"He thinks he must be to counteract the exuberance of the other two," Mrs. Jenkins said while she helped Susanna into the dress. "But when he is relaxed, he is as friendly a man as could be. All three of them are really such dear boys. It is a pity that their situation is so dire."

"Dire?"

Mrs. Jenkins shook her head as she examined the fit of the bodice. "The estate is heavily encumbered with debts inherited from the late baron. A good man, but improvident with his finances. We know where Gawaine inherited *that* trait. His lordship—the current baron—is doing what he can but it is a difficult job."

"That is unfortunate," Susanna said, her apprehension returning. A rich heiress would appear as a godsend to an impoverished baron. She might not wish to tell them who she was.

"You'll see soon enough once you're up and about," Mrs. Jenkins said. "Parts of the castle are virtually uninhabitable. But still, it's a comfortable place. It just needs a woman's hand . . ." She gave Susanna a speculative glance.

Susanna now knew that she needed to be on her guard. She was safe enough here as long as they did not know her identity. But if they learned the truth . . . there was more than one way to force a woman into marriage against her will. Susanna had barely escaped her cousin's trap and she had no intention of falling into another.

It was clear that her "amnesia" was not going to quickly cure itself.

Chapter 3

It was late in the afternoon before Mrs. Jenkins finished altering the dress. Susanna had offered to help, but the housekeeper insisted that she lie down and rest.

Susanna, who was already growing bored in her tiny chamber, paced the floor with growing frustration, wondering how she was going to get herself out of the mess she had fallen into. She could not hide here indefinitely, but her other choices were limited. If she went home, they would surely find her. Yet was she as safe here as she first thought?

The dress, when it arrived, fit nicely and Susanna eagerly followed Mrs. Jenkins into the hall. It was a relief to be out of her room at last and she was curious to see the castle. What must it be like to live in a place with so much history?

Her own grandfather had only erected his fanciful and ostentatious mansion at the turn of the century; it was not even as old as she was. She thought it would be comforting to realize that your ancestors had trod the same steps you did, and provide a sense of security to know that your descendants would be treading these same steps in the centuries to come.

The upstairs corridor and the stairway were paneled in dark, polished wood, but the floor beneath her feet was uncarpeted. Another sign of the baron's financial difficulties, she guessed.

"Where in the castle are we?" she asked.

"Oh, this is the 'new house,'" Mrs. Jenkins explained. "It

only dates back to King Henry's time. The castle proper is not fit to live in."

Susanna felt a stab of disappointment at learning that. How much more romantic it would be to roam amid stone towers and tapestried halls.

"Is that because the castle lacks modern conveniences?" she asked.

Mrs. Jenkins snorted lightly. "The castle lacks *any* conveniences," she said. "Including a roof in some places."

So matters were even worse than she imagined, Susanna realized. It was more important than ever that the brothers did not learn who she was, or about her money.

Mrs. Jenkins halted before a paneled door and Susanna took a deep breath to calm herself before she faced the brothers again. She had nothing to worry about, after all. She had already met them and they had no inkling who she was. She was safe here—for now.

All three men jumped to their feet the moment she stepped into the room. Gawaine was at her side in an instant, bringing her hand to his lips.

"It is such a pleasure to have you join us," he said, flashing her a dazzling smile as he led her to a seat beside the blazing fire.

She glanced about her. It was a long, narrow chamber, with a high-beamed ceiling like the one in her room. But with carpets on the floor, tables, chairs, and sofas scattered about the room, and heavy draperies flanking the tall windows, it was a quite pleasant situation. A fire burned merrily in the grate.

"Dinner will be served shortly," the baron said, greeting her. "We are honored that you chose to join us."

Gawaine immediately took the chair beside her.

"What are we to call you?" he asked. "I fear that 'miss' or 'young lady' are far too impersonal."

"It is so dreadful not knowing who I am," Susanna said with only a brief twinge of guilt at the lie. Even if the baron and his brothers seemed nice, she must protect herself.

"Maybe if we list all the names we can think of, you will recognize one," Harry suggested.

Gawaine looked at her, his blue eyes regarding her intently. "Do you think that might help?"

She nodded hesitantly. "I hope it does."

He gave her hand a comforting pat. "Do not worry. If you do not hear a name that is familiar, you can pick one that you like."

"Wish I could do that," Harry grumbled.

"I'll be more than willing to thump you on the head so you lose your memory," Gawaine said. "Maybe then you wouldn't be so insufferably dull."

"Caroline," the baron suggested, after directing a brief look of annoyance at his brothers. "Catherine. Cassandra. Elizabeth. Edwina. Anne."

As he said each name, Susanna looked thoughtful, then shook her head.

"Margaret. Phoebe. Penelope. Helen," Gawaine offered.

"Circe," shouted Harry.

Gawaine gave him a withering look. "No one is going to name their daughter Circe."

"No one should have named a son Gaheris or Gawaine, either, and look at us." Harry gave her an encouraging look. "How about Lydia? Hermione. Calista. Philomena."

"Susan. Sarah. Sally. Thisbe."

"Thisbe?" Susanna, who'd been holding her breath for fear she would show some kind of reaction if her own name was mentioned, could not suppress a giggle.

"Oh?" Gawaine arched a brow. "You like Thisbe?"

"Of course not," she said, then clapped an embarrassed hand to her mouth. "That is—it is not a family name, is it?"

Gawaine laughed. "In this family? You would be named Guinevere or Elaine."

"That's it!" Harry jumped to his feet. "Since she doesn't know who she is, we can pretend she's one of us. Let's call her Guinevere."

"I think you might allow the lady to decide her own name,"

the baron suggested lightly, although there was a glint of amusement in his blue eyes.

Susanna flashed him a grateful smile. She did not relish being called Guinevere. "I am not well versed in the Arthurian tales. What other names may I choose?"

"Oh, there's Igraine, and Enid and Elaine." Gawaine ticked them off on his fingers.

"Morgana," Harry added.

"Morgana's a witch, you dolt." Gawaine gave his younger brother a disdainful look. "She doesn't want to call herself after a witch."

"Elaine might be nice," Susanna said. "It is shorter than Guinevere, at any rate."

Harry looked disappointed. "We could call you 'Gwen.' That is even shorter."

"If the lady wishes to be called 'Elaine,' we shall call her Elaine," the baron announced.

"That is," he continued, "if you do not mind the informality. We can call you 'Miss Elaine' if you prefer."

"She should be *Lady* Elaine," Harry grumbled.

"Heavens, plain Elaine is quite suitable," Susanna said.

"Then you must call us by our Christian names, as well," Gawaine said. "I would much rather be Gawaine than Mr. Stavely."

"And call me Harry," his brother pleaded.

She looked at the baron. "And what do you wish me to call you, my lord?"

Gawaine laughed aloud. "*My lord?* I wager you love to hear that, don't you, Gareth? Someone finally is showing some respect for your position."

Susanna sensed the baron's discomfort and she instantly regretted teasing him. "Your name is Gareth, isn't it? I will call you by that, if it is what you prefer."

"Yes," Gareth responded and shot both brothers a withering look. "Otherwise those two would never let me hear the end of it."

Susanna wondered if Gawaine and Harry were jealous of

their elder brother, then decided not. There was an affectionate undertone to their jibes. It was the type of teasing siblings indulged in.

Or, at least, she assumed it was. Being an only child, Susanna had no knowledge of how brothers—or sisters—treated each other. At least now she'd have the opportunity to make a firsthand study.

Dinner was a simple affair, served in the small dining room across the hall. For the rest of the evening, all three brothers took great pains to entertain her with stories, jokes, and games. There were no more awkward questions, no attempts to force her to "remember" any details of her life. Instead, they treated her as if she were made of fragile china. Susanna thoroughly enjoyed herself in male company for the first time in many months.

The following morning, she took breakfast in her room and was descending the stairs when Harry rushed up to her.

"There you are," he said. "I've been waiting for you for ages. I wanted to show you around the castle this morning. I know you're eager to see it."

"Of course," Susanna replied with a pleasant smile. She was curious to see the rest of the building.

"Unfortunately, several of my ancestors were not historians and they made modifications to the original structure that destroyed the historical authenticity," Harry said while he crossed the main hall. "But there are still a few places which are undisturbed."

A doorway off the hall led to a narrow corridor, paneled with the same dark wood as the rest of the house. Harry pulled open a heavy, oaken door and the sudden transition to gray stone walls made Susanna realize they were now in the castle proper.

Their steps echoed hollowly in the high-roofed chamber. No carpets muted their footsteps; no elaborately woven tapestries hung on the walls. She shivered, more from the sense of emptiness than any chill. The empty hall possessed an air of sadness.

How different from the gaudy brilliance of home, which was piled top to bottom with paintings of landscapes, expensive porcelain, thick carpeting over rich parquet flooring, and blazing chandeliers. Her grandfather loved to acquire things, and loved to display everything that he had acquired.

Susanna looked at massive beams overhead. "Those must date from the old times."

"The ceiling is original"—Harry swept his hand to encompass the room—"but as for the rest . . . The big fireplace in the far wall was bricked over, and both those doorways were cut into the original walls. Once, this was the heart of the castle, where the lord and his retainers gathered and even slept. But now it's just a huge, empty space."

"How long has your family lived here? Did they come over with the Normans?"

He snorted derisively. "The Stavelys were here long before the Norman invaders," he said with a proud tilt to his chin.

Susanna smothered a smile at his obvious familial pride. "Is the castle that old?"

He shook his head. "None of these buildings go back that far—but there were some sort of fortifications on this site from time immemorial, as close as I can make out. The oldest part of the castle—the cellars—dates back to the 1200s." He took her arm. "Come, that's what I want to show you."

"Cellars—or the dungeon?"

Harry laughed. "It's possible someone might have been lodged there against their will. But it was never a formal dungeon, with an oubliette or a torture chamber. My ancestors were not that ruthless."

"I'm glad of that."

She followed him through a narrow door in the wall beside the fireplace and down a short hallway. He stopped outside a heavy oaken door and lit the two candles sitting on the table beside it. He handed one to her and Susanna was grateful to have her own light. She did not particularly like dark places.

"Stand back while I open the door," he said. "There's a draft."

Dutifully, she stepped back and cupped her hand protectively about the flame. She could only imagine the pitch blackness of the cellar below. If both of their candles went out . . .

"Perhaps we should come back with a lantern," she suggested, trying to hide the tremor in her voice.

"We'll have no trouble," he assured her and pulled open the heavy door. Susanna felt a gentle swirl of air tug at her skirts, but the candle flame held steady.

"Follow me," Harry said and ducked through the doorway. Susanna scurried to keep close behind him.

They went down a steep and narrow spiraling stair. Susanna kept one hand on the wall to guide her as she descended into the darkness. She marveled at how the stone steps were worn deep in the center, and tried to imagine how many feet had passed over them in the hundreds of years the castle had stood.

When she reached the bottom, Harry held his candle high overhead to illuminate the space. It was a simple vault, which stretched off into the darkness. Surprisingly, the cool air did not feel the least bit damp.

He pointed at the wall to their right. "That staircase once led to the main hall but it was blocked off centuries ago."

Susanna walked over to examine the large wooden casks that lined the other wall. "What is in these?" she asked.

"Wine," Harry said. "Or vinegar. Some of the barrels haven't been opened for over a hundred years."

Since nearly inch-thick dust covered every cask, Susanna had no way of judging which were the oldest. It was obvious that none of them had been disturbed for some time.

"Follow me," Harry said and took off down the corridor. Susanna hurried to keep up with him.

"How far do the cellars go?" she asked.

"They extend beyond the length of the hall on either end," he said. "In previous times, when the castle was full of family and retainers, they needed a great deal of storage for provisions."

He suddenly darted into a niche on their right. Susanna saw it was another stairway, this one even more narrow and twisted than the one they'd come down at the far end of the cellar.

"Where does this lead?" she asked.

"Back to the hall," he said.

"You shall have to draw me a map," Susanna said, shaking her head with dismay. "I am thoroughly confused."

His expression brightened immediately. "There are several of them in the library."

"Is that in the castle?"

"No, it's in the main house."

"Is there a large book collection here?" she asked as she followed him down another dark corridor.

"Not as many as I'd like. But there is an exceptional collection of family documents. Everything from the land titles to the original grant of the barony. Many things are so old I dare not touch them, but most are still legible." He regarded her doubtfully. "If you read Latin."

"I don't," she said.

He took her arm and pulled her toward the other door. "You can read the maps, at least. There's even one paper that dates back to Henry the First's days—well, it's a copy, not the original, but you can see how things have been changed over time."

Susanna suppressed another smile. Harry obviously loved to talk about the castle. She had the feeling she would learn more than she ever wanted to about the history of each and every building and room before he was through with her.

But what else did she have to do? Learning the history of the house was better than sitting quietly in her room, bored to tears with no one to talk with. And as long as Harry was busy talking about the house, he wasn't going to be asking questions about her life.

He just might be the safest brother with whom to spend time.

Susanna was ready to revise her opinion a few hours later, after listening to a lengthy discourse on the history of the castle, the family, and the barony of Lindale. Had anyone dared to demand her true identity, she would have willingly admitted everything—anything—to break Harry's lecture.

Harry was very sweet—but the boy could prose on . . . He would make a marvelous university don, but as a companion to a lively young lady, Susanna declared him sadly deficient.

She glanced up with relief when the door opened and Gawaine strode into the room.

"There you are!" he exclaimed. "Where have you been? I've been looking everywhere."

"Harry's been showing me some of the family documents," Susanna replied.

Gawaine groaned. "I thoroughly apologize to you on my brother's behalf, my dear Elaine. You must be bored to tears."

"No, actually, it was rather interesting." The fib came readily to her lips. "And he showed me the Great Hall and the cellars."

"You took her into the cellars?" Gawaine glared at his brother. "What were you thinking? A chunk of stone fell from the ceiling just last week."

"I didn't see any damage," Harry retorted. "Besides, we weren't there long."

"Don't take her down there again." Gawaine glowered at his brother. "It's rather inhospitable to allow your guests to be killed."

"There wouldn't be any problems if Gareth would open his purse for some repairs," Harry fumed.

"For once I agree with you," Gawaine said. "But that's not likely to happen." He held out his arm to her. "May I escort you back to civilization, my lady? I am certain you are hungry."

Susanna took his arm.

"Don't let Harry's enthusiasm fool you—this place is not worth saving," he said once they were in the hall. "Tomorrow, when there is more time, I will show you what I mean."

The next morning, Gawaine was waiting for her in the drawing room when she came down after breakfasting.

"Now I will show you what a disaster this castle really is," he said. "And you will understand why I think Gareth should give it up."

They crossed over to the Great Hall and quickly traversed its echoing length. Gawaine opened a heavy oak door and stood aside while she stepped into a long, narrow hall. Tiny slits high in the walls provided the only illumination, and Susanna was glad they both carried lanterns.

"According to the expert—Harry—this part was built shortly after the barony was established." Gawaine's booted feet echoed loudly on the stone floor.

"How many times has the original castle been added on to?"

He shrugged. "Even Harry hasn't been able to puzzle that out. It's been torn down and rebuilt too many times to count."

The corridor took a sudden turn to the left and he stopped before another door. From his pocket he pulled out a key and unlocked it.

"You will have to be very careful from here on," he said. "I don't know how much more damage there's been since the last time I was here."

She felt the immediate change in temperature as he opened the door. A blast of cold air poured out of the opening and Susanna shivered, wishing she'd brought a heavy cloak with her. She peered through the doorway, wondering why the room was so much brighter than the hallway.

With a gasp, she realized the light was coming from a gaping hole in the roof.

Gawaine glanced upward and shook his head. "The hole's getting bigger."

"Shouldn't it be patched before there's more damage?" she asked.

He shrugged. "Why throw good money after bad? This whole wing is ready to collapse. It would be a waste of time to try to save it now. The smartest thing Gareth can do is pull it down." He patted the wall. "The stone's solid. It'd make a lot of strong fences."   •

Susanna thought of her own sturdy home, where a crew of workmen were always on hand to fix the most minor problem. Why, when the wind blew some shingles off the roof last winter, they had the whole thing repaired within a day.

How many years of neglect did it take before a roof caved in like this? Ten? Twenty? This had started long before Gareth came into the title.

"Seen enough?" he asked.

Shivering, she nodded.

"How much of the castle is in such a bad state?" she asked while he relocked the door.

"That's the worst of the lot," he admitted, "except for the outer wall. Another section in the back collapsed last week."

"Well, you hardly need a wall for protection these days."

He laughed. "True. But for that matter, who needs a castle? I keep trying to convince Gareth that we'd all be better off if he got rid of this monstrosity."

"Where would you live?"

"A house in town would be easy to come by."

"It would be difficult to manage the estate from town."

"Manage what? A few measly fields? A bunch of sheep? He doesn't need to do it firsthand. Hire a manager, I say."

"But if there is no money . . ."

"That's always the problem, isn't it?" He frowned. "Sometimes I think it would be better if he abandoned the whole venture. It's not as if we are growing rich from it."

"You must have some income to live on—and somewhere to live."

"The only thing Gareth owns of any value is his title," Gawaine said. "He'd be better off going to London to look for an heiress rather than remaining here. It's a losing proposition."

A flash of fear jolted through Susanna before she remembered that Gawaine had no idea who she was.

"Are there that many heiresses looking for husbands?" she asked innocently.

He laughed harshly. "Any number of rich cits would mortgage their lives to get their hands on a title. Gareth wouldn't have any problems."

Having been pursued all her life by fortune hunters, Susanna did not think highly of Gawaine's plan for his brother. "Don't you think Gareth would rather marry someone he cares for?"

"He can't afford to," Gawaine said bluntly. "And the sooner he realizes that, the better we all will be."

"How would it help you if Gareth marries?"

"I'd be sure he marries enough money that he can provide for me—and Harry—as well. I might even be able to find an heiress of my own, then."

"Well, I wish you good luck."

He brought her hand to his lips and gave her a melting smile that caused her stomach to give a strange lurch. "A pity you're not an heiress, Lady Elaine. I wouldn't mind marrying you."

To her dismay, she felt heat rise to her cheeks. It was a rather offhand compliment—but the first compliment she'd ever received that was not tied to her fortune.

Gawaine released her hand and sighed. "But, of course, you're not."

"How can you be so sure?" she asked teasingly.

He laughed. "You wouldn't be here if you were an heiress—they are guarded far too closely to ever get lost in the Yorkshire hills."

Knowing better, Susanna gave a deep sigh. If only his words were true.

He misinterpreted her response, for he took her hand again and gently patted it. "I'm certain someone is looking for you, my lady. They will come knocking at the castle door and spirit you away from us in no time."

Susanna cringed at his words. She could not imagine a worse thing happening.

Pray that he was wrong.

Chapter 4

"How could you have been such a fool?"

Jonathan Wilding shrank before his father's wrath. "How was I to know she would hit me over the head and bolt?"

"You never should have allowed her to set foot outside that carriage until you were over the border and safely wed," George Wilding replied scathingly, shifting his bulk in the chair.

"She can't have gone very far," Jonathan said sullenly.

"Oh, no, she only has your carriage and your purse. She could be anywhere in the island by now."

"A single woman on her own? Where would she go?"

"Home, if you are lucky." His father grabbed the brandy decanter and refilled his glass, deliberately not offering any to Jonathan. "Devil of a time finding her before the deadline."

"Where else could she be?" Jonathan asked. He jumped to his feet and began to pace the floor of his father's study in the London town house. "It's not as if she has any other place to go."

"She could be comfortably lodged at any inn on the island."

Jonathan's spirits rose. "Not for long. I didn't have *that* much money with me."

"How encouraging." His father's florid face darkened. "We have to find her as soon as possible."

"Should we place an advert in the papers?" Jonathan suggested.

George Wilding shook his head. "Not enough people will see. Hmmm. I know, handbills! Distributed at every coaching stop, inn, and tavern between Yorkshire and Suffolk."

"With a sketch of her!" Jonathan exclaimed. "She'll be found in no time."

The elder Wilding nodded. "Good idea. You get started on that sketch while I work on the wording."

Jonathan smiled to himself. He may have underestimated his cousin's determination not to marry him, but he wasn't going to let this golden opportunity slip through his fingers. And the one thing he did well—drawing, a talent his father had always disparaged—was going to make their fortune.

He'd find Susanna before her birthday if he had to search every inn between here and York. Her inheritance was far too valuable to let go.

And once he had it in his grasp, he was not going to let anyone tell him what to do ever again.

Especially his father.

Susanna was surprised to find Gareth sitting by himself in the dining room when she came down the next morning. So far she'd seen him only at dinner, and later in the drawing room. He'd treated her with exquisite politeness whenever they were together, but they had not developed the easy comradery that she shared with both Harry and Gawaine. She was pleased to have caught him alone. It would give her a chance to encourage their friendship.

"Have your brothers abandoned you?" she asked teasingly as he held out a chair for her.

"I fear so. I would offer to give you a tour of the place, but I think you've seen everything."

"Oh, I'd like to hear it described from your viewpoint," she said, eager to hear how he viewed his home. "Both your brothers have rather strong opinions on the place."

He grimaced. "I can only imagine what Gawaine says."

"Harry wants the place restored to its medieval grandeur, while Gawaine thinks you should tear it all down and build something more modern."

He laughed. "Each equal in his impracticality."

She regarded him curiously. "What would you do with the castle, if you had the money?" she asked quietly.

"Well, I'd certainly make some repairs. And add a few more modern conveniences. But I rather like the place the way it is—odd additions and all. I think it has character."

"Wouldn't you like to have a house in town? If you could afford it?"

He shook his head. "I can't see any reason to. Gawaine would be the only one to use it and God knows he doesn't need the temptation to spend any more time in London than he already does."

"Is he really so improvident?" she asked. Gawaine seemed far too nice to be a reprobate.

"He suffers more from boredom than anything else," Gareth explained, toying with his fork. "He doesn't want to be a farmer and he hasn't the interest or the money to buy a commission in the military."

"There is always the clergy . . ." She caught his incredulous expression and they both laughed.

"He'd be happiest running his own gambling hell and fleecing all the customers," Gareth said with a wry smile. "But that's hardly the occupation for a gentleman."

She leaned her hand on her chin and eyed him closely. "What is your favorite part of the castle?"

"The ramparts."

"Are they safe to stand on?"

"The front wall is."

"Then take me there. That is one place I haven't seen."

He looked uncertain. "It's rather cold this morning."

"I am not a hothouse flower to wilt in a chill," she said spiritedly. "I did survive a thorough drenching the other night, you will recall."

He insisted she bundle up in the warmest cloak he could

find before he escorted her out-of-doors. They crossed the cobbled courtyard and she followed him as he ducked into a niche next to the front gate.

"The steps are steep and narrow," he warned her, extending a hand. "I pity the poor knights who had to race up them to defend the castle."

"Was the castle ever under attack?"

"Oh, several times, I think." He paused. "You will have to ask Harry for the details—careful, there's a chunk missing in the next step."

In a short while they came out onto a small, enclosed landing. To the left was the near gate tower. To the right, a stone walkway angled off toward another tower, where the wall turned sharply to the right.

The strong wind whipped the folds of her cloak around her legs and she put a hand on the wall to steady herself.

"I warned you!" Gareth grinned at her.

She grinned back bravely. "I don't mind!"

She walked toward the outer wall and tried to peer down to the moat below, but the wall was too thick for her to see over. How had the ancient defenders managed to pour boiling oil on their attackers?

"When was there last water in the moat?" she asked.

Gareth shrugged. "I don't know. Quite a while. It was empty during my father's lifetime, I know."

"I think it would be rather fun to live here, surrounded by a wide moat, with only a drawbridge to allow access. It would make me feel quite secure to know I could keep everyone out if I wished."

He laughed. "As long as you had an army of retainers to keep the moat clean and to raise and lower the drawbridge every time you chose to go out."

She grabbed his arm. "Let's walk down to the corner tower. Does this walkway go all around the castle?"

He shook his head. "Most of the rest is damaged—including that tower."

"Worse than the north wing?"

Gareth grimaced. "Who showed you that ruin? Gawaine, I suppose?"

She nodded.

"Well, at least I cannot be blamed for that. The roof began leaking before my great-grandfather's time. When they built the new house, they decided to close off the old section and it's been neglected ever since."

"But surely it would not be that difficult to put on a new roof."

"The whole wing is a hazard—Gawaine is right about one thing—that corner should be torn down."

"Couldn't you use the stone from there to repair the walls here?"

"If I could get stonemasons who knew how to do the work and *if* I had the money to pay them. But it's more important to buy seed and sheep than to fix an unneeded wall, no matter how picturesque."

Susanna regretted his plight and wished she could do something to help. Why, she suspected her monthly pin money would go a long way toward either restoring the roof in the old castle, or repairing the outer wall. But she couldn't give him the money, not without revealing her identity. And she suspected Gareth would not accept it even if she did. Already she recognized his deep sense of pride.

She would have to find some way to help him. It was dreadful for him to be so poor that he was unable to repair the castle he obviously loved. He was far too nice to have to worry and struggle like this.

But how could she give him money without him knowing? Perhaps there were some valuable treasures hidden in the castle. Harry's precious documents might be worth something to a collector. She might try to broach the subject later with Gareth.

For now, she would enjoy spending time in his company. He might not be as voluble as Gawaine, or as full of historical knowledge as Harry, but she enjoyed his steady calm and wry humor. Stepping closer, she tucked her arm in his. "Tell me more about the crops you are growing . . ."

That evening, after dinner, while Susanna plied her needle to the seams of another gown, Gawaine lured Harry into a game of vingt-et-un and Gareth built up the fire. When the coals were properly glowing, he took a chair beside her.

"We have to face the fact that your memory is not returning," he said. "I think we should make some effort to try to find out who you are."

"How?" Susanna tried to hide her apprehension. What did he plan to do?

"I propose sending a letter to my solicitor in York, asking if he has heard of anyone searching for a lost young lady."

Susanna relaxed. What were the chances that a Yorkshire lawyer knew that Jonathan and his father were searching for her?

Then her optimism died, replaced by sheer terror. Knowing her uncle and Jonathan, they were scouring every shire in the land. York and every surrounding village were no doubt awash with handbills with her likeness upon them. It was very likely that Gareth's solicitor *would* know about the search.

And if he knew, Gareth would learn the truth. Once her secret was out, they'd insist she return to her family. And if she told them everything, they'd know about the money. Either way, her safe haven would be gone.

Susanna forced a smile, even though her insides were in knots. "That is so kind of you. This memory loss makes me feel so . . . helpless."

"Don't worry, you can always stay here if you never remember who you are," Harry piped up. His brothers glared at him but he returned their stares undaunted. "Well, she can, can't she? You're not going to throw her out into the cold now that we know what fun she is."

"I appreciate your invitation, Harry," Susanna said, touched by his spirited defense of her. "But it is right that your brother search for my identity. I would hate to think that there are people out there looking for me, not knowing if I am alive or dead." She could almost feel her eyes misting at the sorrowful picture she painted.

"I will send the letter tomorrow," Gareth declared. "He could have news for you in a few short days."

Susanna certainly hoped he wouldn't. And to make certain, she intended to see that Gareth's letter never made it to York. This was the perfect hiding place for her and she intended to keep it that way.

Later that night, while the rest of the house slept, Susanna crept down the stairs. She had no qualms about wandering about alone in the middle of the night. If there had been even the hint of a mysterious presence or a haunting spirit, Harry would have eagerly regaled her with the tale. No, the only nocturnal wanderers she need fear were the brothers, and she prayed they were all fast asleep. Her task could be accomplished in a few minutes.

She crept into the drawing room and hurried over to the table by the fire. To her dismay, no letter lay on its surface. She'd watched Gareth place it there only a few short hours ago. Where had he put it?

A quick search of the room told her it was no longer here.

If Gareth had taken it to his bedroom, she'd never be able to intercept it.

Susanna sank into a chair, forcing herself to concentrate. Where else could she look? Earlier that night, she'd carefully questioned Gareth, and he'd said that one of the farmworkers usually took the mail to the village, where it would be sent on to York.

At home, mail was always placed on the table in the entry hall, for the footman to carry. But there was no table by the door in this house. Susanna feared that Gareth intended to hand it directly to the worker in the morning.

She pressed her fingers to her temples. *Think.* Where would one put a letter so a farmworker had easy access to it?

The kitchen.

Jumping up, she grabbed her candle and hurried as quickly as she dared down the corridor, through the connecting passage and into the Great Hall. She'd had yet to visit the kitchen, but from Harry's explanations, she knew she must take the doorway at the far end of the hall and descend the stairs.

When she entered the kitchen, to her great delight, she saw the letter lying on the great oak table. She snatched it up and read the address: William Banks, esq., 25 Walton Street, York. Gareth's frank was neatly inscribed in the corner and the letter was sealed with a wax wafer.

Her first impulse was to toss it onto the fire, but then she thought better of it. Gareth might ask if the letter had been picked up. She carefully examined the folded papers. It looked as if there were two sheets—one for the letter and the second for the cover. If she could open the seal and take out the letter, then reseal the sheet . . .

She glanced around the kitchen, looking for a small knife. If she warmed the blade, she might be able to pry up the wax seal without causing too much damage. After pulling open several drawers and cupboards, she finally found what she was looking for. She heated it on the stove and carefully slipped the point of the knife under the edge of the seal. The red wax started to soften, the seal popped off, and the letter lay open on the table.

Quickly she scanned the missive inside. Thank goodness there was no other business discussed. Gareth merely asked his lawyer to make inquiries about a young woman, meeting her description, who had become separated from her family and was suffering from a loss of memory.

She wadded up the letter and tossed it onto the coals, then reheated the knife and carefully warmed the wax. There was no way she could avoid damaging the seal, but she didn't think anyone would notice.

When she finally finished her handiwork, she put the letter back on the table, returned the knife to the drawer, and slipped out of the kitchen.

She was safe again—for a while. Gareth would not wonder about a lack of reply for a week, at least. That gave her time to plan anew.

Gareth tossed and turned on his bed. Sleep proved elusive tonight. "Lady Elaine's" plight tore at him. How could she remain so calm in the midst of such a tragedy? To have no knowledge of who one was, or where one came from. She was a remarkable lady to bear up under the strain so well.

He wished he could afford to spend more time in her company. From their conversation today, he sensed that she understood him better than either Gawaine or Harry; knew why he worked so hard to keep the estate going. It had been a long time since anyone had lent him a sympathetic ear.

He hoped his solicitor would not be too prompt in discovering her identity. Gareth would like to enjoy her company longer. In her presence, he could almost forget all his pressing concerns.

Finally accepting that he was not going to get any sleep, he threw off the covers and pulled on his slippers and night robe. Perhaps after eating something, he'd feel more like sleeping.

He nearly ran over the object of his thoughts when he turned to descend the stairs. She gave a squeak of surprise.

"I am sorry," he said, holding out a hand to steady her. "I did not mean to frighten you."

"You startled me," she said.

"What are you doing about at this hour?"

"I should ask the same of you," she said. "I imagine we both could not sleep."

"You are right. I was going to the kitchen for a light snack."

"Oh, no." She shook her head. "Eating is the last thing you should do when you cannot sleep. It stimulates the digestive system and will keep you awake for hours."

"What then do you suggest?" he asked.

"A glass of brandy or claret can be very soothing," she said. "Or else a very dull book."

Gareth laughed. "I would much rather have a glass of wine. Would you care to join me, or have you found a dull tome?"

She spread her empty hands. "I have not, as you can see. And yes, I would like a glass of wine."

He held out his arm and led her to the drawing room.

"I'll build up the fire," he said and moved toward the hearth. Coaxing the banked fire back to life, he added more coal until it was blazing merrily.

He pulled two chairs close and motioned for her to sit. Then he poured them each a glass of claret and sat facing her.

"Does this come from one of the casks in the cellar?" she asked.

"Good God, no." He shuddered. "That stuff probably turned to vinegar a hundred years ago. Those casks should have been tossed out, but now Harry insists that they have 'historical' value and he won't let me touch them."

"It must be comforting to live in a place with such a long history."

"Comforting?" He snorted derisively. "It's more of an inconvenience if you ask me. No matter what you do to modernize the place, it is still a castle. And castles are most inconvenient to run."

"But you don't mind living here."

He smiled. "No, I don't. I know Gawaine detests the country, but I like it here. The city is too busy, too noisy, too dirty. And too full of people who are only concerned with their consequence."

She smiled at him. "As a baron, you certainly have consequence of your own."

"I'd rather be known for the way I manage my land, or the fine wool from my sheep, than a title I inherited," he said.

"The farm looks prosperous."

"I try to make it so." Gareth gave her a rueful grin. "But Yorkshire cannot compete with the southern counties when it comes to corn. The one thing we do well is pasture animals. If anything can save us, it will be sheep."

"Is your situation really that dire?"

"The estate has been heavily mortgaged since my grandfather's time. The household books were such a mess when my father died that I didn't realize how truly bad things were until years later. But I am determined to get the debts paid off."

"I could help you, while I'm here," she said. "With the account books, I mean. I'm very familiar with estate management and—

He looked at her with amazement. "You're starting to remember!"

She paled at his words.

Seeking to reassure her, Gareth leaned forward and clasped her hand. This was the progress they'd been waiting for. "Tell me more. What else do you remember?"

"It is all so vague," she said slowly. "I can see myself going over columns of figures in a large ledger—that must have been what I was doing."

"Think!" he commanded. "Can you picture the room around you? Do you recognize any objects?"

She shook her head. "It is gone. It was only a fleeting image."

"Well, it is a start," he said, giving her an encouraging smile. "I'm sure if we are patient you will eventually remember even more."

"I do hope so," she said, then set her glass down. "I thank you for the wine, Gareth. I feel I shall sleep much better now."

He set down his own glass and rose. "Then let me escort you back to your room, my lady. I do not want you to get lost."

"And find myself doomed to spend the rest of my life

wandering the endless corridors of Belden Castle?" She laughed. "I am certain that someone would find me."

"You've already been lost once," he said. "As long as you are under my roof, I promise to see that nothing untoward happens to you."

She turned toward him and flashed him a radiant smile that warmed him to his toes. "Thank you, Gareth."

The look in her eyes was so trusting that he again praised the fates that had brought her to his door. He shuddered to think what might have happened to her otherwise. Here, at least, she was safe. He'd do everything in his power to keep her that way.

Chapter 5

Susanna spent the following morning with Mrs. Jenkins, making an inventory of the linen press. Most of the cloths were in sad shape, but she set aside a few that were worth mending. It was nearly noon when she went downstairs to seek her hosts.

The drawing room was empty so she headed for the study, guessing Gareth could be found there. When he saw her enter, he rose quickly to his feet.

"Ah, the fair Elaine." He greeted her with a welcoming smile. "I trust you were finally able to sleep last night."

"Like a baby," she replied, laughing.

"Perhaps we should share a glass of claret every night."

"Are you hard at work?" she asked. "I do not wish to disturb you."

Gareth stepped out from behind the desk. "I am easy to disturb today. Come, I shall take you on an adventure to the most interesting part of the castle."

"I think all of it is interesting," Susanna said.

Laughing, he took her arm. Then you are a lady after my own heart."

Susanna followed him to the Great Hall. No matter how many times she crossed it, Susanna could not help but feel sad at its barren appearance. What had it been like in the castle's past, when it was packed with the lord's family and his retainers?

She wrinkled her nose. No doubt smelly and dark. Poets and authors could romanticize all they wanted to about the

Middle Ages, but Susanna suspected the reality had been far from pleasant, with knight, servants, and dogs living and eating in the same room.

She gave Gareth a sidelong glance, wondering what he thought whenever he walked through the barren hall. Would he like to see it restored to some semblance of its former grandeur, with colorful pennants and tapestries hanging from the walls? Even though Gareth struck her as the most practical of the brothers, she guessed that he would. It was his home, after all, and he would want it to appear at its best.

Before leaving the hall, Gareth lit two lanterns, handed her one, then took her down the corridor which she knew led to the ruined north wing. But instead of entering the chamber with the collapsed roof, he walked past and continued down the hall until they came to an open stair.

"Are we going to the cellar?" she asked.

Gareth shook his head. "The cellars lie behind us. This tunnel leads to the front tower."

"Tunnel?" Susanna asked weakly. In her mind, tunnels were dark, dank, and crumbling—thoroughly unpleasant places to visit even with such a handsome escort. But he started down the narrow passage and she had no choice but to follow him.

To her relief, the "tunnel" was very similar to the cellars, made of sturdy stone, with ample room for two men to walk abreast. No water dripped from mossy walls; no furry creatures skulked in corners.

Susanna guessed they must be nearing the front wall when he stopped in front of a massive door. It was fastened of thick wood, its frame crossed with studded metal braces. Judging from the cobwebs festooning the corners, it had been years since anyone last opened it.

"What is in there?" she asked as Gareth brushed the gray webbing from the latch and shoved the bolt open.

"You'll see."

"The treasure room?" she teased.

"I once thought it was." Gareth handed her his lantern and

shoved the door, but it would not budge. He gave it a hard kick, sending a cloud of dust into the air. Susanna jumped back.

He glanced at her. "It's stuck," he said with a rueful grin. He pushed against it with his shoulder and this time it gave way. With a creaking groan, the door fully opened.

Stepping aside, he made a flourishing motion for her to enter the dark chamber.

Susanna remained where she was. "I'm not going in there first."

Stepping past her, Gareth held his lantern high and walked into the room. Reluctantly, Susanna took a few steps after him. Faint light come from two slits high in the wall but the rest of the room lay in deep gloom.

"Look at this!" he exclaimed from the far end.

Holding her own lantern in front of her, Susanna reluctantly picked her way forward through the clutter littering the floor, trying to make out shapes in the darkness. She finally realized that the dull glint came from pieces of metal, strewn about the floor. She bent down and looked more closely.

Weapons. The entire room was filled with weapons. She glanced around her with growing amazement. Pikes and swords hung on the walls in spider-wrapped racks. Was that a mace on the far wall? And a crossbow beside it?

"Was this the armory?" she asked.

Gareth nodded. "Gawaine and I used to spend all our time here—at least, whenever we could sneak down."

"I should have thought your parents would have kept the door securely bolted."

"We always managed to find a way in," Gareth said, with a grin. He gingerly prodded a pile on the floor. "There used to be mail, helmets, even a suit of armor here."

He set the lantern down and inspected another heap. "I think this is some of it." He bent down and picked up a tarnished hunk of metal. "This looks like an elbow plate." He held it out for her.

The eager look on his face as he handed her the battered

piece surprised her. She realized she was catching a glimpse of Gareth as he must have been as a boy, carefree and full of fun like Gawaine. Before the weight of his responsibilities had sobered him. She wished she could relieve him of his worries, to give him the freedom to enjoy himself again.

Susanna looked at the blackened piece of metal, which did not resemble anything recognizable to her. Carefully lifting her skirts, she worked her way across the littered floor and examined a rack of swords on the wall.

"How old are these?" she asked.

"I don't know," Gareth said. "Harry's the historian."

"I'm surprised he hasn't taken everything out of here to put on display in the main house," Susanna said.

He laughed. "Harry does not have much interest in old weapons. He much prefers his books and documents."

"That seems odd."

"In case you haven't noticed, Harry *is* odd. To him, weapons have no story to tell—they're not made of words." He lifted a heavy sword from its brackets. "Now, if some ancestor inscribed their exploits in detail upon the blade, he might be more interested."

He brandished the heavy sword.

"Of course, it might have to do with the fact that we would never play here with him—he was too young. It's hard to have a sword fight with yourself."

"You and Gawaine actually fought with these weapons?" She stared at him, incredulous. "You could have killed each other."

"Which is why we were not supposed to come down here." He grinned. "That made it all the more attractive. The worst thing that happened was I once knocked Gawaine unconscious. They put a more secure look on the door after that. But we eventually grew out of our interest. I can't even recall the last time I was down here."

Susanna poked among the debris on the floor. A pile of cloth in one corner turned out to be a moldering tapestry, so worn and disintegrated that she could not even make out the design. Had it once hung in the Great Hall?

In another corner, under a heap of rusted chain links, she found a small wooden box, banded with metal.

"Come look at this," she called to Gareth, excited about her discovery. "Look at this box I found!"

Gareth came to her side. "I don't ever remember seeing this." He squatted down and picked up the casket. "Let's see if I can get it open."

He grabbed a small scrap of metal and worked at the lock, but it resisted his attempts to open it. Finally, he stood up, scowling in frustration. "We'll take it back to the house with us. I want to see what's inside."

"Perhaps there's a treasure after all," Susanna said.

He laughed. "More likely some rusted daggers. Or forks— Harry says those were once prized items."

Shaking his head, he slowly surveyed the room. "It does not look like much now, does it? But to a young lad, it was a treasure room."

His foot brushed against a hard object and he picked it up.

"Look, it's the helm from the armor." He rubbed the edge of his sleeve across the metal faceplate. "This might not look bad once it's shined up." He turned and held it out to Susanna. "Carry this for me, will you? I want to take a few more things back to the house."

"Don't forget the box."

"Drat." He selected another sword from the wall and set it beside the one he'd first chosen. "I'll come back for these later—unless you want to stay and wait for me here."

Susanna gave a mock shudder. "Not with all these cobwebs. I'm quite content to return to the house."

He handed her the helmet, which was far heavier than she'd expected, picked up the box and headed out the door. Instead of taking her back the way they had come, through the tunnel, he led her a short distance in the other direction and guided her up another flight of stairs. The door at the top opened into the cobbled courtyard.

They crossed the yard and marched into the drawing room. Gareth set the box on the table.

"I'll go back for the swords. Ring for Mrs. Jenkins and see if she can find something to clean that helmet with." He darted out the door before Susanna could answer.

She looked more carefully at the piece she carried. The metal was black with tarnish and dented in a few places, but she had to agree that once it was polished, it would look impressive. Harry would no doubt claim it for a fanciful paperweight, but she thought it should go into Gareth's study, on his desk.

Setting it gingerly on a chair, she went back to the table and inspected the box. It did not look to be a complicated lock mechanism; perhaps an ordinary key would open it. She'd remembered seeing several keys in the curio cabinet the other night when she'd been looking for that letter. She crossed the room to it.

Yes, there in the top drawer. Susanna grabbed the plainest looking key and tried it in the lock. It twisted around in a complete circle, not engaging anything. Sighing, she retraced her steps and took another key to try.

"Where in the devil did this come from?"

She glanced up with a start. Gawaine stood by the chair, hefting the helmet.

"Gareth was showing me the armory," she replied.

A wide grin split his face. "I haven't been down there in years." He shook his head and held up the helmet. "Can you believe this once fit on my head?" With a last, skeptical look, he set it down and came over to her.

"What do you have there?" he asked, gesturing toward the box.

"We found this in the armory, too," she said. "I was trying to see if one of these keys might work in the lock—I don't think it's a very complicated one."

"Gareth must have the key somewhere. Is he getting it?"

"Gareth went back to get the swords," she said.

"The swords?" Gawaine glanced eagerly at the door. "I'd better see if he needs help. As I recall, they were rather heavy." He was gone before she could say a word.

Sighing, Susanna went back to the frustrating lock.

She'd had no success when Gareth reappeared, lugging one of the swords.

"Still puzzling with that lock?" he asked. "Allow me . . ." He took the box from her. "I used to be rather good with locks in my youth."

He examined the box for a moment, then rummaged in the drawer again. He pulled out a flat piece of metal and poked it into the lock. He twisted and turned it from one side to the other at sharp angles until she heard the sharp click of the lock being sprung.

Gareth stepped back. "Do you want to do the honors?"

She shook her head. "It is your box, after all. What do you think is inside?"

"Let's hope it's full of treasure," he said, lifting the lid, his expression hopeful.

Susanna could hardly contain her excitement as she peered around Gareth's shoulder. Wouldn't it be wonderful news for the brothers if it did contain a treasure, or at least something of value.

But, to her disappointment, all she saw were papers.

Gareth lifted them out slowly, one by one, as if he too hoped to find something of value hidden between them. But at last the box was empty and the papers spread over the table.

"I think Harry is the only one who will think this a treasure," he said with a rueful smile.

"I wonder what these say?" Susanna picked up one of the sheets and tried to read the cramped, unfamiliar writing. "It looks to be in English, at least." She nudged him and pointed to a word. "See, here is 'beefe.' And 'meade.'"

"The menu for a grand banquet?" he suggested. "Or some cook's market list?"

"It could be an inventory of some kind," she said, still trying to make out more words from the old script. "These squiggles look like numbers."

"I cannot make any sense of it." Gareth glanced at several more sheets. "We shall have to defer to Harry in this; he is the expert at documents."

"Won't he be surprised to see what we found!"

"Found what?" Harry stood in the doorway, a slightly suspicious look on his face.

"Look at this," Susanna said. "We found this box of documents in the armory."

"Documents?" Harry's eyes widened with interest. "Let me see!"

He quickly came over and picked up one of the pages, eagerly scanning its contents, then Susanna saw the excitement drain from his face.

"It's merely an inventory of the food stores," he said in a dismissive tone.

"Isn't that important?" she asked.

"No one cares about food stores," he said scornfully. "History is about battles and political intrigues. These are women's matters."

Susanna put her hands on her hips and glared at him. "I'll have you know that 'women's matters' are very important. What would have happened to your knights if they didn't have food to eat? Or clean clothes to wear? Or a pallet to sleep on? You can be sure that it was women who were responsible for that!"

The sound of clapping came from the doorway. Susanna glanced over and saw Gawaine standing there, applauding, a wide grin on his face.

"Well said, Lady Elaine!"

She felt her face flushing. "I think it's just as important to know how the people lived their daily lives as to know how many battles they fought or how many documents they signed."

Even Gareth grinned. "Sounds like you're going to have

to take those matters into consideration when you write the family history, Harry."

"I'll think about it," Harry mumbled.

Gawaine brandished the sword he carried and looked at Gareth. "Remember how much trouble we got into over these?"

"Did you and Gawaine really fight with them?" she asked.

Laughing, Gareth picked up the other blade and walked over to Gawaine. " 'Fight' is putting it too fine. At the time, we could barely lift them. I think a match was judged a success if we even touched blades."

"But that is still so dangerous! You could have hurt yourselves!"

"That's what our parents said, too." Gareth shook his head and lifted the heavy sword. "They went through a number of locks on that door before they finally found one that could keep us out."

"And I was never allowed to touch them," Harry said glumly. He grabbed the other sword from Gawaine and tried to lift it into the air, but lowered it so fast the tip hit the floor with a thump. "That *is* heavy."

"That's why you were not allowed, youngling." Gawaine took the sword from him. "Stand back and watch how a *real* knight does it."

He clasped the sword with both hands and lifted it to point straight at the ceiling. He tossed a challenging glance at his older brother. "Ready for a duel?"

"No!" Susanna exclaimed.

"Of course," Gareth replied, ignoring her protest. He brought his own sword up in a two-handed grip.

"Stop them." Susanna nudged Harry. "Someone could get hurt."

Harry shrugged. "Maybe they'll kill each other and then *I'll* be baron."

"No chance," Gawaine said as he circled Gareth, eyeing him warily.

Gareth lunged forward but Gawaine jumped out of reach.

"Come closer." Gareth was already panting with exertion from holding the heavy sword. "I can't keep this blade up much longer."

"What, you cry defeat already?" Gawaine laughed.

"Never!" Gareth shouted back.

Susanna wanted to cover her eyes but she could not tear her glance away. She couldn't bear the thought of Gawaine hurting Gareth—or the other way around.

Harry grabbed her hand and squeezed it. "Those blades are so dull they couldn't cut butter in August."

"A blow from one of them could break an arm," she protested, her eyes never leaving the two men who circled each other warily.

"There is that," he admitted. "But that's the chance they take."

"Getting tired, brother?" Gawaine taunted as he continued to dance out of Gareth's reach.

Susanna had to admit this was the strangest demonstration of swordplay she'd ever seen. Except for that first lunge, neither man had made a move on his opponent. At least no one was going to get hurt this way.

She saw that the blade of Gawaine's sword was quivering as he struggled to keep it aloft. This "battle" would not last much longer.

Then, with a grunted cry, he dropped his sword and it fell to the floor with a thump. Gareth quickly dropped his own sword and bowed his head. Both men looked equally exhausted.

Gawaine held out his hand. "You win again, brother."

"Age triumphs," Gareth said, grabbing his hand. "Although I have to admit that nearly killed me."

A knock sounded on the door. Mrs. Jenkins poked her head in.

"The mail's come," she announced and set a pile of letters on the side table.

Susanna felt her stomach tighten at the mere mention of letters. What if there was a message from Gareth's solicitor? Her brief period of safety might be over.

Chapter 6

While she anxiously watched Gareth thumb through the pile of letters, Susanna tried to reassure herself that it was far too soon for a reply to have arrived; she had a few more days of safety, at least. But it was a strong reminder that she had to come up with a new plan. Sooner or later, Gareth was going to find that his letter had gone amiss and write another one.

More and more she debated about throwing herself on Gareth's mercy and telling him everything. He was no brute; he would not return her to her uncle and cousin. Yet she could not rely on him permitting her to stay here, once he knew she had a home to return to.

Susanna admitted that she liked it here. Despite their constant teasing and jibes, it was obvious that the three brothers held each other in great affection. Already they were including her in their little jokes. She almost felt like she belonged here.

Even in this rundown castle, she felt more at home than she ever had in her grandfather's elegant mansion. She tried to imagine what it would be like to live here instead, and the idea cheered her. Was there a way she could remain here?

"Damn and blast!"

Gareth's outburst startled her.

"Easy brother," Gawaine said, "There is a *lady* present."

Gareth looked up from the letter he held in his hand, a guilty look on his face.

"I beg your pardon, Elaine. I forgot you were here."

Gawaine gave her an ostentatious wink. "You can see, with remarks like that, why my brother has such a way with the ladies."

"What is wrong?" Susanna asked, ignoring Gawaine.

"It's from Murchison, the corn merchant in York. He's canceling the contract to buy our crop. Apparently, he's found a cheaper source."

"Oh, happy day," Gawaine said, his voice dripping sarcasm. "Now the impoverished Stavelys can become even poorer."

"Can he do that?" Susanna asked. "Cancel a contract?"

"Not without a fight," Gareth vowed, his expression determined.

"With swords. To the death," Gawaine suggested.

"Solicitors at twenty paces," Gareth retorted. "I'll have to let Banks look into it."

Banks. The solicitor. Susanna sucked in her breath. She had to keep Gareth from talking to him. He'd be sure to mention the missing letter and then Gareth would tell him about her and ask if there was anyone searching.

"Is that necessary?" she asked quickly, hoping to forestall him. "Surely, this fellow would be willing to honor the contract if you insisted."

"The insistence would carry more weight if it came from my solicitor," Gareth said.

"But think of the expense!" Susanna was desperate to keep him away from Banks, and York. "You can always go to your man if your own efforts fail."

"Look, she's trying to save you money, Gareth." Gawaine laughed. "A woman after your own heart."

Gareth fixed him with a scathing look. "You are not helping matters."

"What could I do to help? I've told you for years, it's not worth the effort to keep this place. Face it, Gareth, it's a losing proposition. You'll never have enough money to pay off the mortgages and keep the place running no matter how many bushels of corn you sell."

"So what do you propose I do?" Gareth demanded.

"Sell off everything."

"And where do you propose we shall live? In the streets?"

"Lower your damnable pride a notch and marry some rich cit's daughter," Gawaine said. "I'm sure any number of them would pay handsomely to be a baroness."

"I am not going to sell myself like a piece of cloth," Gareth returned stubbornly. "I will find another buyer for the crop—or take this fellow to court to enforce the contract we have."

"And for what? So you can go through the same struggle next year? Face it, Gareth, no amount of grain is ever going to get us out of debt." Gawaine threw up his hands. "It's time to give up."

"This land has been in the Stavely family since before the Conqueror," Gareth said, his voice tight. "I am not going to go down in history as the one who gave it up."

"Fine." Gawaine started for the door. "But don't expect me to lift a finger to help you." He stalked out of the room.

An uneasy silence descended. Susanna gave Gareth an apprehensive glance.

"Are matters really that bad?" she asked.

"Gawaine exaggerates," Gareth replied. "He thinks that money is to spend and cannot understand that forced economies now will bring us more money in the future."

"But losing the contract . . ."

He ran a hand through his sandy hair. "It will not help," he admitted. "But it is too early to tell if all is lost. Something may still be done. I'm not going to concede without a fight."

Susanna admired his sense of purpose, his loyalty to the family name and history. He worked so hard; this was all so unfair. If only she could help him in some way.

Gawaine's words came back to her—"Marry some rich cit's daughter." It would be the perfect solution to his problem.

And Susanna just happened to know where he could find one.

She clapped a hand over her mouth to keep from laughing. It was so simple, she did not know why she hadn't thought of it before. Over the years, she'd concentrated so hard on avoiding marriage to a man who wanted her money, she had never thought about marrying to please herself.

Now, suddenly, she found herself in the company of three handsome young men who would all make suitable husbands.

Young men who knew nothing of who she was, or what she could bring to a marriage. They had no reason to believe she was anything other than what she claimed—a confused young lady with no family. If one of them would be willing to marry her under those circumstances, she would know that they cared only for her.

In the short time she'd been here, Susanna had been happier than she had in years. She'd had a glimpse of what it was like to belong to a real family and she longed to have it last. All three brothers were honorable gentlemen.

She'd resigned herself to losing her grandfather's money by refusing to marry—she would face a modest future but she would not starve. But for the first time, she saw what that money could mean to another. She did not know the extent of Belden's debts, but she could not imagine that they would severely deplete her grandfather's vast wealth. There would be money left over to repair the castle, put in more modern conveniences. Money to send Harry to Oxford. Money for Gawaine to spend without worry in London.

But how could she hope to persuade one of them to marry her? A woman about whom they knew nothing? Susanna must put herself in the unfamiliar role of pursuer, rather than the pursued. Now she had to flirt and flatter and do all she could to attract their attention. It would be a challenge to one who'd never sought male attention.

But the rewards—a house and family to call her own and the financial benefits of her inheritance could not be sneered at. Both she and the man she married would benefit greatly.

Yet how to accomplish that without making a complete fool of herself? Susanna had never pursued a man in her life; she'd spent all of her time trying to avoid annoying suitors. She didn't know the first thing about attracting a man's attention.

Talking to them was one method, she supposed. That would be easy enough with Harry—she was already helping him with cataloging his precious documents. If she expressed a deeper interest in his work, a lifelong desire to live in a real castle . . . he would certainly pay attention. Harry would be the easiest conquest.

Then came Gawaine, who had no apparent interests other than indulging in outrageous flattery and flirtation. But she did not think his attentions meant he seriously cared for her; he would behave the same way with any lady. It would be easy, at least, to flirt with him. And perhaps that would be all she needed to do to spark his interest.

Gareth would be the most difficult of all. With all his worries, marriage was not foremost in his mind. Yet he did need help managing the estate books. She'd managed her grandfather's affairs for years and knew all about investing in the funds. Perhaps after examining his books, she could find ways to save him money. He would appreciate that. And from appreciation could come attraction.

Susanna laughed aloud at her conceit. She certainly had a high opinion of herself if she thought that all she had to do was crook her little finger and men would come running toward her.

Then she sobered. That was exactly what she needed to have happen if she intended to marry one of the brothers before her birthday.

Which one of them would it be?

In the morning, Susanna descended the stairs, eager to put her plan into effect. She was disappointed to find only Gawaine sitting in the dining room. She'd hoped to have all

three of them together so she could begin the task of decid-
ing which one was the best choice for her.

"Where are your brothers?" she asked.

"Harry is off playing with his moldering documents and
Gareth went to York. May I pour you some tea?"

Susanna's knees buckled and she quickly sank into a chair.
"York? He said he was going to wait before he consulted
with his solicitor."

"He changed his mind." Gawaine handed her a cup.

She grasped it firmly to hide her trembling hands. This
was terrible news.

Gawaine must have noticed her confusion for he looked
at her intently.

"Would you like to go to York? I'll be glad to escort you.
I'm certain you would like to do some shopping."

"N-oo." Susanna fought back her rising sense of panic.
Once Gareth talked with his solicitor, he would hear about
the missing letter. She prayed they would merely regard it as
another failing of the Royal Mail.

But that letter was the least of her worries now. If her
uncle or Jonathan had initiated a search, Bates would surely
have heard. Her secret would be revealed.

She could only hope that Gareth would be so worried about
the corn contract that he would forget to ask about her. She
must cling to that faint hope. Until she knew the worst, she
would continue to put her plan into action. Gawaine was here
with her now; she must take advantage of the situation. And
if Gareth came back from York still ignorant of her identity,
she would try her wiles on him as well.

"The weather looks good today," she said, giving him what
she hoped was a flirtatious glance over the rim of her teacup.
"Would you like to take a walk along the wall?"

Gawaine was on his feet in an instant. "I am always eager
to escort you wherever you wish to go, my lady."

Smiling, Susanna rose and took his offered hand. Gawaine
spoke with a gilded tongue, and she knew he was not at all
serious about his fulsome compliments. It was a long step

from that to a declaration of marriage. Still, of all the brothers, he had shown her the most interest. He might be her best hope. And at least time spent in his presence was most enjoyable.

Despite his early start, it was still past noon when Gareth arrived in York.

Ordinarily, he wouldn't mind a day in town, but there was too much to do back at the castle. He'd have to work all the harder to account for the time spent here. But if he managed to force Murchison to live up to the terms of their contract, it would be time well spent.

He stabled his horse and started to head for the solicitor's office, but the smell of roasting meats that poured from the door of one of the taverns reminded him that he had not eaten anything all day. Gareth ducked inside and ordered sausage and a tankard of ale.

There were times—like today—when he admitted he was tired of trying to keep the castle and the farm going. Perhaps Gawaine was right—they should get rid of the castle and lease out the land. Yet the thought of abandoning nearly a thousand years of Stavely history made him queasy. Duty to his family and his heritage had been ingrained in him since birth; it guided his every action. Gareth knew he had to keep plodding on, making minuscule reductions each year in the debt he'd inherited. With luck and care, he might have the mortgages paid off before he died.

He stared dolefully at the tankard in his hands. It was not the most inspiring future. But he refused to be the man who lost the estate; he would never be able to live with himself if he did. Gareth knew he must provide for the generations of Stavelys who would follow him.

If there were any. In his impoverished state, and busy as he was with the farm, he was not in any position to seek out a wife. No, far more likely that one of his brothers' offspring would reap the rewards of his efforts.

Gareth knew, from bitter experience, that there were few

women who would have him, up to his ears in debt as he was. He'd found that out two years ago when Miss Caroline Sunderland suddenly called off their betrothal once the full extent of his financial woes became known after his father's death.

He also realized that he no longer had the luxury of marrying for love. If he married at all, he had to marry money. Yet no one with money would have him, unless they were hunting for a title. The thought of marrying the daughter of some rich man just to get his hands on her money was repugnant to him. No, if he ever persuaded someone to marry him, it would be a woman who knew exactly what she was doing and married him willingly, debts and all.

He took a long drink of ale. Most likely it would be Gawaine or Harry's families who would reap the rewards of his toil. He hoped his future nieces and nephews appreciated the sacrifice he was making for them.

After draining his mug, he stood and headed for the door. He'd wasted enough time in his morose meandering.

A poster on the wall caught his eye, the word REWARD printed in large black letters. Was someone plying the highwayman trade again? He thought they'd eliminated that nonsense last year. He walked closer and peered at the poster, then stumbled back in shock.

It was a drawing of the woman he called Elaine.

Gareth glanced over his shoulder, to see if anyone was watching, then he stepped closer.

"REWARD for information leading to the return of the young lady pictured below. She became separated from her family during a trip to Yorkshire. Please send all information and inquiries to D. Haines and Sons, 25 Sloop Street, York."

Gareth reread the words a second time, and a third. He felt an enormous sense of relief in learning there was someone looking for her—and a flicker of disappointment as well. He'd known she wouldn't be staying with them forever, still . . .

At least he could bring *her* a welcome surprise when he returned from York.

He pulled the poster from the wall and went out the door. After asking directions, he headed toward Sloop Street, wondering just how much the reward might be.

D. Haines and Sons was, as he'd guessed, a solicitor's office, only a few streets away. Gareth pushed open the door and stepped in.

A thin-faced clerk looked up from his work at a paper-strewn desk.

"May I help you?" he asked.

Gareth held up the handbill. "I would like to speak with someone about this young lady."

"You and everyone else in town." The clerk sighed and pointed to a straight-backed chair outside the inner door. "He's with a client right now. You'll have to wait."

"Have there been many people making inquiries?" Gareth asked as he took his seat.

The clerk snorted. "Offer people money and they'll claim to have seen a three-headed goat with blue wool."

"It is unfortunate what people will say," Gareth agreed.

The clerk shrugged, then lowered his voice. "Of course, it doesn't help that the woman's an heiress."

An heiress? Gareth's head shot up. He'd been playing host to an heiress?

"How do you know that?" he demanded.

"Oh, I was here when they came in to make the arrangements," he replied. "'Twas her uncle and a cousin, or so they said."

Gareth tried to quell his amazement. "Does this woman have a name?"

"Miss Susanna Chadwick," the clerk replied. "From Somerset, and last seen in a rather disreputable inn north of here."

"Whatever was she doing in that place?"

The clerk leaned closer. "They were rather vague on exactly how they 'lost' her"—he grinned—"but they were adamant on her being found as soon as possible."

Gareth frowned. The tale grew more puzzling with each new detail.

"Naturally, as her relatives, they would be worried."

"That's what I thought," the clerk replied. "But then, when they were leaving, the older gent turned and told Haines that if she wasn't found by a certain date, not to bother."

"That seems odd," Gareth said.

"Indeed," the clerk said, "so I asked Haines about it. He told me the girl stands to inherit a tidy sum of money."

"So she really is an heiress, then," Gareth said, half to himself.

The clerk nodded. " 'Thousands of pounds' is what Haines said."

Gareth shook his head, hardly believing what he heard. She seemed so unassuming, so good-natured. Not at all like an heiress. Then again, with no memory of who she was, perhaps the true Susanna Chadwick was not as amiable as the Lady Elaine.

He shook his head again. No, that would not change her true nature. Elaine or Susanna, she was still the same sweet girl.

"I can see why they wish to find her," he said.

"I'd like to find her myself," the clerk said. "And soon— apparently the money goes elsewhere if she's not married by her birthday. It's only a fortnight or so away. That's why they're in such a lather to find her." He glanced again at the closed door. "I suspect she's making it her business not to be found."

"Why?"

"My guess is she eloped with some unsuitable fellow."

Gareth nodded thoughtfully. "The money would all go to her husband, then—if she marries."

The clerk grinned. "Long as it's before her birthday."

Gareth stood and started for the door.

"Say!" The clerk called after him. "I thought you wanted to talk to Haines about this person."

"I fear I was mistaken." Gareth pulled open the door. "I don't know this woman at all."

He kept walking until he was around the corner, then sagged against a wall.

"An heiress." "Thousands of pounds." Living in his house, with no idea of who she was.

But now he did.

Miss Susanna Chadwick, from Somerset.

How on earth had she ended up on his doorstep? And what was he going to do about it? Contact her uncle? Tell Elaine—Susanna—that he'd uncovered her identity?

Or keep the whole thing to himself for a while longer?

The decent, honorable thing to do would be to tell Susanna who she was and restore her to her family. But why had she been wandering about the Yorkshire countryside by herself? Young ladies rarely strayed from home without an escort—unless they were running away. Had she been running away? From whom? Or what?

And how would he ever find out, unless he asked her? Would she even remember?

The letter. He'd almost forgotten that he'd written Banks and asked him to investigate any reports of missing young ladies. Perhaps he knew more and could advise him.

At the solicitor's, the clerk ushered him into Banks's office.

"Lindale." Banks extended his hand. "Good to see you. What brings you to York?"

"I'm having a problem with Murchison and the corn contract," Gareth replied as he took a seat. "He wishes to cancel our agreement. This late in the season, I won't be able to find another buyer."

"Hmm." Banks looked thoughtful. "I'm not certain that anything can be done."

Gareth looked at him with growing panic. "I have no recourse?"

"I cannot be absolutely certain until I have looked into the matter. But my advice to you is to spend your efforts on finding another buyer."

Gareth gripped the arms of his chair. There *were* no other

buyers. Unless Banks found a way to persuade Murchison, Gareth's corn would be worthless.

"Was this why you wrote me?" Banks's brow furrowed. "Damndest thing—the cover was there, but no letter. You know how horrible the Mail is these days."

Gareth hesitated. Did he want to tell him about the heiress?

"A young lady showed up at the castle," he said tentatively. "She arrived in a rainstorm and has no recollection of who she is or where she came from. I hoped you could help us find her family."

The solicitor's eyes widened. "Not the Chadwick heiress? My boy, you might just have found your fortune!"

"What are you talking about?" Gareth strove to sound casual, but his heart was racing.

"One of the wealthiest young ladies in the land," Banks said. "Disappeared under what we shall call mysterious circumstances about a week or two ago. They've been looking for her ever since."

"You mean this girl?" Gareth showed him the handbill.

Banks glanced at it. "Yes, that's her. Don't tell me she's the one at the castle?"

Gareth felt a sudden reluctance to reveal the truth. The law clerk's story still bothered him. He didn't want to tell anyone that he knew where she was—not until he'd had a chance to talk with her, and find out why she had fled.

If she even remembered.

"The lady at the castle doesn't look like this woman," he said emphatically.

"Pity," Banks said. "Marry that one and your troubles would be over—for generations to come."

"She's that rich?"

"She could buy and sell The Golden Ball three times over, from what I hear."

"How could she have disappeared without a trace? Do they suspect foul play?"

Banks spread his hands. "There's something odd about the whole story. I suspect she's eloped and the family is trying to hush things up." He shrugged. "But enough of that. What do you want me to do about your lost female?"

"I hoped you would make some inquiries," Gareth said.

The solicitor took up his pen. "Very well, what can you tell me about her?"

Gareth swallowed hard. "She's . . . short. And blond. And rather plump . . ."

It was nearing six when he finally left the solicitor's office. Gareth resigned himself to spending the night in York before starting home in the morning.

He took a room at the usual inn and dined in the taproom. Then he retreated to his chamber to wrestle with the dilemmas facing him.

"Elaine" was really an heiress, who had vanished from her family in a cloud of mystery. She had an uncle and a cousin searching for her. An uncle and a cousin who wanted her back by a certain date—or else she would lose her inheritance.

But did they really want her back—or was their real concern for the money?

Gareth wondered if he would ever discover the truth. Elaine—Susanna—certainly couldn't tell him. She presently had no recollection of what had happened to her.

The logical thing to do was return to Belden and tell her everything he'd learned in York. That information might be enough to restore her memory. And if she still did not remember, then he could contact her relatives.

Yet a niggling doubt still remained in the back of his mind. Why had she been wandering the countryside in the middle of a torrential rainstorm, on foot? She'd last been seen on the other side of York. So how had she ended up at the castle, miles away from anywhere?

Unless that had been her intention. Had she been running away?

Gareth felt an enormous sense of responsibility for her. She'd arrived on his doorstep, after all. And admittedly, she was an attractive young lady. Coupled with her fortune, it was a tempting combination.

He didn't want to turn her over to this uncle and cousin without knowing more. Money made people do strange things; he wanted to make certain that her relatives' motives were honorable.

Yet if she couldn't answer his questions, how could he find out the truth without telling her family where she was? If they were unscrupulous, he would only be handing her over to them.

He wrestled with the issue all evening and through the night, his sleep fitful. Gareth woke with the dawn and after grabbing a quick breakfast of bread, cheese, and ale, he had his horse saddled and headed back toward Belden.

He had to make a decision before he reached home.

Should he tell Susanna who she was? Or keep the knowledge to himself?

Chapter 7

By the time he'd caught the first glimpse of the castle, peeking over the treetops, he'd decided.

He simply did not trust this uncle and cousin. Their story sounded far too suspicious; he did not think they had Susanna's best intentions at heart. They wanted the money—or else they would not have put such an emphasis on getting her back before the deadline.

But if he kept her at the castle, she would still lose her money, and he could not imagine that she wanted that. There had to be some other way to solve her problem.

The solution was simple.

One of them could marry her.

She seemed happy at the castle and her presence had certainly brightened their lives. It would not be a sacrifice to have her remain with them forever.

Gareth swallowed hard. Sacrifice? He'd tried not to dwell on her attractiveness—those smoldering dark eyes and shapely curves—she was a guest under his roof, after all. But it was not difficult at all to think of her as a prospective bride.

Then he laughed. She probably had no desire to marry him. Gawaine was always the one who attracted the ladies' interest. No doubt Susanna would prefer him, instead. Or even Harry.

He frowned. He would have to let his brothers in on the secret, to give her the chance to choose between them. It would be a competition, in fact. One which they would all win, for in the end, it would save Belden.

Gareth had resigned himself for so long to not being married that it was hard for a moment to imagine what it would be like. But then he thought of the sound of children running through the corridors of his home and he realized that marriage and family was something he still wanted.

And Susanna Chadwick was a remarkably pleasant woman. He'd only known her a short while, yet felt confident she would be a suitable partner. Many marriages were arranged with even less forethought. And he knew he would be a good husband to her. She would be safe, and protected.

Gareth realized he wanted to take care of her, wanted to keep Gawaine and Harry in the dark while he courted her on his own. But he dare not take that risk. What if she did not want to marry him? What if she loved living in the city? Thrived on the entertainments there, the theater, the opera, shopping and dinner parties, fetes and dances? Gawaine would make her a far better husband.

Well, he would leave that decision up to her. She might not remember the details of her life, but he refused to believe that her lack of memory had altered her fundamental personality. If she wanted the city, she would be attracted to Gawaine. If she enjoyed the quieter life of the country, she would prefer him.

And if she enjoyed working in dusty libraries with moldering documents, she would opt for Harry, although he could not imagine that any woman would eagerly embrace that life. But she had cheerfully helped Harry with his work, so perhaps she was a scholar at heart.

Throwing Gawaine and Harry into the pot tripled their chances of winning her as a bride. Surely, she would accept one of them.

He would have to find a way to "reveal" the truth to her eventually, of course, so she could claim her inheritance. But it would be easy enough to do that after marriage. Her uncle and cousin could howl all they wanted to, but once she was married, they could do nothing about it. And Susanna's fortune would remain in her hands—and her husband's.

He wasn't going to take it from her. If what his solicitor said was true, she had more than enough money to save Belden and still live comfortably. He had no intention of wasting it on extravagant rebuilding projects or ostentatious displays of expensive art. He merely wanted to pay off the debts, repair the damaged portions of the castle, and continue to operate and enlarge the farm. Free from debt, it might actually make money.

He straightened in the saddle. Gareth felt confident that he was doing the right thing for all four of them.

And he intended to be the victor.

"What I have to tell you is of the utmost importance—and you cannot breathe a word of it outside these walls."

He looked into the faces of his two brothers, closeted with him in the study, but they only regarded him with mild curiosity.

"While I was in York, I learned Elaine's identity."

"You did?" Harry jumped to his feet. "That's superior. I'll go get her."

"Sit down," Gareth said.

"Who is she?" Gawaine asked.

"Will you both listen to me for a minute?" Gareth took a deep breath. "She's an heiress."

"You're joking." Gawaine stared at him open-mouthed.

"How can she be?" Harry asked. "She came here all by herself."

"I don't know how she came to arrive on our doorstep, but she is here, and she is rich."

"How rich?" Gawaine's face took on a calculating look.

"Rich enough to save Belden, and the farm, with plenty left over," Gareth replied.

"Are we going to hold her for ransom?" Harry asked.

"No!" Gareth looked at him with exasperation. "She has an uncle and a cousin looking for her, but I think they are after the money."

"Then she should stay with us," Harry said. "We'll keep

her safe. Fill up the moat and pull up the drawbridge and they can never get to her."

"There is more," Gareth continued. "The money only goes to her if she is married before her birthday."

Harry looked at him blankly, but Gareth saw a flash of understanding in Gawaine's eyes.

"Well, that problem's easily solved," Gawaine said with a grin. "Wish me happy, brother."

"Why should anyone wish you—oh!" Harry glared indignantly at Gareth. "You aren't going to make her marry Gawaine, are you?"

"No," Gareth said. "I mean—only if she wishes to. What I propose is that all three of us should woo her."

Gawaine laughed. "Really, Gareth, why go to all the bother? No doubt she will choose me in the end."

"Because we can't take the chance of her taking you into aversion and saying no," Gareth snapped, irritated by his brother's smug arrogance. "Not every female thinks you are the greatest gift."

"Elaine does, I'm sure."

"Did you learn her real name?" Harry asked.

"I did but I'm not going to tell either of you. She must not know that we know, or we'll have to tell her everything."

"But what if she never remembers who she is?" Harry demanded. "She won't remember that she has the money."

"I think we can safely deal with that *after* she's agreed to marry one of us."

Gawaine jumped to his feet and clapped Gareth on the shoulder. "I didn't think you had it in you to mastermind such a clever scheme, brother. My hat's off to you."

"What if she decides she doesn't want to marry one of us?" Harry asked.

"That is not an acceptable outcome," Gareth said. "One of us must convince her that he is the only man for her."

"As I said"—Gawaine brushed a piece of lint off his coat—"I will be honored to have the two of you stand up for me at the wedding."

"Why would she want to marry you?" Harry demanded. "You don't have any interests outside of horse racing and cards."

"Perhaps she enjoys those pastimes."

Harry snorted. "You're the last person who should have his hands on a fortune. You'd spend it in a week."

"We would make certain that he'd do no such thing," Gareth said. "And she does seems to have shown some partiality toward you, Gawaine. You might be our best prospect."

"It's obvious she wouldn't see anything attractive in you," Gawaine said. "Always worried about money and complaining about expenses and how we have to economize. She'll think you want her for an unpaid housekeeper."

"My economizing is keeping what is left of this roof over your head," Gareth retorted.

"If *I* marry her, I can oversee the restoration of the castle," Harry said with sudden realization. "I think this is a rather good idea."

"We are agreed, then?" Gareth asked. "We will each do our best to win her."

The other two nodded.

"May the best man win," Gareth said.

Susanna paced her room, too agitated to sit. Gareth had returned from York several hours ago, yet she had not seen hide nor hair of either him or his brothers. Where were they? She'd been on pins and needles ever since she heard Gareth had returned.

She tried to reassure herself that if Gareth had discovered anything in York, he would have come to her immediately. Her secret was still safe.

But she was not—that would not happen until she was married—or her birthday came and went. She *had* to entice one of them into marrying her before then. She wanted them to have her money.

She could go to Gareth and propose a purely business arrangement. She would settle a substantial amount of money on him in exchange for his hand in marriage. It sounded rather cold-blooded, but many marriages were arranged in that manner.

Yet she stubbornly held to the dream that one of them would want to marry her for herself. This was her only chance to ever discover if that was possible. Was she the kind of woman a man could love?

All her suitors had been after only one thing—her money. She wanted to be wooed by a man who desired *her*. Was that too much to ask? A man whose feelings she could trust, whose words she could believe?

If it drew too close to her birthday, and no proposal was imminent, she might reconsider. But she still had time to convince one of them that she would make a suitable wife.

And to decide which one would make her a suitable husband.

Which she was not going to accomplish by sitting in her room waiting for them. She grabbed her shawl and walked to the door.

As soon as he left the study, Gawaine headed for the stair landing, trying not to look like he was waiting for Elaine to appear. He did not want to waste any time getting the lead on his brothers. He intended for Elaine to marry *him*.

For an instant, he wondered if Gareth was playing an elaborate hoax on them. After all, heiresses were not supposed to be as attractive as Elaine. They were tall and thin, or short and fat, or spotty and ugly to boot. Elaine was nothing like that. Oh, she would not stop traffic in the center of London, but she was certainly pleasant to look at, with those big brown eyes and soft chestnut curls.

And pleasant to be with as well. Not arrogant or demanding, as spoiled rich heiresses should be. Of course, if she did not remember that she was an heiress, perhaps she had forgotten how she normally behaved.

But no. She might not recall the details of her life, but he refused to believe that would change her innate nature. No, she was a genuinely sweet-tempered miss.

And one he would not mind marrying.

They'd have a house in London, of course, where they would entertain during the Season. She'd be his hostess for witty dinner parties and elegant soirees. They would have a box at the theater, where they would see and be seen by all of society. No doubt they'd be invited to all the fashionable parties and balls.

And in the summer . . . Perhaps she already owned a lovely country estate, and all their friends would come to visit for weeks on end. They would travel, too. Paris, Rome, Egypt . . . There was no end to the things they could do with money.

He shook his head ruefully. When he'd climbed out of bed this morning, marriage had been the furthest thing from his mind. Now, it was all he could think of. That—and making certain that he was the one she chose.

Not that he thought Harry would offer much competition for her hand. No lovely lady would want to marry someone whose only interest was ancient history. Living with Harry would bore her to tears.

His older brother, however, was a different matter. Gawaine knew that he was far more handsome than Gareth, who did not have a gift for the sweet words and little attentions that ladies loved. But he had one thing that Gawaine lacked—a title.

Elaine seemed a very levelheaded young lady, not the type to be swayed by such a superficial concern. But Gawaine knew that women were often full of surprises. She might find the idea of being a baroness appealing.

That was why he had to take charge from the beginning and make sure that Gareth did not have a chance to insinuate himself into her affections.

Light steps sounded on the floorboards above, signaling her descent, and he jumped to action, striving to make it appear as if he were coming up the stairs. They met a few steps below the landing.

"Elaine!" He greeted her with a warm smile. "How fortuitous. I was hoping to encounter you."

"Oh?" Her eyes lit with curiosity.

"I thought you might like to take another stroll around the ramparts—at least those parts that are not crumbling. At this time of year, it always is wise to take advantage of any decent weather."

"Has your brother returned from York?"

"Gareth?" Gawaine gave an indifferent shrug. "Well, yes, he returned some time ago. By now he's up to his eyebrows in the estate books; he said he didn't want to be disturbed."

He wondered why she looked so relieved.

"Then I would love to join you for a walk," she said. "Let me get my cloak." She turned and ran lightly up the stairs.

Gawaine felt a smug sense of satisfaction as he escorted Elaine across the courtyard. If he played his cards right, he'd have this matter nicely wrapped up before Harry or Gareth even knew what had happened.

They were halfway across the courtyard when Harry came running up behind them.

"Where are you two going?" he demanded, glaring suspiciously at Gawaine.

"For a walk." Gawaine gave his brother a dismissive look.

Harry fell in step beside Elaine. "Oh good. I'll join you."

Gawaine frowned. He'd intended to be *alone* with Elaine. Having Harry tag along was the last thing he wanted. "I do not believe you were invited."

"Oh, Elaine won't mind, will you?" Harry gave her an eager look. "Don't they say 'the more the merrier'?"

Elaine laughed. "Of course you can join us if you wish, Harry."

Irritated, Gawaine took Elaine's arm to make it clear just whom she was walking with. Even so, he couldn't exactly court her with Harry here—who no doubt had come after them with exactly that intention. He'd have to find a way to get Elaine alone, later, so he could work his magic on her.

They climbed the winding stairs and stepped out onto the

walkway, where she peered through one of the arrow slots in the outer wall. "Were the castle defenses ever tested in battle?"

"Several times," Harry said. "The Scots had the castle under siege more than once."

"Did it ever fall?"

"Not ever," he said proudly. "The Stavelys always fought gallantly. They say that during one siege, they grew so hungry that they boiled saddle leather to make broth, and the women—"

Gawaine deftly turned Elaine's attention to the vista spread out below them.

"Harry does go on," he said, giving her a sympathetic smile. "I believe a lady should never be bored."

He stayed close to her as they walked along the wall while Harry stumbled after them. "I wish we could devise some sort of entertainment to please you, Lady Elaine. But unfortunately there is little opportunity for entertainment in this isolated spot."

"You miss London, don't you?" she asked.

He started to nod, then shook his head. He did not want her to think him a mere pleasure-seeker. "Not at all. I find the country most relaxing."

Behind them, Harry gave a loud, derisive snort.

"Do you have any recollections of ever being in London?" Gawaine asked hopefully.

"I don't think so," she replied slowly. "Do you think I would enjoy it there?"

"Oh, yes," he said, eager to convince her. "It's a place of endless amusements—you can visit friends, shop, attend the theater—or any number of balls."

"Or gamble in low dens, wager on horses, and drink blue ruin," Harry added.

Elaine glanced at him. "What's blue ruin?"

"A very cheap form of gin that only fools drink," Gawaine said, fighting the urge to toss Harry over the wall. He was going to spoil everything if he didn't pipe down. "London has beautiful gardens, museums, art galleries." He smiled at her. "Someday I would like to show them to you."

She smiled back. "Perhaps one day you will."

"I could do a much better job of showing you around London than he could," Harry protested. "Gawaine doesn't know anything about the history of the city."

"I don't think she wants to spend her days looking at tumbledown buildings and moldy old documents," Gawaine retorted.

Something on the parapet caught Harry's attention and he stopped to examined it. Gawaine took Elaine's arm and hustled her toward the far tower, and the stairs that led to the courtyard.

"Harry means well," he said, when they were back on the ground, "but his presence makes it rather difficult to have a romantic interlude."

"Oh?" She gazed at him with her wide, dark eyes. "Is that what this was meant to be?"

"I had hoped it would," he said, taking her hand and bringing it to his lips. "Unfortunately, it can be difficult to find a private spot at times."

"There are plenty of rooms in the castle."

"Ah, but I said 'romantic.' Ducking the birds in the north wing is hardly conducive to romance."

"True," she replied with a laugh.

He took her hand again and started across the courtyard. "Come, I know just the place. Full of romance—and we can be alone."

Susanna smiled to herself as Gawaine led her through a maze of corridors and doorways. He seemed most attentive this afternoon. Were her attempts at flirtation having an effect on him? Or was he merely turning to her out of boredom? If he was accustomed to the excitement of life in London, no doubt he found the isolation of Yorkshire particularly wearing.

Yet that might bode well for her. Even a flirtation started out of boredom might turn into something serious. Her birthday came closer with each passing day. She must work diligently if she intended to be married in time.

He cut left down a narrow corridor, then shoved the bolt aside on a wooden door. It creaked open on its rusty hinges; then he stepped through, turning back to take her hand.

Susanna followed and looked about her in amazement. They were outside again, standing in a small, rectangular courtyard. Three of the surrounding walls were built of stone, but the fourth was timbered and incut with diamond-paned windows like the ones in her room.

A large, empty stone basin encircled a statue that sat atop an ornamental pillar. Both were so begrimed and moss covered that she could barely make out their shapes.

"What was this?" she asked.

"That was once a fountain, or so I've been told," Gawaine replied. "I've never seen it with water flowing."

"This place must have been lovely, once," she said. Brushing off some dirt, she sat gingerly on the ledge surrounding the pool. "It should be restored."

"I would do it if I could," he said. "Just to please you."

She laughed. It was just the sort of thing she would expect him to say. "And what else would you do to please me?"

"Take you away to distant lands," he said emphatically.

"Really?" Susanna regarded him with some surprise. She'd expected him to say he'd buy her a big house in London or some other grand present. "Where would you take me?"

"Paris, of course," he said. "The Continent. Egypt. Even Russia."

"Why Russia?"

His smile was self-conscious. "Because it sounds like an interesting place."

Susanna considered. She had always longed to travel, but her grandfather insisted it was not necessary. "An Englishman has no need to go elsewhere," he always said. With Gawaine at her side, she could visit all those places she'd dreamed about . . .

If she chose to marry him. Which she was not at all certain she wished to do—at least not until she'd had more of a chance to talk with him, and with his brothers as well.

She gave a little sigh. She feared it was not going to be an easy task to decide which one of them she wished to wed. But she was going to have to choose—and soon.

Chapter 8

With growing annoyance at his own stupidity, Harry watched from the ramparts as Gawaine and Elaine ran laughing across the courtyard. He should have known Gawaine would find a way to keep her to himself.

Well, he'd learned one thing—if he expected to make any kind of impression on Elaine, he'd have to do it when neither of his brothers was around. He must find something novel to capture her attention—something that Gawaine or Gareth would never think of. Something that would set him apart as the best of the brothers.

Suddenly, Harry smiled with new resolve. He knew exactly what to do. He'd go back to the library and look over those papers she'd found. He still didn't think they contained anything of importance, but she'd be pleased if he pretended otherwise. He would read them and write up a little article about his findings, which he would then present to her.

Now *that* was a thing that Gareth or Gawaine could not do.

It might even be smarter to enlist her help now, before starting on the work. That way, she'd see that not only was he interested in her discovery, but that he valued her assistance as well. That he knew she was more than just a pretty ornament. Gawaine could spout all the flowery phrases he wanted to, but a sensible girl like Elaine would prefer to be valued for more practical reasons.

Harry dashed down the stairs and headed toward the house. Gawaine might be handsome and full of sweet words, but

Elaine would soon see that Harry was the smart one. Women admired that trait in a man. It was his main advantage and he intended to make full use of it.

To his growing frustration, he was not able to immediately approach Elaine and put his plan into action. She and Gawaine returned to the drawing room quickly enough, but his brother settled into the chair beside her and showed no signs of leaving. Harry gritted his teeth each time Gawaine launched into some new tale designed to impress or amuse her.

But just when he thought he'd have to postpone his plan until another day, Gareth peered in the door and said he needed to speak with Gawaine. Harry could hardly contain his excitement as they both left. Eagerly, he slid into the chair vacated by his brother.

"I've been looking over those papers that you found," he began. "I think there is a great deal of important information in them."

"Really?" Her expression brightened and he knew he'd said the right thing.

"Since you were the one who found them, I thought you might like to help me examine them in more detail." Harry tried to look sincere. "It would be a treat to have someone working with me. You've seen how neither Gareth nor Gawaine show much interest in what I do."

Elaine gave him a warm smile. "I should like to help."

"Good." He stood up. "We'll start immediately." He saw the look of surprise on her face and his confidence faltered. "That is, unless you would rather wait until another time."

She stood and moved toward the door. "No, I should like to do this now."

"I've been working on an article to submit to the Royal Historical Society on the history of the castle," he said as they walked toward the library. "I'm hoping those papers might supply some nice details."

"I don't know how much help I will be," she said, her

expression doubtful. "I wasn't able to read much of that old handwriting. And I certainly do not know any Latin."

Harry pulled open the library door. "You can take notes for me."

He scurried around the room, looking for paper, quill, and ink. Finally, he managed to settle her at a corner of the desk and he took the papers out of the box.

"I wish I knew when these were written," he said, frowning as he perused them. "I'd like to put them in the proper historical context."

"Can't you tell from the types of items on the lists?" she suggested.

Harry darted her an approving glance. She might be more helpful than he'd anticipated. "You are a clever girl. Perhaps I can do that." He glanced more carefully at the first sheet, curious to discover just how clever she was. "Now, this seems to be a list of food. What do you think that will tell us?"

"What they ate," she replied.

He nodded, pleased by her quick response. "And what else?"

"Does it indicate quantities? That might tell you how many people were living in the castle at the time."

"And knowing what I do of the castle's history, that might give me enough information to fix an approximate time period." He nodded again, his excitement growing. "I think you have the makings of a fine historian, Lady Elaine."

She grinned at him. "Why, thank you, Harry."

He glanced in her direction and for the first time, really examined her closely. She was a pretty thing, with those rich brown eyes, tip-tilted nose, and rosy lips. He'd never really thought about it much before, but there were certainly advantages to having a handsome wife. Gazing at her countenance would provide a welcome break from his books and documents.

She had a neat hand, too, he noticed as he glanced at the notes she was making. That would be particularly helpful—more than once he'd been unable to decipher his own atro-

cious scrawl after a time. It looked more and more as if
Elaine would make a useful assistant—and, of course, a
wife.

"What do you intend to do if your memory never re-
turns?" he asked abruptly.

She set down her pen and looked pensive. "I do not know.
I shall have to find work of some sort."

He stared at her. "Whatever for?"

Elaine laughed. "I must have food to eat, and a roof over
my head."

"There's no need for you to go out and earn a wage," he
said, dismissing her concerns with a wave of his hand. "You
can simply stay here."

She shook her head. "I cannot remain here forever."

"Why not?"

"I have already imposed on your family's hospitality for
far too long," she replied.

"I don't mind," he said. "It would be nice to have another person around here." He saw her forced smile and realized he'd said something wrong. "That is . . . I mean, I
would like to have you stay."

"That is sweet of you to say, Harry."

He thought he saw a hint of fondness in her eyes as she
looked at him and he felt himself reddening. For the first
time in his life, he wished he had Gawaine's easy way with
women.

Tentatively, then with more purpose, he reached out and
clasped her hand. "You could really help me with my work."

Once the words were out of his mouth, Harry wanted to
pull them back. Gawaine would never have said anything so
stupid. He would have praised her charms, complimented
her on the color of her eyes, or her hair.

"Y-you're very pretty," he stammered.

"Why, thank you."

The smile she gave him warmed him to his toes, and emboldened him further. "Do you think . . . ?" he began. "I
mean, is it possible . . . ?"

She regarded him quizzically. "Is what possible?"

"That you would . . ." His voice trailed off as he realized it was far too soon to speak to her of marriage.

"Harry?"

He looked at her expectantly. "Yes?"

"You're squeezing my fingers too hard."

He jerked his hand away as if scalded and grabbed the first piece of paper he could reach.

"Let's see what we have here . . ."

Once Harry became absorbed in deciphering the old documents, Susanna slipped out of the room, easing the door shut behind her. How long would it take before he even realized she was gone? She shivered with delight. It was such a delicious feeling to be *ignored* by a man.

But being ignored was not going to get her closer to her goal—marriage to one of the brothers. So far, Gawaine had shown her the most attention. But even Harry, in his rather bumbling way, had demonstrated a spark of interest before his mind had again been captured by his precious history.

Only Gareth had ignored her completely, barely saying a word to her since he'd come back from York. She knew he was worried over the future of the estate, trying to hold on to what his ancestors had created. But if she wanted to make a fair choice between the three, she had to get to know him better, too.

And if he would not come to her, she would have to go to him.

Gareth glanced up from his ledgers when he heard the door to the study open. To his surprise, Susanna stood in the doorway.

"You look to be working far too hard," she said, her smile light and inviting. "I thought you might enjoy some company."

He pushed back the pile of papers before him. "I don't know that you could say I was working hard. Mostly, I'm staring at these columns of figures and realizing what a disaster is facing us."

She sat down on the other side of the desk. "How did you fare in York? Was your solicitor able to take care of the problem?"

"It was a dismal trip, as far as the corn contract goes. He says there is little that can be done."

"Surely, you can find another buyer . . ."

He shook his head. "It is not that simple. There is too much corn on the market right now and no one wants it."

"What do you intend to do?" she asked.

"Pray." Gareth set down his quill and gave her a rueful smile. "There is no point in working at this any longer; the numbers will not change simply because I wish them to. Is it still pleasant outside? Would you care to go for a walk?"

She shook her head. "I have been walked around the castle twice today. I'd much rather sit and chat."

Gawaine and Harry had not wasted any time, Gareth realized with a start. If he wasn't careful, they would cut him out before he even had a chance to woo her.

And he did not want that to happen. Not because he wanted the money, he told himself hastily. It was merely that he did not think either Harry or Gawaine suited her. Harry was too young for one thing, and certainly not ready to marry. And as for Gawaine . . . Gareth admitted he was not at all comfortable with the idea of his brother getting his hands on all that money. Susanna's interests must be protected.

No, as the eldest, he would be the best choice for her. Now he only needed to convince her of that.

He stood and stepped from behind the desk, gesturing toward the sofa. "Why don't we sit here, then? It is far more comfortable for chatting."

"What shall we discuss?" he asked, when they were comfortably situated. "The weather? The latest popular novel?"

"Tell me about York," she said. "I've never been there—or at least I don't think I have."

"I wish I could snap my fingers and bring all your memories back." Gareth felt a twinge of remorse at keeping the truth from her. Was he really doing the right thing? "I cannot imagine how you can remain so calm."

"There is nothing I can do," she replied. "I can either dwell on my misfortune, or try to live the best I can."

"You're a remarkable woman."

She gave a little laugh. "Not remarkable at all. Just realistic. There is no point in struggling against something I cannot change."

"Are any memories coming back to you?" He watched her carefully, waiting for her response. How much simpler it would be if she did *remember.* Yet it would dash all his hopes. She would never want to marry him if she knew who she was. An heiress could aspire to a far higher match than an impoverished baronet.

"Sometimes I feel as if I only walked around one more corner, I would walk straight into my past—but it always remains just outside my grasp."

"Do you think a doctor might help? We could consult one in York. He may know of some methods for hastening the process."

"I think that there is little anyone can do," she said. "Either my memory will return in its own time, or it won't."

"If there is anything I can do to help . . ." He gave her a self-deprecating smile. "As if I have any medical experience."

"I think talking about everyday matters may be the best way," she said. "I never know when a word or a remark will trigger a memory."

"Then we shall talk. How did you spend your time while I was away?"

"I helped Mrs. Jenkins with the mending and—"

He glared at her with dismay. "You are here as a guest, not an employee," he said.

"But I like having something to do," she protested. "I

don't know how I will ever be able to repay you for your kindness . . ."

"I have told you before that there is no need. Everyone— my brothers and I—enjoy having you here. You've brought a bit of fresh air into our rather dull lives."

"I wouldn't say life here was dull."

"Unexciting, then."

"There is nothing wrong with that. I find it restful to be away from the city—oh!"

She clapped a hand over her mouth.

"You remembered something!" he said, not knowing if he was pleased or not.

Her brow furrowed in concentration, as if she was trying to capture the memory, but her expression slowly turned to one of disappointment.

"It is gone," she said with a sad little smile.

"Still, you remembered something. That is good."

Her eyes brightened. "Do you think there is hope?"

"Of course there is," he said with as much confidence as he could muster. "What did you remember just then?"

"It was not so much a memory as a sensation. The feeling of being tired and harried from too much activity."

"It does mean that things are coming back to you." He gave her a wary look, wondering how far he dare encourage it. "I cannot help but fear that you have a family somewhere who is worried to death about you."

She glanced down at her hands. "I . . . I do not know. I have no clear memory of any person or persons in my life. Just brief flashes of places or things. Perhaps I am alone in the world."

The sadness in her voice tore at him. "You need not fear that," he said gently. "You will always have a place here."

"That is so kind of you," she said. "But I cannot impose on your hospitality forever. Why, what happens when you marry? I doubt your bride would wish to have a strange woman living in the house."

He laughed. "That day will be long coming, I fear. Few

women want to marry a man whose fortunes are in such disarray."

"Money is not everything," she said.

"No, it is not," he agreed. "But there are not many people in this world who believe that."

"Family," she said. "That is what I think is far more important."

He gazed at her sadly. If she only knew how ruthlessly her own family treated her. "I agree. It is why I keep struggling here when a sensible man would have given up long ago. I have to keep Belden intact—in memory of all those who came before—and those who will come after."

"You must marry one day if you want to have heirs to carry on the name—and the estate."

"I was engaged, once," he said. "To a lovely young lady. But she broke the agreement when my father died, and the extent of the family's debts became known."

She bristled with indignation. "How horrid of her! You should count yourself lucky not to have been saddled with such a shallow female."

Gareth laughed. "You have a way of going to the core of matters, don't you?"

"What do the vows say? 'For better for worse, for richer for poorer'? Those words are there for a reason."

"Love should be strong enough to overcome all obstacles?"

"I'm not certain that love can overcome anything," she said. "It is more a matter of love enabling a man and a woman to share—or endure—the bad with the good."

"A woman would have plenty of opportunity to do that here," he said, shaking his head. He wished he could be open and honest with her. The words she'd spoken today almost gave him hope that she would consider living here—that she would be a willing partner at his side.

"That is the type of woman you should marry," she said softly. "One who is willing to share all that comes with life."

"And where do you suggest I find such a paragon?" He chuckled to hide his avid interest in her answer.

The door flew open and Harry dashed in.

"Lady Elaine, you'll never guess what I found in those papers! Come, you must see!"

Chapter 9

"Harry, if you don't shut up about your dashed discovery, I'm going to toss those blasted papers onto the fire."

Susanna watched with growing dismay as Gawaine stalked across the drawing room and tried to snatch the documents out of Harry's hands, but Harry nimbly leaped out of reach.

"You're just jealous because I'm the one who found these," Harry taunted him.

"*You* found them? As I recall, Gareth was the one who went to the armory, and brought the casket up here."

"And *I* am the person who found it in the first place. So I should be the one to receive the credit," Susanna said, hoping to smooth their ruffled feathers. They had been at each other's throats ever since Harry triumphantly announced his big discovery before dinner.

Harry frowned, as if considering her argument. "But I discovered their importance. Without me, no one would have known what they meant."

"Which you never would have done, either, if you hadn't been trying to impress the lady," Gawaine retorted. "You first said the papers were worthless."

Susanna smothered a smile. In a roundabout way, they were arguing about her—or at least, their attempts to impress her. It was not perhaps the most romantic battle, but it at least showed that they had some interest in her.

She darted a quick glance at Gareth, who sat on the sofa with his arms folded across his chest, making no attempt to hide his amusement at his siblings' bickering. He had taken no sides—was that because he thought the whole argument silly, or that he was not interested in impressing her?

"I can't help it if you don't have the brains to recognize an important piece of history when you see it." Harry gave Susanna a smug smile. "And I certainly intend to give Lady Elaine equal credit for finding these papers."

"Unless those papers contain the alchemical formula for turning them into gold, I think Gawaine is right." Gareth looked skeptically at Harry. "They would be best used for starting a fire."

"But Gareth"—Harry dashed to his brother's side—"you must know how important these are. Why, it shows that when everyone thought the Stavelys were supporting the king, they were really—"

"Oh, now you want to taint the family with the label of treason," Gawaine drawled sarcastically. "That would certainly be an admirable revelation."

Harry drew himself up stiffly. "I am trying to right a historical misunderstanding."

"One that I am certain no one outside of a few moldering dons even knows or cares about," Gareth said. "Do what you will with the papers, Harry, but for God's sakes, leave off with the arguing, both of you."

Harry shot Gawaine a triumphant look, then beat a hasty retreat into the hall, clutching the precious papers to his chest.

Susanna glanced again at Gareth and they both burst out laughing.

"What's so amusing?" Gawaine demanded.

"Arguing about something that happened hundreds of years ago," Gareth said. "None of it means anything to anyone, now."

"I'm tired of Harry walking around feeling so puffed up with himself because he's a *scholar.*" Gawaine turned to Susanna. "Tell me honestly, my lady, does Harry's work send you into raptures of excitement?"

"Well . . ." Susanna was reluctant to take either side; after all, she still had not decided which brother would best suit her. "He does get rather absorbed in his work, at times. But it is admirable that he has such an abiding interest."

Gareth clapped his hands. "Bravo, Lady Elaine! A truly diplomatic answer."

She gave him a nod of acknowledgment and they shared a conspiratorial grin.

"Is that what you admire in a man?" Gawaine demanded. "A worthy interest?"

Susanna realized she was going to trap herself in a corner if she was not careful. Gawaine might not have a grand passion like Harry, but he was an amusing companion. Life with him at her side would never be boring. And she need not worry that he would constantly forget her presence while he buried his nose in a book.

"I think what I admire the most in a man is honesty," she said quickly, then felt more than a twinge of guilt at the reminder of her own deception. *But it was necessary,* she told herself. She had to protect her future.

Gawaine gave her a puzzled look, as if he'd been expecting another answer.

"An admirable virtue, indeed." Gareth nodded his head in agreement.

"Yes, but nearly every man could fit into that category. Can't you think of a more particular quality? Something more unique?" Gawaine looked at her with a hopeful expression on his face.

Susanna considered for a moment. What did she want from a husband? Companionship, of course. Respect. A shared appreciation for the same things. But there was one special thing she valued most.

"A love of family," she said at last. It was what she wanted the most, after all, was why she had decided to set her cap at one of these men; they gave her a place to belong.

Family was the one thing that she did not have, the one thing that all her money could not buy. Even when her grandfather had been alive, they had not been a family. Only a few dim memories remained of her life before her parents' death.

But somehow, she knew that she wanted to recapture that feeling.

She glanced at Gareth, surprised to find him looking at her with a sympathetic expression on his face.

"It must particularly pain you not to know if you have any family," he said.

Guilt stabbed at her more sharply. But she could not tell them, not now. It wasn't protection she wanted from them, but affection. Affection that would always be in doubt if they knew the truth. She wanted them to want her for herself and not her money. And she would never know that for certain if she revealed the truth. Not until she had made up her mind which one to marry—and had been asked by that man.

Until then, she would keep her secret, no matter how guilty it made her feel.

"Somehow, I have the sense that there is no one close to me," she said, giving Gareth a wan smile to cover her discomfort. "Perhaps all my near relatives are dead."

"That would be a pity," Gareth said softly. "You deserve to have a family to return to."

"All the more reason that she should stay here," Gawaine said.

"Then perhaps you and Harry should stop your bickering, before you drive her away," Gareth said dryly.

"Hmmph. I see I will get no sympathy here tonight." Gawaine bowed to Susanna and sauntered out of the room.

"I fear that my presence here is disrupting your life," Susanna said.

"Nonsense." Gareth smiled warmly at her, his eyes bluer than ever in the candlelit room. "Those two are always arguing with each other. You merely give them another topic to squabble over."

Susanna felt rather deflated by that remark. Perhaps they really did not care for her, and her plan to spur their romantic interest was not working as well as she'd hoped.

She looked back at her host and saw that he had turned his attention back to his account books. He certainly seemed impervious to her attempts at flirtation. He was treating her with the same polite courtesy as he had from the first time she'd met him.

She sighed. Perhaps there was something to be said for Gawaine's glib way with compliments. She might not believe all that he said, but at least it meant he was interested in her as a woman. Harry only wanted someone to help with his research. While Gareth . . . Gareth seemed to regard her only as a pleasant houseguest.

Of course, he had so many other things to worry about. Susanna wished there was something she could do to help him, to ease his immediate concerns. The burden of responsibility weighed heavily on him.

But unless she could find a way to spark his interest in her, she would have to marry one of the others, and only help him indirectly through them. Would Gareth even accept her help under those circumstances?

It was all becoming far too complicated, she told her reflection in the mirror as she readied herself for bed. But she had to unravel the tangle and settle on a husband before time ran out.

Harry smiled with smug satisfaction as he examined his reflection in the dressing-table mirror in his room. He'd taken great pains with his attire this morning and thought he looked rather dashing in his green coat and the yellow striped waistcoat he'd pilfered from Gawaine's wardrobe. Surely, Lady Elaine would be impressed.

He wanted her to be impressed, for he'd decided last night that his best chance to win her hand came from acting quickly. He would ask Elaine to marry him today. Wouldn't his brothers be surprised when he announced the news? That he, Harry, would be the one to save the castle.

But first, he had to get Elaine all to himself. His experience yesterday showed him that it would not go well if Gawaine was also around. His flattering words had a way of distracting women from examining him too closely. Harry knew that if his superior intellect was to shine, he had to be alone with her.

He knew his brothers were waiting in the morning room for her to come down to breakfast. Harry planned to get the march on them by going directly to her and inviting her to the library, instead, to see the new things he'd learned from the papers.

He'd worked long into the night going over those papers she'd found and each new tidbit of information added more to the fascinating tale he'd discovered. She'd be eager to hear about his new findings. Then, while she was impressed with his scholarship, he'd pose the question.

After giving his cravat one last tug, Harry went into the hallway and followed the corridor to her room. He rapped tentatively on her door, then knocked again with a firmer hand.

"Who is it?" she asked.

"Harry," he replied. "I've something to show you. In the papers."

She pulled open the door. "What have you found?"

"In the library," he said, jerking his head toward the stairs. "Come, you must see."

She looked at him doubtfully. "Cannot it wait until after breakfast?"

"It will not take long," he said.

"All right." She turned back to retrieve her shawl, then joined him in the hall.

"I really owe it all to you, for finding those papers," he said as he led her down the back stairs. No sense in risking an encounter with Gawaine or Gareth. And, after all, this *was* the quickest way to the library.

"Someone would have found them eventually."

"It's a good thing it wasn't Gawaine," he said. "They'd be ashes by now. He has no appreciation for the history of this place."

"Think how complicated matters would be if you had more

than one historian in the house," she said. "This way, you are the acknowledged expert."

Harry considered her comment. He'd never thought of it that way before. His life would be a nightmare if he had to compete against Gareth or Gawaine to carry out his research. This way, he had a free hand in everything—and a natural way to impress Elaine.

"I think history is important," he said. "It tells us who we are, where we came from."

"Have you ever thought about writing a book about the castle?"

Harry glanced at her in surprise. He'd dreamed of doing exactly that—it was his deepest desire. But he feared that no one would be interested in the work of an unknown scholar from Yorkshire who'd never even been to university.

He shrugged with feigned indifference. "It might be an amusing pastime," he said.

They reached the library and he pulled open the door, smothering a groan as he scanned the interior. He'd forgotten the extent of the disarray he'd left when he'd finally blown out the candles and gone to bed.

"Goodness, you have been busy," she said. She frowned doubtfully at the nearest chair, filled high with books and papers. "Can I move these?"

"Let me." Harry leaped in front of her and grabbed the stack, then looked frantically for a new place to deposit his armload. There, beside the far bookcase, was a free spot of floor. He hastily set down the pile, then turned back to his guest.

She sat in the chair, an expectant look on her face, and Harry suddenly felt rather silly. He thought his discovery was important, but would she agree? Would it impress her enough to consider him as a husband? He swallowed hard.

Yet if she was as rich as Gareth claimed, there'd be no end to what he could do. Repairing the castle was the first task, then he would take his time and restore it to its full medieval grandeur. There'd be books to buy for his library, antiquities to acquire—

"Harry?"

Her voice interrupted his reverie.

"What is it you wished to show me?"

Susanna waited for Harry to explain his newest "discovery," hoping he would hurry since she really did want her breakfast. He'd seemed so earnest when he came to her room that she hadn't wanted to dampen his enthusiasm, but her patience was not endless.

Harry perched on the edge of the desk facing her. "I was looking over those inventories again when I found a brief mention of some drawings of the castle floors." His eyes glowed with anticipation. "And if I am right about the age of these documents, it means there are plans of the castle before the last great rebuilding. I have searched for years looking for something like that, but to no avail. And now . . . well, that was just the clue I needed."

He strode to the tall cabinet by the door. "The records have grown sadly disorganized over the centuries—very few of my ancestors were interested in preserving history, I'm afraid. But they did keep nearly everything. It's merely a matter of finding the right collection."

He rummaged through the heaps of papers and pulled out a large roll.

"Then I found this!" He unrolled the massive chart and spread it at her feet, kneeling beside it. "See? It's a complete plan of the entire castle, floor by floor, drawn up in the fourteenth century! I could barely believe my eyes when I realized it. I've seen this several times but never knew how old it was—we always thought it was far newer than that."

Susanna felt caught up in his enthusiasm, awed that a building could be so old and yet still be a home. A home with history, tradition. The very things she wanted.

"And look." He pointed to the corner of the plan. "See where the wall juts out here? I've always thought that there should have been another defensive tower on that side, but

I'd never found any reference to it. But this clearly shows that it was there."

"How wonderful," Susanna said. His ardent enthusiasm amused her, but she admired his single-minded determination. Harry would be a first-rate scholar, given the opportunity.

An opportunity her money could provide.

Harry sat back on his heels, a look of triumph on his face. "With this map, I'll be able to show that the castle fortifications were far more significant than anyone thought."

"Is there a society devoted to history in Yorkshire?" Susanna asked. "I feel certain they would be thrilled to have an article about your studies."

"The local society?" Harry sniffed disdainfully. "I would consider nothing less than the Royal Historical Society for this article."

"Oh." Susannah concealed her grin with difficulty. Harry did know what he wanted. "I think that is an admirable goal."

Harry carefully rolled up the fragile plans and set them on the desk. He came toward her and suddenly sank to his knees.

"Without your efforts, I never would have made the connection."

Susanna raised a hand in protest. "I really did nothing."

"You brought these papers to my attention and I feel I must repay the favor." He blinked, and his expression suddenly turned shy. "I could marry you, if you like."

"What?"

"It would be the best thing to do in your situation," he went on. "Someone has to look out for you. You can't stay here as a guest forever."

"I realize that," she said. "There is a still a chance I will get my memory back."

"But what if you don't? You'll need a husband to take care of you."

She gave him a dimpled smile. "Are you offering to take on that role?"

"Well, er, yes. Definitely."

"Oh, don't be silly. I am only teasing you, Harry."

"But I am serious," he protested. "I should like to marry you."

Susanna stared at him with growing dismay. This was what she had wanted, wasn't it? A declaration from one of the brothers, a marriage that would make her future secure? But she had not expected this so soon—and from Harry.

"I do not know what to say, Harry. This is all so surprising." She struggled to find the right words, ones that would put him off without hurting his feelings. Whatever was she to do? "Your declaration honors me. But don't you think it is perhaps rather precipitous?"

"Have you been talking to Gareth and Gawaine? 'Harry's too young.' That's what they always say." He regarded her glumly.

Susanna took pity on him. "I did not say you were *too* young," she corrected him. "I only . . . I had not realized you were considering such a serious step as marriage."

"Well, someone has to marry you, if they're going to take care of you."

"Is that what you want? To take care of me?"

"Of course. We get along well enough."

"But . . ." Susanna was at a loss for words. Did Harry really care for her? He'd never given any indication of having strong feelings—yet now he was asking for her hand.

And she realized that, despite her plans, she was not yet ready to take that irrevocable step.

"You do me a great honor," she said at last. "And I will certainly give your offer serious thought. But I would like to have time to consider it."

"Of course," he said, and rose to his feet, dusting off his knees. "Dammed uncomfortable on the floor."

Susanna stood.

"Shall we get started?" Harry asked, turning back toward the desk.

"Get started on what?" she asked.

"Working on the article. I'll need you to take notes for me."

Susanna shook her head. One moment he was proposing to her, the next his attention was firmly focused on his historical studies. It was a clear indication of what life with him would be like! "I am going to have some breakfast before I do anything more today."

Harry bent over the desk. "Hurry back. There is a great deal of work to be done."

Susanna's steps were slow as she headed for the drawing room and her breakfast.

What a surprising morning. The suddenness of Harry's offer had startled her. He was so absorbed in his work that she never expected him to notice her as a woman—let alone consider her for his wife. Perhaps there was more going on behind those scholarly eyes than she'd first thought.

He was right—they did get along well together and she enjoyed helping him with his work. And she would be glad to see her money go to the restoration of the castle.

But was Harry the right man for her?

Chapter 10

"There you are!" Gawaine peered at her from the doorway as Susanna popped the last piece of toast into her mouth. "I waited here for you for the longest time. I didn't think you were going to come downstairs until noon."

"Harry had to show me the new papers he found," she explained, wiping her fingers on a napkin. "He's excited because he found some old plans of the castle."

Gawaine shook his head. "Will that boy never learn?" He sauntered into the room, grabbed a chair, and swung it around before straddling it. "I fear he has no sense of how to impress a young lady."

"And what would you do to impress one?" she challenged him.

"I would first inquire as to what the lady wished for," he said. "Then do my utmost to satisfy her every desire."

"What if the lady wished for something madly impractical—like snow on a summer's day? Or a dog with blue fur?"

"Dogs can be dyed," he said, and grinned. "But I do not expect such impracticalities from you, my lady. I only wish I was possessed of musical talents, so I could write sonatas dedicated to you. If I could put words to paper, I would pen sonnets to your lips."

"What exactly can you do?" she asked, amused by his flirtatious banter—so different from Harry's offhand compliments.

He pulled a small volume from his jacket pocket. "Merely read the words of others," he said with an almost sheepish expression.

"That would suit me nicely." Susanna pushed back her chair and stood. "I intended to do some sewing. You can read to me. But let us move closer to the windows, where the light is better."

He followed her over to the sofa that sat between the tall windows overlooking the courtyard and made a great fuss over seeing her seated comfortably, a pillow at her back. Then he settled himself at her feet and pulled out the book and began to read:

> She walks in beauty, like the night
>   of cloudless climes and starry skies;
> And all that's best of dark and bright
>   Meet in her aspect and her eyes:
> Thus mellow'd to that tender light
>   Which heaven to gaudy day denies.

"Byron," she said, recognizing the familiar words. "That is one of my favorites."

"I am glad to have pleased you, my lady," Gawaine said.

She prodded him gently with her toe. "Go on, read more. I have a great deal more sewing to do."

"I will, if you grant me a boon."

Susanna glanced down at him. "Oh? And what is that?"

His blue eyes darkened and his expression grew serious. "A simple kiss, my lady."

She dropped her gaze to the sewing in her lap to hide her surprise. A tiny shiver of anticipation shot up her spine. Kissing a flirt like Gawaine might prove an interesting experience.

And perhaps give her an inkling if he was the one for her.

"A reasonable request," she said.

In a swift, fluid motion he was off the floor and at her side, his arm slipping around her shoulders.

"I have wanted to do this since the first moment I laid eyes on you."

Susanna laughed. "Wrapped in my bedcovers with my hair all disheveled?"

"You were an angel," he said and bent his head to hers.

If she'd been expecting some shock of discovery, or sense of rightness when his lips touched hers, Susanna was disappointed. It was a simple kiss, nothing more, just like countless others she'd received. No bells rang out, no voice told her, "He is the one."

Gawaine leaned back, his arm still around her shoulder. He gazed into her eyes.

"I think it must have been providence that brought you to my door," he said.

"Or a miserable rainstorm." She gave an awkward laugh.

"No, I think it was meant to be." He ran a finger across her cheek. "I may not know your name, but I know that I care for you. Deeply."

He took a deep breath. "It was my greatest fear when Gareth went to York that he would find someone searching for you. I know it is terribly selfish of me, but I cannot help it. I do not want you to leave here."

Gawaine squeezed her fingers. "You would make me the happiest man on earth if you would agree to marry me."

Two proposals in less than an hour . . . Susanna's head whirled. She had not been expecting this from Gawaine any more than she'd expected Harry's declaration. It was so soon, so—

"Gawaine, I—"

He put a finger to her lips. "Do not say anything yet. I know that this is sudden, but do not see me as rash. It is only that I . . . well, after fearing I would lose you, I felt I had to speak."

"I am surprised," she admitted.

He jumped to his feet and stood before her. "I know you have not seen the best of me, but I am not as improvident as everyone thinks. I have a modest income from my mother. We can live here at the castle, and I could help Gareth manage the farm."

He sat down beside her again and took her hand in his. "I know it is not the life of wealth and ease that you deserve, but you will never want for your comfort. And we will be able to go to the city once or twice a year."

"Are you so certain that this is what you want?" she asked. "To stay here at the castle?"

"It is my home," he replied with a negligent shrug. "And it is not as isolated as it appears—Gareth merely does not bother to keep company with our neighbors. You must travel a distance, but there is some society even in this small corner of Yorkshire."

Susanna stared at her hands. What was wrong with her? She should be ecstatic at her situation. Both Harry and Gawaine wished to marry her, wished her to stay here with them. Her future would be secure; theirs would be as well. Why was she suddenly paralyzed with reluctance?

She glanced at Gawaine, who was looking at her expectantly.

"You must allow me time to consider," she said slowly. "And I wish you to take some time to think, also. Remember, you know nothing about me. I may not be the kind of person you wish to have for a wife."

"I could not imagine anything that would change my mind," he said, squeezing her fingers. "I am not some callow youth to transfer my affections at a whim."

"I promise then, that I will consider matters carefully," she said.

He bowed his head. "That is all I can ask."

Harry burst through the door. "I thought you were coming back to help!" he cried, then stopped in mid-stride and stared at the two of them for a moment before he sprang forward at Gawaine.

"Unhand her, you cur!"

Gawaine laughed and did not move from Susanna's side. "Down, youngster. Nothing untoward has occurred. I merely asked this gracious lady to make me the happiest—"

"You what?"

Gawaine's hand tightened around her fingers. "And if I am lucky . . . she might agree."

"She's not going to marry you!" Harry sneered at his brother. "She's going to marry me."

"You?" Gawaine laughed. "She may have lost her memory, but she hasn't lost her mind."

Susanna jerked her fingers from Gawaine's grasp and clapped her hands over her ears. "Both of you, stop it! I do not want to hear any more of this!"

Harry whirled toward her. "Did you say you were going to marry Gawaine?"

"No," she replied.

"See?" Harry gave his brother a triumphant look.

"I never said I was going to marry you, either," she pointed out. "I have not agreed to marry anyone."

"But you said—" Harry's voice rose in protest.

Susanna silenced him with a quelling look. "What exactly did I say?"

"That you were honored and . . ." his voice trailed off.

"Then you *are* going to marry me!" Gawaine crowed with triumph as he looked at her.

"I have not said that I would," Susanna replied.

The door crashed against the wall and an irate Gareth stood in the doorway. "What in the blazes is going on in here?" he demanded. "I can here you yelling clear down the hall."

Gawaine laughed. "Harry actually thinks that this gracious lady is contemplating the idea of marrying him."

"And why wouldn't she?" Harry demanded with a sullen expression. "I'm just as good as you are. Better, even. I'm smarter. And I don't waste all my money gambling."

"Which is neither here nor there," Gawaine snapped.

"Quite so," Gareth said. He turned to Susanna. "Do you intend to wed Harry?"

"No," she said.

"Exactly." Gawaine preened. "The lady intends to marry me."

Susanna thought she saw a flash of dismay cross Gareth's eyes, but when she looked again, there was no trace of it.

"Then let me be the first to wish you happy."

Susanna sank down into a chair, not knowing whether to laugh or cry. "I have not promised to marry anyone," she insisted.

"Well, you have to marry one of us," Harry said. "You said so yourself. How else can you stay here?"

"Harry does have a point," Gareth said, then he smiled at her. "I think, my lady, that you need to make a choice."

With sudden clarity, Susanna realized that the one proposal she wanted was the one she had not received. *Gareth's.* That was why she had been so stunned by Harry's offer, and bemused by Gawaine's. Because somewhere, deep inside, she had known that Gareth was the one she wanted.

What was she going to do now? Accept Harry or Gawaine, and forget about Gareth? Or try to forestall the other two, and give him time to discover that he wanted her?

"I am overwhelmed," she said slowly. She had to find a temporary solution that would please everyone. Susanna glanced desperately around the room, seeking inspiration. All she saw was furniture, windows, walls.

Walls. This was a castle. The very name conjured up images of knights in shining armor, battling foes, observing the rules of chivalry, rescuing damsels in distress.

And did not knights have to go on quests to prove themselves worthy of the lady they loved? She could set a complicated challenge before them, one that would take more than a few days to accomplish. A quest that would give her time to convince Gareth to marry her.

"Before I can give an answer" she spoke in her most elegant tones—"you each must prove yourself worthy by going on a quest."

"A quest?" Gawaine asked. "What kind of quest? You aren't going to ask me to slay a dragon or some such silly thing?"

She laughed at the idea. "Nothing so complicated—although if you do find a dragon, I should like to hear of it! No, it is not a dragon you shall seek, but something . . ." She racked her brain to think of a suggestion. "Something . . . for the castle. Something that will improve the castle."

"The only thing that would improve the castle would be a large pile of money," Gawaine drawled.

"Not everything of value is made of gold," she said. "Use your imagination and see what you can discover."

"How much time do we have?" Harry asked.

Susanna considered. Her birthday was a mere ten days away. She dare not dally long.

"Five days," she said. "You must be back within that time. I will then grant my hand to the one who best satisfies the quest."

"That isn't much time." Gawaine looked dubious.

"*I* shall have no trouble." Harry gave him a superior look.

"What about Gareth?" Gawaine demanded. "He must go on the quest too."

He shook his head. "I do not have time to play silly games. There is too much work to be done here."

Susanna's heart sank. Even though he had not spoken, she'd hoped that he might participate, indicating he had some interest in her.

"Well, that should make things easier," Gawaine said with a satisfied grin. "Now I only have to beat Harry and that is a thing easily accomplished."

"Don't be so certain," Harry snapped.

"The best man will win," Gawaine prophesied.

Harry dashed for the door. "I'm going to start right now."

Gawaine raced after him.

Susanna dared not look at Gareth. "What have I done?" she mumbled, half to herself.

"It is an admirable idea," Gareth said.

"I am only sorry that you do not wish to participate," she said, trying to keep her tone light.

"I must see to the day-to-day running of the estate. I dare not leave the castle, unless to seek new buyers for the crops." He smiled at her. "But I am sure Gawaine and Harry will do an admirable job of fulfilling your quest. Perhaps I shall also benefit, since you wish them to help the castle."

In her dismay, Susanna wanted to shake him. *She* was the

answer to all his financial problems, if he only knew it. But she could not tell him that. And now it looked as if he did not even care for her.

Bitter irony flooded her. This was the first time ever that a man had shown her the slightest bit of indifference. *The man she wanted did not want her.* It was a shock to one who had been pursued all her life.

With Gawaine and Harry gone, she had to work to change his mind, had to convince him that she would make him a good wife. She had to try, even if the odds were against her. She was an unknown woman with no past, no history—and no money, as far as he knew.

She must show him what else she had to offer—companionship, and the skills needed to manage a household. Affection and respect. And she could give him a family.

And if she became totally desperate, she had one last alternative—reveal the truth to him and tell him she wanted an arranged marriage—one in name only that would benefit the two of them. She would share the money with him, in return for his name and a home.

But she could have that sort of arrangement with anyone. Now that she had determined to marry for love—Gareth's love—she wanted nothing less. Somehow, she had to make him fall in love with her. Otherwise her future was bleak. She knew there was no way she could marry Gawaine or Harry now—not when she wanted Gareth.

Five days. Five short days to convince Gareth that he needed her in his life, wanted her at his side forever. Could she do it? It would be the strongest challenge of her life.

But Susanna was determined. She knew this was her one chance at happiness and she was not going to let Gareth's stubbornness deter her.

Chapter 11

Gareth lay awake long through the night, staring at the ceiling above his head.

Why had he been such a fool? The moment he heard that Gawaine and Harry had offered for Susanna, he should have stepped in with an offer of his own. Three brothers, three offers. An equal contest.

Instead, he'd stood there like a tongue-tied fool while his brothers stole a march on him. Now she would think that he had no interest in her. Which was not true at all. He wanted her for his wife.

He wished he could go gallivanting about the countryside to prove his devotion, although he didn't think anyone had a chance of successfully fulfilling the quest. Only a dragon's horde of treasure would accomplish that.

Then he smiled. Miss Susanna Chadwick *had* a dragon's treasure and more. And while his brothers were engaged in a fruitless search, he would be here, alone, with the true prize. By the time his brothers returned, she would have already made her choice.

It was up to him to get the result he wanted.

She had given them a deadline of five days. Five days in which he must convince her to marry him. It would not matter what Harry or Gawaine found—*he* would save the castle—and give Susanna the home and family she said she wanted.

He bit back a bitter laugh. Who was he to think he could win her hand in such a short time? He was no Don Juan, to have women falling at his feet at the merest glance. No doubt a rich heiress like Susanna had been pursued by any number of men. She would be inured to the most fulsome compliments, the sweet words, the gallant declarations.

Well, he could not pretend to be what he was not. No, if Susanna chose him, it would be because she felt he was the type of man she could spend her life with. A rather ordinary man with a mountain of debts, and a crumbling castle, but a dedication to his family and his heritage, and a true desire to see her happy.

Many good marriages had been based on less.

The one thing in his favor was proximity. With Gawaine and Harry gone, Susanna would have to spend all her time in his company. A closeness that might take weeks of polite social visits to achieve could be accomplished in less than a day or so here.

And while he wooed her, he would show her what life here would be like, if she chose to stay. He'd show her the fields and the farm, let her examine the ledgers that ruled his life, to see that he was doing his best to keep the estate solvent. He wanted her to come into this marriage with her eyes open.

Gareth winced at that thought, remembering the larger truth he was holding from her.

He would have to tell her who she was, of course, once they were wed. In such a way that she would have no inkling that he already knew. But if matters went as he planned, it would not make any difference. By then she would care for him, and want to stay no matter what.

At least, he hoped she would. Else his plan would lead them both into disaster.

Gareth hated the deception; hated taking advantage of her trust in him; hated the circumstances that forced him to make such an unpleasant choice. It would take a long time before he could forgive himself.

Susanna's happiness would be his one consolation. He intended to do everything and anything to make sure she was.

*   *   *

Susanna half expected to be waylaid by either Gawaine or
Harry on the way to the drawing room for breakfast the next
morning, with pleading importunings to tell them what she
really wanted to find. To her surprise, only Gareth sat
at the table.

He must have noticed her expression for he gave her a
teasing smile.

"Your beaus have departed already, I'm afraid. Harry tore
out of here at the crack of dawn and Gawaine was not far
behind."

Susanna smiled with genuine pleasure. Now she had Gareth
all to herself. Certainly, she could elicit an offer of marriage
from him in the next few days.

"I hope you will not find life here too dull with only myself as company," he said, handing her a plate of freshly
baked scones.

"Oh, I think I will endure." Susanna gave him her most
innocent look. "Goodness knows, there is plenty I can do to
keep busy."

He shook his head. "I've told you before that you are a
guest here. I do not wish you to feel obligated to help."

"I like having something to do," she said.

"Well, then, you certainly came to the right place."

"What are your plans for the day?" Susanna hoped he
would be engaged in some project that she could help him
with. She had to convince him of her value. "Any matters
in which I can assist? Letters to write perhaps, or papers to
organize?"

He looked startled for a moment, then a warm smile spread
over his face. "As a matter of fact, there are. I've a whole
set of estate papers that I've been meaning to organize but
I have not had the time." His expression turned doubtful.
"That is, if you would not mind helping with such mundane
matters."

"I think that sounds like an interesting project." Susanna
leaned forward and added in a confidential whisper, "And, I

must confess, that I am a bit tired of sewing. I welcome the chance to help in some other area."

"Organizing the papers it is," he said. "That is, when you are ready." He lifted the teapot. "More tea?"

Susanna beamed inwardly with self-congratulation. Gareth had played right into her hands and now she was committed to spending the better part of the day with him. She would do her best to make him see what a help she could be.

Once again she reflected on the oddity of her situation, having to convince a man of her value. No one had ever bothered to look past her inheritance; now, when she needed to show Gareth the advantages marriage to her would bring, she could not rely on her money as an enticement. Instead, she had to convince him that he was making a good decision to take a penniless, amnesiac woman into his house.

A lesser woman would have shrunk from even making the attempt. But Susanna was determined. She had been searching all her life for something like this—a home, a family, a place where she belonged. A man she could talk with, a good, honest man who wanted her for herself. Now that she had found him, she was not going to walk away. In the next few days, she intended to make Gareth wonder how he had ever gotten along without her—and to make certain he asked her to stay.

Gareth knew his papers were not in such a state of disarray as he pretended, but he wanted to convince her that he needed her help. Women loved to feel needed, and wanted. He shook his head ruefully. She would never lack for that around here. It would take an army of helpful hands to set the castle right again.

But it gave him the perfect reason to stay at her side for the remainder of the day.

He was determined to make her forget all about Gawaine and Harry. His family's future—and the future of the castle—depended on it. He could not rely on either of his brothers to do everything that was needed. No, Gareth knew the responsibility for the estate rested solely upon his shoulders.

And on his ability to convince Susanna Chadwick to spend her life here—with him.

"The ledgers themselves are in reasonable order," he explained when they entered the study. "But there is a great mass of other papers to be sorted and filed." He gestured to the desk. "Would you like to work here, or near the window?"

"Are you going to be working at the desk?" she asked.

He nodded.

"Perhaps it would be best if I sat near you, then, in case I have any questions."

"An excellent idea." Gareth wrestled the heavy Queen Anne chair from its spot near the fire and placed it by the desk.

From the cabinet behind him, he lifted out a pile of papers—bills, letters, and torn scraps with who-knew-what written on them. He'd seen all of it, and knew there was nothing terribly important, but it would help to have it organized.

"How do you want me to sort things?" she asked. "By type of document, or the matter to which it pertains?"

"What would you suggest?" he asked.

"I would categorize things by subject," she said. "For example, papers regarding sheep would go into one pile; those that pertained to the castle in another."

"An excellent idea," he said, not caring in the least how she did things, so long as she was here with him.

Gareth sat down on the other side of the desk, facing her, and he suddenly realized he had not given a thought to what he was going to do while she worked. Gareth stood back up and pulled the current ledger from the cabinet. He had to look busy.

After giving her an encouraging smile, he watched as she bent her head over the pile of papers, her brow furrowed in concentration.

The silence rapidly grew agonizing, the rustling of paper

the only sound in the room. Gareth began to wonder if he'd made a mistake in dreaming up this task, for she was applying herself with great industry. He'd imagined that they would talk and laugh their way through their work.

Instead, while he could barely keep his eyes off her, she was thoroughly intent on her job.

He admired the shapely hand that held the sheet of paper. A lock of hair had come unpinned and dangled beside her cheek. He wanted to reach over and tuck it behind her ear—or pull out all the pins and have her hair cascade over her shoulders, as it had the first time he spoke with her. He wanted to pull her into his arms and whisper sweet words to her.

She looked up and caught him gazing at her.

"Would you like some tea?" he asked hastily, to cover his embarrassment, then rose without even waiting for her reply. He pulled the bell for Mrs. Jenkins and glanced out the window. The day was overcast, gray, hinting of rain.

"Are you cold?" he asked her. "Shall I build up the fire?"

"I think the tea will warm me well enough." She set down the papers she was holding.

"Bored already?" he asked, half-hoping that she was, so he could devise a different task—one that would require that they work more closely together.

"Oh, no." She smiled. "Just surprised at all the expenses involved in running the estate. Are you quite sure that the merchants in York are charging you fair prices?"

"I am sure that they are charging exactly what they think I am willing to pay." He shrugged. "But you must remember that we are a great distance from town, and everything must be brought out by carter."

"Still . . ." she began, then paled and hastily picked up another paper. "I am sure that is quite true."

When the tea arrived he insisted that they take a break and he turned her chair around so it faced its partner. The tea tray sat on the table between them.

"Do you ever get lonely, living out here so far from any neighbors?" she asked.

Gareth shook his head. "I do not have much time for socializing, in any case."

"Still, you must have some acquaintances with whom you visit. Gawaine mentioned that there are some not-too-distant neighbors."

He suddenly realized what—and why—she was asking. Wondering if she would be isolated here at the castle with no one but the family to speak with, day after day, if she stayed.

"There are several families within visiting distance," he said. "Dinner parties and musical evenings are common."

"Yet you do not attend."

"Only because it is awkward," he said. "Most of the guests are married couples—or have eligible daughters and sons. As a not-very-eligible man, I am not particularly necessary."

He saw the disappointment on her face and quickly went on. "I am still invited everywhere, if I chose to go. And York is full of all kinds of delights—nothing like London, of course. But there is a small theater, with plays and musical performances. There are lectures and several cultural societies that meet often."

Laughing, she held up her hand. "Enough, enough. You have convinced me of the virtues of York."

"Would you like to go there? I can hire a carriage and we could go within the week." He flashed her a false smile. "We might even discover that someone is making inquiries for you."

She looked suddenly apprehensive.

"I am certain that your solicitor is doing a thorough job of investigating," she said. "If he has not discovered anyone searching for me, it must be because no one is."

"Then we could turn it entirely into a pleasure trip," he said. "You could do some shopping. I am certain you are growing weary of wearing all these altered clothes."

She ran a hand over her skirt. "These dresses are quite lovely," she said. "Perhaps when your brothers return we can all go . . ."

Gareth suppressed a sigh. He'd thought to provide her with a treat by going to York, but she did not seem interested. Well, that was all to the good. There was always the chance that the search would still be on, that those posters would still be on display. It would be nothing short of disaster if she saw one, or someone recognized her. He dare not risk that; not until they were married.

"Do you ever travel to London?" she asked as she refilled their cups.

"Not above once—or rarely twice—a year. I have neither the inclination nor the funds." He chuckled. "Apparently only Gawaine thinks he can live in the city on nothing but air."

"Is he truly a inveterate gambler?" she asked.

Gareth hesitated. With a word, he could destroy his brother's suit.

Yet he could not bring himself to lie. And, after all, if he could not win Susanna's heart during this week, Gareth still fully intended that she would wed one of his brothers instead.

"He gambles out of boredom—and with the desperate wish that he will increase his funds," he said. "I am certain that if he were contentedly wed, he would feel no need for it."

"Are you recommending that I accept his offer?" she asked.

Gareth sat frozen. What could he say? Yes? No?

"I intend to neither encourage nor discourage you," he said finally. "But I do not wish you to think he is an idle gambler. Occupied properly, Gawaine will make a suitable husband."

"While Harry could use a little less preoccupation," she said, her expression rueful. "I hoped perhaps you could give me some guidance in the matter."

"I am the last person you should ask," he said. "They are my brothers, after all. Of course I would speak highly of them."

"Of whom shall I inquire, then? Mrs. Jenkins?"

Gareth laughed. "Only if you wish to know of every

naughty escapade from their infancy on. No, I fear you are going to have to rely on your own mind in this matter."

"That was why I sent them on their quest," she said. "So I could have time to consider matters carefully."

"I think you should," he said. "Marriage is a serious matter. It should not be entered into lightly."

"Have they spoken at all with you about this? I am flattered by their attentions, but . . . well, I cannot imagine why anyone would want to marry me."

Any man in his right mind would want to marry you, he thought.

"Why ever not?" he asked. "You are a lovely young lady, with spirit, grace, and poise. You came to us in the most dreadful circumstances yet you have never complained about your fate."

"Goodness, you make me sound like a paragon of virtue. I assure you I am not."

"I do not believe anyone thinks you a paragon," he said. "But we have all seen how you have handled your situation with courage and acceptance. You would make an admirable wife for any man."

She looked as if she intended to say something, but then took a sip of tea. He grabbed his own cup and started to take a drink, before he noticed it was empty.

Why couldn't he be more like Gawaine, who was always at ease in female company? Trying to talk like this with Susanna made him feel tongue-tied and awkward. His words of praise sounded trite to his own ears; surely, she must find them so as well.

"I should get back to work," he said.

"And I, too." She stood while he moved his chair, then she resumed her seat facing him across the desk.

Susanna paid scant attention to the papers she was sorting into piles, her emotions in turmoil. She wanted to grab Gareth by the shoulders and shake him. How could he go on about how courageous and virtuous she was—and yet not make the slightest attempt to woo her for himself? It was a slap in the face. It was as if he thought she was a suitable wife for his brothers, but not good enough for him.

Only your pride has been damaged, she told herself. *You are so spoiled that when a man fails to throw himself at your feet, you take offense.*

Pride or no, at her feet was where she wanted Gareth. Somehow she had to convince him of that.

She looked at the pile of papers before her and redoubled her efforts. If he wanted someone to organize his office, she would organize it. She would scrub his floors, polish his boots, starch his cravats if it meant she would become indispensable to him.

But somehow she did not think that any of that would matter to Gareth. His first obligation, his main interest, was to his heritage and his family.

Family. Perhaps that was why he did not speak—because Gawaine and Harry had asked before him. *Of course!* Being the elder brother and a baron, Gareth was very conscious of his superior position and he would not do anything to undermine his brothers. His earlier defense of Gawaine showed her that.

Would he go so far as to give her up, in order to maintain the appearance of playing fair?

That was carrying gentlemanly conduct too far.

She needed to show him—with exquisite subtlety—that Gawaine and Harry were not her first or even second choices for husbands. Which, now that she had resolved not to marry either, would not be so difficult to do. But it would require careful wording—she did not wish to insult them either. And not make it too obvious to Gareth that she was setting her cap for him.

She sighed. Every step dragged her further into the morass she had built around her plan.

"Tired?"

She glanced up and saw Gareth looking at her, concern on his face.

She flashed him a warm smile. "I fear I have been in Yorkshire too long. Even on such a gloomy day I feel the need for some fresh air. Would you care to walk around the courtyard?"

"With pleasure, my lady."

Susanna smiled to herself. It was too difficult to converse with Gareth while they were both working. It would be far easier to talk while they strolled.

And she would let him know, carefully, that she really did not wish to marry Gawaine or Harry. That her interest was fixed on another. To let him know that the door was open—all he had to do was step through it.

Chapter 12

The next morning, Gareth entered his study with a cheerful step. He'd barely spent a minute apart from Susanna yesterday until they finally retired for the night and he felt matters were going well. After dinner, he'd read aloud while she sewed and the domesticity of the setting gave him hope.

He looked up with surprise—and delight—as Susanna danced into the study. The room brightened instantly with her arrival.

"You look unusually cheerful," he said. "Has something momentous occurred?"

She gave him an impish smile. "Not yet—but I hope it shall."

He set down his pen. "Oh?"

She walked over to the desk and put the lid on the inkwell. "You have worked in here long enough today. The sun is shining and it is a lovely day. You are taking me for a walk."

He sat back, arms folded across his chest. Gareth knew there was a fatuous grin on his face, but he didn't care. A walk with her would be pure delight. "I am, am I?"

She held out her hand. "Come. The day is passing without us."

He stood up, marveling how such a simple thing as a walk with her could cheer him so. But then, anything done in her presence was a delight. He could never have imagined that a woman could bring him such joy by merely walking into the room.

In the hall he helped her with her cloak and grabbed his

own coat from the peg. "Nice day" was a relative term in Yorkshire, where it could be warm and sunny one moment, and gray and rainy the next. Still, he thought, surveying the sky after they stepped outside, this did look to be a marvelous day, with only a few fat, fluffy clouds scudding overhead.

She locked her arm in his and led him toward the castle gate.

"I have a surprise for you," she said.

He glimpsed it at once after they'd passed between the gate towers. A wicker picnic hamper sat on the far end of the bridge.

"A basket of kittens?" he asked, trying to sound as if he believed his jest.

She waggled a scolding finger at him. "It is a picnic, silly."

"I never would have guessed."

Susanna gave him a withering look. "At least try to appear pleased."

"I am pleased," he said. "Where do you propose we eat this picnic?"

"Is it far to the stone circle?" she asked.

"Too far with such a heavy basket." He lifted it, testing its weight. It *was* heavy. "What is in here?"

"Mrs. Jenkins prepared it," she said.

"Then I know I shall not be able to carry it that far. She is always too optimistic about the amount of food a person can consume."

"Do you think you can get it to those trees?" She pointed across the field to the copse by the stream.

He lifted the basket again and put on a strained expression. "I am not . . . certain, my lady. It is so . . . heavy."

She laughed. "It cannot be *that* bad or you would not have the strength to protest so vehemently."

Gareth held up the basket with one hand and held out his arm to her. "Alas, I have been exposed for the fraud I am. To the stream it is."

How clever of her to come up with such a delightful plan.

Gareth knew he never would have thought to take her on a picnic. Clearly, he was sadly out of practice when it came to wooing a lady. Today, he intended to put his best foot forward. For a short time, at least, he would put all his worries behind him and enjoy Susanna's company—and pray that she enjoyed his.

At streamside, behind the protection of the trees, it was warm enough to remove their wraps and spread them on the grass.

"After carrying this basket all this way, I am eager to see what Mrs. Jenkins has fixed for us." He lifted the lid and spread the food out before her. Bread and slabs of cheese, meat pies, a packet of cakes, and some tarts, plus a bottle of his best claret and two tumblers.

"She seems to have thought of everything—and then some," he said. "There's enough food here for six."

Susanna picked up one of the meat pies, broke it in two, and handed him half.

"This was a wonderful idea," he said as he struggled to open the bottle of wine. "What made you think of it?"

She shrugged lightly. "It was such a lovely day—I wanted some excuse to drag you away from your ledgers."

"Am I such a dullard as all that?" he asked.

"You are a conscientious landowner," she said. "But one who needs to learn to enjoy himself more."

Gareth poured them each a glass of wine, then leaned back on his elbow. "There are times when I wish I didn't have to work so hard," he said. "Days when I think it would be easier to just give up—"

"Oh no, but you can't," she exclaimed.

He grinned ruefully. "Deep down, I know that I could not. I am too stubborn to realize when I am beat."

"You must remain optimistic," she said. "Your circumstances could change in an instant."

How could she retain such optimism after what had happened to her? Gareth wished he could borrow some of her cheerfulness, when matters looked bleak.

But matters would not be so bleak—for either of them—
if she married him.

Gareth fixed her with his warmest smile, vowing to court
her with what skills he had. He liked the idea of having her
here permanently with him. She was like a shaft of sunlight
piercing the gray Yorkshire clouds.

Gareth waved his hand over the food spread out before
them. "I cannot remember the last time anyone did anything
this nice for me. Thank you."

She lowered her gaze, but he saw a flush of pleasure cross
her cheeks. "It was nothing."

"On the contrary. I am flattered to be the object of your
attention. And it makes me aware of how remiss I have been
in my treatment of you."

"Remiss?" She looked at him with a puzzled expression.

"I've been thinking so hard of my own problems, and
you've been such a willing helper, that I did not stop to think
you deserved a rest."

"I do not mind helping you. I find it interesting."

"Then I shall have to find something even more interesting to lure you away. Perhaps when we finish eating, we'll
leave the basket here and I will take you to the stones."

Her eyes lit with excitement. "Oh, would you? I should
so like to see them. I've always wanted to see Stonehenge
and—"

"There's another memory!" He tried to sound enthused,
but the thought filled him with alarm. She couldn't recover
her wits now, not before he'd bound her to him.

"But not a very useful one," she said with a rueful shake
of her head. "Perhaps seeing the stones will lead to more."

"I fear that there is little comparison between the two,"
Gareth said. "If it were not for the fact that these stones are
clearly arranged in a circle, they differ little from the out-
croppings of rock that dot the hillsides. You will be vastly
disappointed."

"Nonsense. How many people can say that they have an
ancient pagan temple on their land?"

"I fear someone's been filling your head with exotic tales," he said.

"Well . . ." She laughed. "It was Gawaine, actually, who claimed that all manner of pagan rituals were performed there."

"As if he knows anything about pagans or rituals."

"Oh, I am certain he made most of it up. But he is a marvelous storyteller." She tilted her head and glanced at him with a trace of apprehension. "Did you really find a skull there?"

"What?" He stared at her, aghast at the nonsense his brother had been spouting. "We never found any such thing."

Her relief was obvious. "I hoped not. I do not relish the chance of tripping over another one."

"Eat up, and I'll take you to your precious 'circle.' I assure you, all your romantic notions will be dashed the moment you see it. It is quite unimpressive."

"Perhaps I should not go, then. I might prefer to hold on to my illusions."

He slowly set down his glass, disturbed by her words. After all, he was surrounding her with illusions at this very moment. "Is that what you really want? To never know the truth?"

She laughed lightly. "No. I would like to see your stones, crumbled and all."

He watched while she quickly packed the remnants of their luncheon into the hamper, and then he placed the basket beside a tree.

"It is a rather arduous walk," he said, giving her a last chance to decline. He feared that despite her word, she would be disappointed in the circle. Disappointed in him, for taking her there.

But unless he wanted to give up and cede her hand to one of his brothers, he must persevere.

He held her hand as he guided her across the narrow bridge—barely a strip of wood—that crossed the stream. Then they climbed the gentle slope before them, and followed along the top of the ridge.

"What is that large hill over there?" Susanna asked, pointing to the green mass to the west of them.

"Grafton Hill," he replied. "It's the highest point in the area."

"Have you ever been to the top?" she asked. "I imagine the view must be marvelous on a clear day."

"It's not made for climbing. You can't tell from here, but the whole hill is limestone, riddled with caves and fissures. You'd as likely fall into one as reach the top."

"Oh." The tone of her voice reflected her disappointment.

"Yorkshire can be a dangerous place," he said. "Especially up in the fells. It's riddled with sunken streams and abandoned mines. It's not a place to wander alone."

"Then I am content to travel with you as my guide." She turned and looked back at Belden, dominating the valley below. "It looks rather impressive from here."

"That it does." He was forced to admit that from a distance, it did not look as tumbledown as he knew it to be.

"Can't you picture a band of mounted knights, riding out across the drawbridge, with their banners waving and the sunlight glinting off their armor?" she asked.

"Now you sound like Harry." His laugh was tinged with a trace of regret, realizing how she'd spent far more time with both of his brothers than she had with him. "Gawaine and Harry have certainly entertained you with their clever tales. I must appear dreadfully dull by comparison."

She stepped closer and looped her arm in his, her expression turning serious. "Perhaps they make up tales because they have not yet experienced life."

Gareth grimaced. "Now you make me feel ancient."

"I do not mean that at all." They strolled along the path. "It is merely that you know what it is to run an estate and keep a household together, and to be responsible for others. They understand nothing of that."

"Their illusions have not yet been shattered, you mean."

"They have not learned to temper their dreams with a dash of reality," she replied. "You have shielded them too well."

"While I have had too many dreams shattered." He shrugged. "That is what growing up is about, after all."

"Is it? Or is it trying to hold on to those dreams, even when everything seems to be set against them?"

"You can only fight and struggle for so long. There comes a time when you have to accept the truth." He glanced over at her, saw her pensive expression. "Perhaps you would do best to marry one of them, while they still have their dreams."

"You still have your dreams," she said. "Else you would not be fighting so hard to keep Belden going. It takes far more courage to continue even when you know it is an up-hill struggle."

"Courage—or foolishness?"

"All you need is someone to remind you on occasion why you are doing this—to remind you what this place means to you."

Would that it were you, he thought. *With you at my side, I would not mind all the hard work.*

"Here comes the difficult part of the journey." He pointed to the hill before them, glad to change the subject. Her words confused him. For one moment, it sounded as if she wanted someone like Gawaine or Harry, who still viewed life with naive optimism. But then she spoke with such understanding of his own needs that he doubted his first impression. "All you need is someone to remind you . . ." Was she offering herself? Could she possibly consider spending her life with him?

He was glad they both had to concentrate on keeping their footing on the steep slope as they scrabbled over the loose rock. There was no more time to delve into such serious matters. At last they reached the top of the hill, and the easier descent down the other side.

He saw the circle now, the weather-worn stones covered with moss and lichens.

"There it is," he announced, pointing to the site at the base of the hill.

She brushed past him and halted beside the tallest stone, which barely came to her knees. Yet to his surprise, she did not look a bit disappointed but glanced around with avid curiosity.

"How old these must be, to be so worn." She started to enter the circle but he leaped after her and pulled her back.

" 'Tis not good luck to enter a circle without first asking permission of those who built it," he said with a trace of embarrassment at still believing the old folk wisdom.

She quickly stepped back. "How sensible. Are there special words I should say?"

"Just a quick request, as you might make of any householder."

She gave him an impish grin. "What if they say no?"

Gareth grinned back. "I've never heard tell that they do."

She closed her eyes for a moment, as if concentrating on her words, then walked into the center of the circle. Gareth, hastily mumbling his own request, followed.

"I do not feel any different," she said, twirling slowly about, her arms outstretched. "So permission must have been granted."

She carefully walked about the circle, examining the stumps of the stones that had once stood tall. "What do you suppose the Roman soldiers thought, when they first glimpsed these?"

"That Britain was full of pagans," he suggested.

"And painted blue, were they not?"

"So they claimed. The old Roman highway crosses the dales north of here."

"Oh?" She glanced at him eagerly. "Can we go there, too?"

"Not today. It's too far."

"Next week, perhaps?" She gave him an expectant look.

By next week, his brothers would have returned. Would she still want to go anywhere with him then—or would her attention have been switched to another?

Gareth realized just how much he wanted her for himself.

"Next week," he agreed, hoping he'd be able to grant her request.

She sat down on one of the stones. "Did you come here often, as a child?"

"No. Yorkshire is covered with stones—ones much closer to home. I didn't need to come this far to see them."

She gave him an exasperated look. "Honestly, Gareth, for someone named after an Arthurian hero, you have such a prosaic view of life."

"I leave the romantic notions to Harry—he has enough of them for both of us."

She stood up and shook out her skirts. "Well, despite your arguments, I still find it a fascinating place. But I imagine we should start back."

"It is time," he said, and turned to leave, then halted, emboldened by the magic of the moment. "There is one more custom, about the stones."

"Oh?"

He stepped toward her. "Any man that finds himself inside the circle with a lovely young lady is entitled to a kiss. It is thought to provide the best of luck."

"Oh." Her eyes widened as she watched him approach.

Gareth took another step toward her and put his hands on her shoulders. "I would not wish to risk bad luck by breaking such a tradition."

"Nor would I," she whispered.

He bent his head and brushed her lips with his, letting them linger for just a moment until he pulled away. To his delight, he saw a slight flush in her cheeks. *She had not minded.*

Then she reached up and pulled his head down again. "I think we can use all the good luck we can make," she whispered, and brought her lips to his.

Gareth eagerly wrapped his arms around her waist, delighted by her eager response. Her own hands were around his neck, clinging tightly as they kissed, and kissed again.

Then she pulled back, a little breathless and gave him a look of such innocent desire that it pierced his heart.

I cannot let Gawaine or Harry have her, he thought. *She must be mine.*

Gazing at Gareth, Susanna's heart thumped so loudly that she feared it might burst.

She'd never kissed a man before. Oh, she'd been kissed, but never had she initiated it. But when Gareth had kissed her, then pulled away, apprehension heavy in his eyes, she'd only thought to reassure him.

A shiver ran though her at the remembrance of how wonderful it had felt to be held—even for an instant—in his arms. She knew she must have this man.

"Cold?" Gareth's eyes were full of concern. "We should start back to the castle."

Susanna wanted to say "no," that she had no desire to leave this place. That he was quite wrong and there *was* something magical about the ruined stone circle and she wanted them both to stay within its confines forever. To forget about everything else but each other.

Instead, she nodded and let her hands drop to her sides, waiting for him to take the first step.

He held out his hand and she took it, and they walked away from the circle together.

Neither of them uttered a word on the walk back toward their picnic site. At first, while she relived those kisses in her mind, she did not notice, but after a while his silence gnawed at her. Had he found her too forward, kissing him like that? Was he regretting the entire incident, thinking it had been a mistake on his part? She wished he would say something—anything—but he continued to walk in silence.

And she was too nervous to speak. She had no experience in these matters, and did not know what to say, how she should act to reassure him that she wanted his attentions. Susanna feared she would say something silly—or stupid—that would offend him somehow and break the fragile rapprochement between them.

She felt relief when they at last they reached the stream, and the waiting picnic basket. Gareth halted to retrieve it.

"I think there are a few cakes left," he said, peering inside. "Should you like one?"

Cakes? I've just had the most wonderful kisses of my entire life and you want to talk about cakes?

"No, thank you," she replied.

He lifted the nearly empty basket with ease and held out his arm to her again. She took it gladly, and they strolled back toward the castle.

They'd just come through the entrance when Mrs. Jenkins burst into the courtyard, her apron billowing before her.

"Thank goodness you two are all right. I was ready to send out a search party. Where have you been? I was afeerd you were lost—or worse."

Gareth laughed. "We walked over to the stone circle on the far side of the dale."

Mrs. Jenkins shook her head. "And now I'm sure Miss is exhausted. Come inside, dearie, and I'll get you a cup of tea." She shot Gareth a scathing glance. "And next time you decide to drag a young lady on such an excursion, take a carriage."

Susanna laughed. "It was a lovely walk; I did not mind it in the least." She turned to Gareth. "Will you join me for tea?"

"I shall be in shortly," he said. "I have a few matters to take care of."

Striving to cover her disappointment, Susanna followed the housekeeper inside. With every minute that he avoided speaking of what had passed between them, she grew more and more fearful that he was not pleased.

Was he thinking about Gawaine and Harry, feeling that he'd taken unfair advantage of their absence. How could she tell him that she'd sent them away for that very reason? Yet she dare not allow him to think that honor required him to retreat in favor of his brothers. *He* was the one she wanted.

Sighing, she poured a cup of tea from the pot brought by Mrs. Jenkins. Why couldn't she just confront Gareth, tell him she cared for him, and hoped that he cared for her? If the tables were turned, and she were a man courting a lady, it could be done. Why then, as a lady, must she wait for him to make the first move? Particularly if he hesitated to take that step out of a misplaced sense of obligation to his brothers.

She would wait and see what happened this evening. If he said nothing, made no allusion to those kisses, to her situation, she would have to take control of matters.

Susanna smothered a giggle. Why, she might even be so bold as to kiss him again. *That* should certainly give him a clue.

Chapter 13

Gareth lingered outside, climbing the steps of the tower to check and recheck the parapet railing until he could not stand it any longer. He knew he was avoiding Susanna, but his emotions were in such turmoil that he had to bring them under control before he dared to speak with her.

How could one kiss turn his whole world upside down?

Before this, it had all been a game—one with a serious goal, but a game nonetheless. A game of "marry the money," with the bridegroom as the winner. And although he wanted to be the victor, he would not have begrudged either of his brothers the prize.

Until that fatal moment in the stone circle. Now, for him, the prize was no longer just the money, but Susanna herself.

A prize he was determined to win.

So why was he standing out here instead of by her side, making every effort to win her to him? Because he was a fool, acting like a giddy schoolboy with his first crush.

How should he proceed? Pretend that nothing had happened and continue to slowly woo her? Or should he throw himself on his knees before her and beg for her hand as abruptly as his brothers had?

Neither alternative appealed to him. She deserved better. But he did not have much time. The longer he dallied, the more he ran the risk that one of his brothers would return, his quest fulfilled, and Susanna would give away her hand. He could not allow that to happen.

Gareth reminded himself that while he had kissed her first,

she had certainly kissed him back. Should he take encouragement from that? Did it mean that she felt *something* for him?

Or had she kissed Harry and Gawaine like that, too?

He shook his head. He couldn't imagine Harry kissing anyone. But Gawaine was another matter. He'd always had a way with the ladies from the time he was in short pants. It was very likely he'd kissed Susanna—more than once. And probably with far more skill and finesse than he had.

Was that what she was doing now? Comparing the two of them? Gareth paled at the thought. He did not have Gawaine's glib way with compliments, or the ability to make witty conversation that attracted the ladies. He'd only courted one girl in his life, and look what a disaster that had been. He was mad to think that he could outdo Gawaine.

But Gawaine was not here and he was.

Gareth turned and started down the stone steps. There was no point in continuing to mull things over while Susanna sat in the drawing room, alone. He would go to her at once, and continue his bumbling courtship. Within the next few days, he would win her to his side, or . . .

She was sitting on the sofa, gazing out the window, a teacup in her hand, the late afternoon light setting golden highlights in her hair. Gareth wished he was a painter, so he could capture the moment for eternity. But then she turned to greet him and he forgot everything except the welcoming look in her eyes.

"Is the tea gone?" he asked. "Or shall I ring for more?"

"There is enough for another cup," she replied, filling one for him.

He took it from her and perched uneasily on the edge of the chair. Gareth took a sip to steady his nerves, wishing he had something stronger than tea right now.

"I hope you are not too fatigued from our long walk," he said at last. "Mrs. Jenkins was right, I should have taken the carriage."

"Nonsense," she replied. "It was an invigorating walk."

Gareth took another sip of tea, trying to summon his courage. He had to know what she thought about him—about what had happened—and what the future might bring. "I do believe that I owe you an apology, however."

"An apology?" Her eyes widened with puzzlement. "For what?"

"I should not have taken advantage of you, while we were alone. For that, I am sorry."

"Advantage of me?" Her expression remained puzzled, then her eyes flashed with surprise. "Are you referring to the kisses we shared?"

He nodded.

To his amazement and dismay, she burst out laughing. "Oh, Gareth, you are a dear. But I assure you, I was not offended."

"You weren't?" he asked, elated by her reaction.

She smiled softly. "It was only a few kisses."

He set down his cup. "I do not wish you to think that I was trifling with your affections. After all, there is Harry and Gawaine to consider . . ."

She put a hand on his arm. "This is not the time or place to talk about them. I am very pleased that you kissed me today."

A slow smile spread over his face. "So am I."

"I think perhaps that stone circle still has some magical power. I feel we are caught in its spell."

He took her cup and set it on the table. "I think the only magic comes from you, my lady. You've woven a spell around me." Gareth clasped one of her hands in his.

"It is I who am spellbound," she said, her voice low and soft. She looked directly into his eyes. "I sent them away on purpose, you know. Your brothers."

His heart leaped at her words. "Did you, now? That was a wise thing to do. Or else very, very foolish."

"I do not think it was foolish at all," she said. "I find their gallantry and attentions flattering, but I know they are not the ones for me."

"You are very lucky, to know your mind so well."

"Perhaps because I have forgotten so much else, this one thing is crystal clear." Her gaze dropped to their hands, linked together in her lap. "I think I have loved you from that day on the ramparts, when you told me all your hopes and plans for the estate. I wish so much that they will come true for you."

Gareth could barely believe his ears. *She loved him!* Not Gawaine or Harry, but him.

He tightened his grasp of her fingers.

"You do me great honor," he said. "I only fear that I will not prove worthy."

"You are the most honorable man I have ever met," she said.

His insides twisted at her words. If she knew how dishonorable he was, she would never speak to him again. "Do not elevate me too high, my lady. Else I might hurt myself when I fall."

He brought her hand to his lips and kissed it. "You could make me the happiest man on earth if you will marry me." He laughed lightly. "I may be the last member of the family to ask, but it is not from lack of feeling for you. I adore you . . . Elaine. You are so brave, and full of hope . . . I need you to share that with me."

"You may take all that I have, Gareth. Everything that I am is yours."

He cupped his hands around her face and leaned toward her. "I do love you," he whispered as he kissed her.

Tears pricked at Susanna's eyes as she lifted her face for Gareth's kiss. At last, she'd found someone who loved her. Loved her because of who she was, and not for the money she had.

She almost wanted to tell Gareth the truth, now, to surprise him with the news that his penniless guest was really rich beyond his dreams, and that his financial worries were over forever. But a last stirring of caution told her to save the news for a while longer.

He broke the kiss and gazed at her, adoration in his eyes. "You will marry me, won't you?"

"Yes, Gareth." Those simple words filled her with indescribable happiness. She'd dreamed so long of being able to say them, feared for so long she would never have the opportunity. Now, Gareth had given her her heart's desire.

He squeezed her fingers, still looking at her with tender regard. "I only wish that we could contact your family, or friends, to share with them our good news."

Not until we are safely married, she thought. She would not give Jonathan or her uncle the chance to spoil things at the last moment. All the more reason to wait to tell Gareth the truth until after the wedding. His sense of honor would demand that he contact her family and she dare not take that chance. She wanted nothing to do with them until her grandfather's money was safely in her—her and Gareth's—hands.

"Perhaps, in my happiness, my memory will return," she said. "We may not be able to invite them to the wedding, but they can share in our joy afterward."

"I think a quiet ceremony is in order, then," Gareth said. "That is, if you do not object."

"The sooner we are wed, the better," she replied, mindful of her birthday, which was rapidly approaching.

"I am not certain—that is, I fear we will need to consult my solicitor on how we shall proceed. We can hardly have the banns read when we do not even know your name."

Susanna frowned. She had not considered that problem. If she was not wed under her true name, would the marriage be legal? She dare not give Uncle the chance to challenge anything. Susanna realized that she might have to "regain" her memory before the wedding, to make certain the ceremony would be legal.

"Write and inquire," she suggested.

He looked relieved at her suggestion. "I shall write this very night." He took her hand in his. "Would you be offended

... would you object ... if I asked him about obtaining a Special License? The banns take three weeks, you know, and I—"

"That would be perfect," she said. "We can get married as soon as Gawaine and Harry return. I do not wish to delay."

He laughed and hugged her tightly. "That is what I find so wonderful about you, my love, you are always agreeable to any suggestion. It is as if we are of the same mind."

Inwardly, she cringed at his false admiration. She placed a hand on his arm. "Gareth, I am not nearly so perfect as you make me out. I fear you will grow disappointed when you know me better."

He brought her hand to his lips again. "I could never be disappointed in you."

She fervently prayed he would not, when she revealed the truth she had concealed from him.

"There is another matter we should consider," he said. "The propriety of my remaining here with you. Many would not consider Mrs. Jenkins an adequate chaperone."

His concern pleased her, but she could not smother a giggle. "I think it matters little after I have already been here alone with you for days."

"I assure you I shall behave with honor."

"If you have not ravished me already, I have nothing to fear," she said. "Or is it that you fear I will ravish you?"

He laughed. "As appealing as that prospect may be, I do not fear you. And I do not fear that anything will be said of your staying here. I merely want to make certain that you are satisfied in your mind that all is proper."

"I have no worries."

"I fear my brothers will be unhappy with me, when they return and hear the news," he said.

"I do not think we need fear that. I think they were far more enamored with the idea of being in love rather than actually feeling that emotion for me."

"How could they help not being in love with you?"

"Because neither of them really wishes to have a wife.

Harry wants to study his history, and Gawaine . . . well, Gawaine may not know exactly what he wants, but it certainly is not a wife."

"While I know my own mind all too well," he said, giving her a gentle kiss.

Sitting here, with his love clasped in his arms, Gareth could hardly believe his good fortune. That she had chosen him among the brothers; that she was prepared to put her future into his hands.

He vowed to make her the happiest woman in the country; she would never want for his attention or devotion. And he would manage her resources carefully, with economy, so she would never have cause to complain that he was wasting money that was rightfully hers. He would be as thrifty after their marriage as he had to be now.

Still, it was an enormous relief to know that their marriage would bring an end to his financial troubles. He was weary of the constant battle to keep the estate going. Now, he would be able to relax, to enjoy life, to spend time with her instead of his account books.

She was right about Harry and Gawaine, too. They would protest volubly when they heard the news, accusing him of taking advantage of Susanna while they were gone. But neither of them was ready for marriage. They would never have even considered the matter if he hadn't mentioned it to them. He was doing them a favor by marrying her.

At least that was how he considered it. Harry, he was certain, would not mind one way or the other. But Gawaine—he would have liked the idea of having all that money. All the more reason *not* to let her marry him.

"I cannot believe it." Jonathan Wilding flung himself into the armchair in his father's London study. "I searched every square inch of that corner of Yorkshire and there is no sign of her. Anywhere."

"I'm holding you responsible for this disaster," his father thundered.

"What difference does it make? We've lost the money now for certain. Thrashing me won't bring it back."

"No, but it might make me feel better." George Wilding picked up the letter on his desk. "This was the last report from the man in York. He claims the investigators have had no luck either, searching farther north. And we know she has not gone to her house in Suffolk."

"That's that, then." Jonathan pulled out an elegant gold-rimmed snuff box from his pocket. Before he could open it, his father leaned across the desk and snatched it from his hand.

"This will bring a tidy sum from the right buyer," he said. "No sense in wasting it on you."

Jonathan gulped. It was a stark reminder of what losing Susanna's fortune meant to him. He was barely one step ahead of the bailiffs as it was, staving off the most demanding of his creditors with tales of his upcoming marriage. Once it became know that she was missing, or . . .

She couldn't be dead. Somehow, somewhere, she was hiding, biding her time until her birthday. He had no doubt the foolish girl intended to give up her grandfather's money, just for spite.

Stupid, stupid girl.

He clenched his fists. He was not going to allow her to do that. An army of men had not found her, but that was not saying that one man couldn't. After all, who had the most to lose? The investigators were getting paid whether they found her or not. While he . . . well, he didn't want to even dwell on his future if he didn't find her in time.

"I'm going back to Yorkshire," he announced.

His father regarded him skeptically. "I admire your tenacity, Jonathan, but don't you think you'd be better off arranging the sale of your possessions? Once it becomes known there will be no marriage, it will all be seized. Better to sell now, while you can."

"She is hiding somewhere, I know it. And I intend to find her."

Shrugging, his father took a pinch of snuff from the box he'd confiscated. "I fear your task is hopeless, but go ahead and try. After all, what more do we have to lose?"

"Exactly. I'll leave now. Starting from that blasted inn, I'll speak to every single person within a two-day's ride. She could not have disappeared without a trace. Someone had to have seen her."

"I wish you the best of luck, my boy. I will do what I can to salvage what is left. But I fear we must both prepare ourselves for a rather lengthy 'holiday' on the Continent should you fail."

"I will not fail," Jonathan vowed. "I'm going to find her and take her over the border if I have to tie her hands and feet to do it."

"You would have been well advised to have done that the first time."

"She won't escape me again. I'm wise to her tricks."

"Best you be off then. Check with the man in York first, in case there has been any news. I wish you good searching."

Jonathan jumped to his feet and strode toward the door.

He had to think like Susanna would. Where would she go to ground? They'd checked every lodging house within a hundred miles, then started with the suitable private homes.

He could not picture her living in some rough farmer's dwelling, not for this length of time. No, wherever she was, she was comfortable and content.

But not for much longer. He would search every dwelling, every barn and shed, dovecote and well house until he found her.

She was not going to cheat him out of that money.

Chapter 14

Sitting in the drawing room, Susanna busied herself with retrimming the large straw bonnet Mrs. Jenkins had unearthed from one of the trunks in the attic. With new ribbon and some extra lace, it would be presentable for a wedding.

Her wedding. It had been two days since Gareth had proposed; two blissful days spent mostly in his company. They'd labored over the estate books, taken long walks hand-in-hand, and spent hours talking in front of the fire in the evenings.

And shared more and more kisses. Never having been in love, Susanna could not have imagined the power of the desire that swept over her at his touch. She could not wait for Harry and Gawaine to return, so they could be wed.

There was a noisy commotion in the hall and she set the bonnet on the sofa, curious to discover the cause of it. But before she could take two steps, the door flew open and Harry burst into the room.

"My lady," he gasped, struggling for breath. He executed a shaky bow, then held out a letter. "Read this."

A shaft of panic tore through her. *He'd discovered her identity!* No, he would have announced that immediately, if he had. This must be something else. Trying to control her still-trembling fingers, she opened the letter and quickly scanned its contents.

"Harry, this is wonderful!" she exclaimed as she read the words. It was from the Royal Society of Historians, attesting to their acceptance of a series of articles written by Harry about the castle's history.

He beamed proudly. "And that is not all. Sir Robert—you see, he's the one who signed the letter—introduced me to Lord Atherton, and he has requested me to take up residence at his estate and make order of all his documents—and to write a book on the family's history."

"Goodness, you will be busy for years," she said, truly amazed at all he had achieved.

"Exactly. And he's going to pay handsomely for it, too." His grin widened. "So you see, my lady, I have dutifully fulfilled your quest. My article will bring fame to the castle—and since I will be earning a living, we will not be a drain on Gareth's purse."

Susanna sat down slowly. No matter how much she loved Gareth, she had not been looking forward to this moment. Harry had been successful far beyond what she would have imagined—and now she had to throw a splash of cold water on his enthusiasm.

"Please, sit down," she said.

Harry collapsed into the wing chair. "I do not have to be at Atherton's until the end of next month. That will give me time to finish the first article for the Society. And, of course, for us to marry."

"Harry, there is something I must tell you." She looked directly into his eyes, knowing she owed him that respect. "I am honored beyond words that you wish to marry me. And I wish that I could accept your offer. But I have given my hand to another."

He jumped out of the chair. "Gawaine is back already? I didn't see his horse in the stable." He clenched his fists. "I knew he would ruin things."

"Do sit down!" Susanna said sharply. She waited until he complied before she continued. "Gawaine has not yet made his appearance."

"Then who are you going to marry?"

"Your other brother."

He looked puzzled for an instant, then his blue eyes flared

with anger. "Gareth? But he didn't even participate in the quest. It's not fair!"

"I cannot argue with the promptings of my heart," she said. "I know you are disappointed, Harry, but look what you have accomplished! Your articles in the Society's journal. And someone who is willing to pay you good money to do what you love. I would say that you are a very fortunate man."

He appeared to consider her words. "You would have been a great help to me," he said, at last.

"And I still can help you, while you are working at the castle. And no doubt, if you need an assistant, you can convince Lord Atherton to get you one."

"Still . . ."

She laid a hand on his arm. "I am sorry, Harry. I am very fond of you. But once I became aware of my feelings for Gareth, I knew that I could marry no other man." She watched him carefully, praying she could prevent a rift between brothers. "Please say that we can remain friends. And that you will wish us happy."

"Of course we are friends. And if Gareth is the one you want . . ." He shrugged.

"Thank you, Harry. Your friendship means a great deal to me."

His expression suddenly brightened. "I can't wait until Gawaine gets back and hears the news. Won't he be stunned?"

"Don't you dare say a word to him until I have had my chance to speak. It would not be fair."

"Oh, all right. Although it would be amusing to see the look on his face when he hears the news." He stood again. "I suppose I should go wish Gareth happy."

"And tell him your news! He will be so pleased." She handed him the letter. "Be sure to show him this. And tonight at dinner we will have a celebration for you. I'll have Mrs. Jenkins fix a special treat."

From the look on his face, she saw that her remarks pleased him and she felt better.

She let out a deep sigh of relief when he had departed.

That had gone far better than she'd feared it would. But she'd also known that Harry did not hold a deep passion for her— his marriage offer had been motivated more by a desire to help her than by true love.

Now he had helped himself, and the castle too. She'd never expected him to come back with such stunning news. He was well on his way to becoming a respected historian.

Now, if things only went as smoothly when Gawaine returned.

They were all sitting at the dining table, lingering over the special cake Mrs. Jenkins had baked in honor of Harry's achievement, when Gawaine strode into the room and slapped his gloves down on the table.

"Congratulate me, brother," he said to Gareth, with a wide grin. "I have saved the castle."

Susanna immediately shot Harry a warning look. He squirmed in his seat, but remained quiet.

Gareth tilted back in his chair. "Do tell."

"In a few short days, we are hosting the first tournament of combat seen in this island in over two hundred years."

Gareth's chair legs hit the floor with a thump. "What?"

Ignoring him, Gawaine turned to Susanna and bowed. "And you, my lady, shall be the Queen of the Joust as I intend to be the victor."

"I am overwhelmed by the honor," Susanna said, trying to keep a straight face. "But how have you arranged all this?"

"And how do you intend to pay for it?" Gareth demanded.

Gawaine grabbed a chair and sat down. "That is the beauty of my plan. It will cost you nothing. In fact, it will earn you a tidy sum—minus my modest charge for organizing services."

"I knew there had to be a catch," Gareth muttered.

"But how can you stage an event like that in such a short time?" Susanna asked. "Who will come?"

"They're on their way already," Gawaine replied with a smug look.

"What?" Gareth exclaimed. "Good God, what have you done?"

"Relax." Gawaine's grin grew broader. " 'Stubby'—the Marquis of Eversdale to those not numbered among his close friends—has been planning this for months. All was set, the knights recruited, armor created, banners sewn, and stands erected—then his father decided he couldn't hold it at the Park because it would frighten the moor fowl or some such thing. Poor Stubby was in utter despair after all his work. I offered Belden and he jumped at the chance to hold his tournament at a real castle."

"Oh, no." Gareth groaned aloud. "Go on."

"We spent the last two days packing everything up. The first cart should arrive tomorrow and most of the guests the following day. The tournament is set for Saturday."

"Did it ever occur to you that we have no place to house these people—and no staff to deal with them?"

"Don't need to," Gawaine replied. "Either they're bringing their own tents—you should see the one St. Lowe had made, all in red silk and gold tassels—or they intend to sleep in the Great Hall, like the knights of old."

"That doesn't answer the problem of the servants."

"Every knight has his own page who can do double duty. And the ladies will all bring their maids."

Gareth glared at him. "Ladies? What kind of ladies?"

Gawaine drew himself up indignantly. "Respectable ones, of course. St Lowe's sister and some of her friends, and Stubby's cousins. You don't think I'd bring anyone disreputable to the *this* house, do you?" He shot a pointed glance at Susanna.

"What are these hordes of people going to eat?"

"That's all taken care of. Stubby's borrowed his father's cook, and he's sending a whole herd of pigs along. I don't suppose we could roast one in the Great Hall?"

"The chimney's stopped up," Harry announced.

"Then we'll have to roast it outside. Everything else will be ordered from York."

Gareth shook his head. "I do not see how you can put on something of such magnitude at the last moment and not expect it to cost a fortune."

"Oh, it will." Gareth grinned. "But Stubby *has* a fortune. He's paying for everything. This will be the talk of the town for years."

"I think it sounds like devilish fun," Harry said. "Are you going to have jousting with real poles?"

"Padded ones," Gawaine replied. "As well as mock sword fights and a grand melee at the end."

"What if someone gets hurt?" Susanna asked.

"That's why everyone has armor—or at least a lot of padding. You should see Stubby's rig—he found a complete suit in his attic. St. Lowe spent over a thousand on his outfit."

Susanna shook her head. A thousand pounds on something so frivolous?

Gareth threw up his hands. "I don't see where I have much of a choice, since people are already on their way. But I warn you, Gawaine, if I have to spend a single penny on this . . . this circus, it will come directly out of your flesh."

"I assure you, it will put money into your pocket." Gawaine leaned forward eagerly. "This is the best part—I'm charging Stubby for using the castle and the grounds."

Gareth's jaw dropped. "You're what?"

"It's no different than if he had to rent a theater to put on a play. He was quite agreeable to the whole idea."

"Dare I ask how much he is paying?"

Gawaine's grin widened. "Two thousand pounds."

Susanna gasped at his words. *Two thousand pounds.* Gareth should be ecstatic. She glanced over at him, but his expression remained impassive.

Ignoring the others, Gawaine turned back to Susanna and clasped her hand. "Now, I have some important business to attend to. May I be permitted to speak with you privately, my dear?"

Susanna darted a quick glance at Gareth, who nodded. She

could not delay this any longer, although she hated to dampen Gawaine's eager enthusiasm. "We can go into the drawing room," she said. "If you two will excuse me."

They all rose and Gawaine held open the door. He followed Susanna across the hall and into the drawing room.

"I was dismayed when I saw that Harry had arrived already," he said, while she took a seat on the sofa. "But then I realized he could not have possibly come up with such a grand plan."

"Harry did very well," Susanna said. "He's going to be writing some articles for the Royal Society of Historians, and he's been commissioned by Lord Atherton to write a book for him."

"That sounds like something Harry would find exciting. But will it bring in a penny to Belden? I think not."

"Money is not everything," she said.

"But you charged us to find something to help the castle. I think I have acquitted myself superbly, if I do say so myself."

"It does sound very exciting."

"The most exciting thing will be crowning you as the Queen of the Tournament. And being able to wear your token while I joust."

"Gawaine, we need to discuss this."

Something in her tone of voice must have given him warning, for his eyes narrowed with suspicion. "You didn't accept Harry, did you? Just because he came back first? I hardly think that fair."

"No, I am not going to marry Harry."

"Good. While I was at Stubby's I had a chance to talk with his uncle—the archbishop, you know. He said our situation is a bit unusual, and if we really wish to make certain that all is done right and legal, he says we should go to Scotland."

"Scotland?"

He nodded. "They don't have much in the way of rules up there. Don't care what name you're married under, as long

as you're willing. So there's no problem with your not knowing who you are."

Susanna hid her smile. Gawaine had neatly solved one of
her problems. Now she would not have to reveal her identity to anyone until she and Gareth were safely wed. It would
be one last little bit of insurance.

But she still had to deal with Gawaine.

"It was thoughtful of you to investigate the matter," she
said. "In truth, I had not thought of the complications it would
cause. But I—"

"That is what a husband is for, to take care of all those
awkward legal matters."

"Gawaine, I—"

"Now, with the tourney being on Saturday, the guests will
probably linger through Monday. Shall we start for the border on Tuesday? It will be a long trip, but we would arrive
late that evening."

"Gawaine, will you listen to me! I am not going to marry
you."

He looked at her with a stunned expression. "Why not?"

"While you and Harry were gone, I . . . well, Gareth and
I realized that we care very deeply for one another and we
are—"

"Gareth?" Gawaine jumped to his feet. "You are going to
marry that stick-in-the-mud? Why on earth would you want
to do that?"

"Gareth and I think very much alike," she said simply.
"We both feel strongly about having family, and a home. And
truly, I am not a very complicated person. I do not mind living here in the country where it is peaceful."

"Wonderful," he grumbled as he sat down again. "Now
how am I going to explain this to Stubby and the others? I
told them this would be our engagement celebration."

"*That* is your problem, not mine," she said. "You never
should have told them such a thing without the matter being
settled."

"I knew you weren't going to marry Harry. But Gareth . . . he didn't even participate in the quest."

"Perhaps, after all, he did," she said. Marrying her would certainly help the castle.

"How?"

"One day, you will understand. Gawaine, I am sorry to cause you hurt, but I cannot go against the wishes of my heart. You, with all your romantic notions, will understand that."

He scowled. "Well, at least you aren't marrying Harry. Don't think I could forgive you that."

She smiled. "I assure you, if I had not fallen in love with Gareth, you would have been my first choice. Harry is a dear, but—now don't you say a word of this to him! He's been quite the gentleman about things. And you should congratulate him for his accomplishments. He is well on his way to becoming a reputable scholar."

"At least if he's working for Lord Atherton, he'll be out of our hair." He stood up and bowed. "I am crushed, my lady, but with all the work I have to do to get ready for the tourney, I won't have too much time to dwell on my loss." He took her hand and raised it to his lips, then turned on his heel and departed.

Susanna sank back against the cushions, relief washing over her. Thank goodness that was over and done with. And Gawaine, like Harry, had taken the news well.

She could not wait to tell Gareth what his brother had learned from the archbishop. Now there was no need to obtain a Special License; why, they could leave for Scotland tomorrow!

And how ironic! This had all started with Jonathan taking her to Scotland against her will. And soon, she would gladly be going there with Gareth. A very satisfactory ending to what had once seemed an insurmountable nightmare. She would be a married lady in no time.

*   *   *

"You plan to leave for Scotland tomorrow?" Gawaine glared angrily at his brother. "What about the castle? And the tournament?"

"We will be back in plenty of time."

"But . . ."

Gareth gave Susanna a questioning glance. "Do you mind if we delay, my love?"

Susanna bit her lip. The tournament was scheduled for Saturday; Sunday was her birthday. Would there be enough time to marry if they waited?

"How long does it take to reach Scotland from here?"

"Most of a day," Gareth replied.

Susanna tensed. It meant waiting until the last minute. If anything went wrong, if they were delayed . . . the risk was too great. She looked at Gareth and shook her head.

"I think we should leave in the morning as planned," he announced. "We will still be back before the tournament starts."

Gawaine's crestfallen look caused Susanna to wince. She knew how much needed to be done to make the castle ready for guests; knew that if they were gone, Harry and Gawaine would have to do it all themselves.

She glanced at Gareth. "If we leave at first light on Sunday, can we still be wed that day? I must admit the thought of being married on Sunday has its charm."

"Are you certain?" Gareth grasped her hand. "It will mean a long day of traveling."

"I want the tournament to go well," she replied. "And I think we will need all the helping hands we can get to set things to right in time."

"Thank you," Gawaine said with a look of relief. "I will follow you all the way to the border, to ensure that your journey goes smoothly."

"Sunday it is, then," Gareth said, with only the hint of a sigh.

Chapter 15

Susanna awoke early the next morning, knowing that despite Gawaine's protests to the contrary, they faced a monumental task in getting the castle ready for guests. The men might be willing to play at being knights and sleep in tents or the Great Hall, but the ladies would want more civilized accommodations.

She had one day—two at best—to get the bedrooms in order. Mattresses needed to be turned, bedding aired, and the rooms swept and dusted. Mrs. Jenkins was arranging to bring in help, but Susanna knew she would have a very busy day.

However, she relished the challenge, for it would further show Gareth how helpful a wife she could be. She wanted to reassure him that he'd made the right choice. He knew she could assist with his accounts; now he would see that she could run a house as well. All those years of supervising her grandfather's staff had made her capable of managing a household twice this size.

But even managing a royal palace was not as important to her as Belden. She vowed to make Gareth proud of her by ensuring that all the domestic details were capably dealt with. The men could worry about their tournament activities; she would see to their comfort.

With one of Mrs. Jenkins's aprons wrapped around her dress, Susanna stepped into the hall and entered the small bedroom across from hers. It was time to get to work. She grabbed a broom and began sweeping.

She did not mind keeping busy. It gave her time to think

about Gareth, and their wedding, which would be simplicity in itself. Her main concern now was how to "regain" her memory without revealing to Gareth that she had been fooling him all along. Perhaps a faked fall with another "bump" to the head would suffice. Yet, remembering how bruised she'd been after the last time, she did not relish being that sore again.

Perhaps she could claim the trip to Scotland had restored her senses.

In fact, the more she thought of it, the better that idea sounded. She could tie it in with the whole terrible story of Jonathan and his kidnapping of her. And do it in such a way that Gareth would never suspect that she'd always known who she was. Now that she'd fallen in love with him, she did not want him to know she had not trusted him enough to share her secret.

And no matter how she tried to pretty the matter up, it was a lack of trust that had motivated her charade. At first, she had not trusted him to keep her safe from her family. Then, when she knew she was safe in that way, she did not trust him with the secret of her money, because deep inside, she did not trust him to really love *her* if he knew of her fortune.

That was the real reason she could never tell him.

Sighing, she turned to the windows and pulled them open, letting the pleasant Yorkshire breeze fill the room. There were worse secrets one could keep in a marriage. They both loved each other, and that was what mattered.

And how surprised Gareth would be when he discovered just how valuable a wife he had taken!

Gareth had expected Gawaine to be at his elbow first thing in the morning, demanding that he provide one item or another that he'd conveniently "forgotten" to plan for. To his surprise, when he went downstairs he learned that Gawaine had left for York at first light to carry out Stubby's instructions.

His brother had left a list, detailing all the furniture that needed to be moved into the Great Hall and a quick sketch of the plan for the tournament field outside the gate. Gareth had never seen his brother exert so much effort in his life. Perhaps this was a sign that Gawaine was turning over a new leaf.

He hoped so. He knew that in a very short time, life at the castle would change. Susanna would take her place as his wife, and the very thought made him grin widely. But once Harry departed for Atherton's, what would Gawaine do? Gareth could not imagine that he would stay here; he craved a more lively existence. But Gareth didn't like the idea of his brother returning to London with money in his pocket. That spelled trouble.

Yet Gareth had enough trouble of his own. He still agonized over how he was going to reveal the truth to Susanna. He wished he'd known Gawaine was going to York, for he would have asked him to look for the handbills. How easy it would be to bring one back and pretend shock and amazement at discovering her identity.

He knew he could never tell her that he'd always known who she was, fearing she would believe he had married her for the money. And he had not. Even at the first, when he'd learned she was a rich heiress, he had been more concerned about her safety and well-being. He did not trust the relatives who'd been searching for her and kept the knowledge from her from the best of motives—to protect her.

And later . . . when he'd feared she'd give her hand to Harry or Gawaine, it had not been the thought of losing the money that had struck at his heart—no, it had been the prospect of losing Susanna.

Even now, he could barely believe that she returned his feelings. That she was willing to share her life with him.

Would she still have made that choice if she knew who she was? Gareth did not want to think about that. He knew they would be happy together, and that was what mattered. He would take the lie with him to the grave.

With a sigh, he realized he had a great deal of work to do if the castle was to be ready for guests on the morrow. He still was not convinced that Gawaine's friends were that eager for the "authentic" experience as he claimed, but they would have no choice. Simple straw pallets in the Great Hall were all that he could provide.

And if anyone complained, he would lock them in the cellars. It was only a pity that Belden had no dungeon.

Gareth laughed. Knowing Gawaine's set, they would probably think it a privilege to be imprisoned in some dank, dark hole. As long as it was "authentic."

Gareth found Harry in the Great Hall, pacing off distances and jotting down numbers on a square of paper.

"I wish Gawaine had given us more time," he said. "We could have tried to unblock the chimney. And found some tapestries to hang on the walls . . . I fear it will not look like a real hall."

"Strew some greasy rushes on the floor and toss spoiled food about and it will take on the right atmosphere," Gareth observed dryly.

"I did tell Mrs. Jenkins to start baking bread so we can serve the food on trenchers," Harry said.

"What is a trencher?" Gareth asked.

"That's what they used for plates," Harry replied. "Flat, dried bread."

"And I suppose you intend for everyone to eat with their fingers—"

"Well, they can have knives," he said. "But no forks!"

"Harry, I don't wish to discourage you, but I really doubt Gawaine's guests want to experience medieval life as it really was. They still want all the comforts of the nineteenth century."

"Why bother to have a medieval joust at all, then?" Harry said sarcastically. "They should just stand about and shoot at each other with pistols. *That*'s the modern way of combat."

"Unfortunately, it's far too deadly. I'm worried enough that someone will get hurt as it is."

"I wish I was small enough to fit into the armor we have," Harry said. "Gawaine's friend is sure lucky."

"Ask him how lucky he feels after he's been wearing it for a while." Gareth frowned. "I suppose this means you want to participate in the tourney?"

Harry looked at him eagerly. "Can I? Oh, I do want to."

Despite his reservations, Gareth didn't have the heart to say no. "Just be careful not to break an arm or a wrist. You don't want to have to give up Atherton's commission."

"Oh, I'll be careful," Harry said. "Can I take whatever I need from the armory?"

"If Gawaine left anything."

The look of alarm on Harry's face was almost comical. "If he took all the good pieces, I'll . . . I'd better go see right now." He raced from the hall.

Gareth grinned widely. It had been wicked of him to tease Harry so, but he could not resist. He suspected Harry was even more excited about this event than Gawaine. The biggest problem would be putting a damper on his insistence of authenticity during the activities. These people were looking for entertainment, not real history.

Ah well, Gawaine would surely keep him in line if he became too overbearing.

He'd check back with Harry later, to be certain that the contents of the armory had not totally distracted him from his task of preparing the Great Hall. Gareth turned and went back to the new house, to see how Mrs. Jenkins was faring in getting the bedrooms readied for the ladies.

To his surprise, he found Susanna sweeping one of the small bedrooms, a large white apron wrapped around her dress and a kerchief tied about her head.

"What are you doing?" he asked.

She greeted him with a smile. "Sweeping."

He took the broom out of her hands. "You shouldn't be doing such menial tasks. Where is Mrs. Jenkins?"

"She's down the hall in the other room, showing the girl what to do. We've only the one helper so far, but she says her sister will be by later."

She took the broom back. "We need all the hands we can get if the rooms are to be habitable by tomorrow."

Gareth knew she was right but he did not like to see her working at a housemaid's tasks. "Can't you—?"

"Gareth, I truly don't mind helping. You work about the farm. The house is my realm of responsibility and I can't expect others to do what I am not prepared to do myself."

For the thousandth time, he thanked whatever fates had sent her to him. He was lucky beyond all measure.

"Then I shall help you," he announced, taking off his coat and rolling up his sleeves. "Has the mattress been turned yet?"

"No. Do you want me to help you?"

"I think I can manage."

Did he imagine it, or did he see a glint of amusement in her eyes? How hard could it be to turn a simple mattress?

He turned toward the bed, which had been stripped of all its coverings. Grabbing the long edge of the mattress, he lifted it off the bed frame and tried to flip it over, but it folded onto itself.

Gareth thought he heard a noise from Susanna, but when he turned to look at her, she was busily sweeping the floor.

He crossed to the other side of the bed and pulled the bottom edge of the mattress toward him, intending to flatten it out. Instead, the whole mattress slid toward him, still folded over like a pancake.

This time he knew she had laughed. He ignored her, jerking and tugging at the flopping material until he finally had it laying flat on the bedstead once again.

"See"—he turned toward her with a look of pride on his face—"that wasn't so hard."

"You still have to turn it around the other way," she said, barely smothering a grin.

He looked at the bed and groaned.

She set the broom against the wall and approached the foot of the bed.

"I'll take this end and you take the other and we shall turn it together. It is far easier."

"You're right," he admitted.

They managed with ease what he now realized would have taken him several frustrating minutes to do alone. He flashed her a grateful grin.

"I see I must learn to rely on your advice for household matters."

"Many tasks are easier when done by two," she said.

He stepped toward her. "You have a smudge of dust on your nose." He brushed it off with his finger.

They stood toe to toe. A few locks of hair escaped from the kerchief, giving her a mischievous look. Gareth thought he'd never seen a lovelier sight.

"I am the luckiest man in the word," he said, pulling her into his arms.

"Not as lucky as I."

He bent his head and kissed her gently. Life with her was going to be so wonderful.

In a few short days, they could start their life together.

"I do love you." He kissed the tip of her nose. "More than you can imagine."

"I can imagine a great deal," she replied, planting her own kiss on his mouth.

He tightened his hold on her, crushing her against his chest. *Oh, how he wanted this woman.* It was agony to hold her like this, knowing they could not be wed for several more days. He was tempted to carry her out of here, set her on a horse, and ride posthaste to Scotland, Gawaine and his tournament be damned.

A cough sounded from the doorway and Gareth lifted his

head. Mrs. Jenkins stood there, bucket in hand, a big grin on her face.

"Don't mind me," she said. "Just a little window cleaning to do."

With a deep sigh, Gareth released Susanna from his arms.

"We must get back to work," she said with a rueful look.

He nodded in agreement. But he intended to get her alone again as soon as he dared.

Exhausted, but pleased with all she had accomplished, Susanna settled beside Gareth on the sofa after dinner. Gawaine had ridden hard and just returned from York, with the news that he had taken care of most of the arrangements.

Harry stumbled through the door, his arms piled high, then dropped his load of tarnished metal into a heap in the middle of the floor. He looked at it disconsolately.

"None of this is any good," he said, darting an angry glance at Gawaine. "You took all the best pieces."

"One sword and a dented shield," Gawaine replied. "The rest of it is not worth the space it is taking up."

"But how am I going to joust without any armor?"

"Don't joust," Gawaine said.

Harry glared at him.

"Gawaine, you don't have armor, either. What are you going to do?" Susanna asked.

"I do not plan to get hit." He gave Harry a smug look.

"Easy to say," Gareth said. "I hope you are planning to wear some sort of padding."

"Of course I am," Gawaine said. "St. Lowe had a whole costume made, in case his armor wasn't completed in time, so he's loaning it to me."

"Well, Harry," Susanna said, "we shall just have to make you some padded garments of your own."

He looked at her joyously. "Would you?"

Gareth frowned. "I hardly think she has the time—"

"Harry must be able to joust," she insisted. "Mrs. Jenkins

can help me. We'll need a coat that's too large for you and
something to pad it with."

"I know just the thing," Harry said and dashed out of the
room.

"You are kind to do this for him," Gareth said.

"I do not mind." Susanna gave Gawaine a dark look. "And
you really must stop taunting your brother. This is as much
his adventure as yours."

"I had no intention of keeping him from the joust,"
Gawaine said with a chagrined expression. "I'd loan him my
own clothes. And he can have the sword and shield if he
wants them so badly."

"We shall see about those. But I intend for Harry to have
his own suit of clothing." She turned to Gareth. "Are you
certain you don't want to join the combat?"

He shook his head. "I have no intention of being a bruised
bridegroom—particularly if we have to travel all the way to
Scotland."

"This will be one for Harry's history book," Gawaine
drawled. "The first Gretna marriage in the history of the family."

"I find it rather romantic," Susanna said, smiling at Gareth.

He leaned closer and squeezed her hand. "So do I."

She felt herself blushing under his adoring gaze.

"Really, you two could show some consideration for my
broken heart," Gawaine said.

"Your heart is not broken," Susanna said. "Only your pride
is bruised."

"I see I shall have to look elsewhere for sympathy," he
said. "Perhaps one of Stubby's cousins will take pity on my
sad plight."

"You should thank me for saving you from a great doom,"
Gareth said, tossing Susanna a teasing look. "You see how
she leads me around by the nose, and we're not even married yet. I shudder to think how she will dominate me then."

"You will enjoy every minute of it," Susanna said.

Gareth grinned at her. "I know."

Gawaine flung up his hands and stood. "Gad. This is getting worse by the minute. I need to get some air."

The moment he shut the door, Gareth and Susanna burst out laughing.

"You are too awful," she said. "Telling him he is better off without me."

"But he is." Gareth's face was a picture of bland innocence. "You would ride roughshod over the boy."

"That will be when we know Gawaine is truly in love—when he allows a female to do that to him."

Gareth was leaning forward, surely intending to kiss her, when Harry dashed back into the room, his arms piled high with clothing and bedding.

"I think this will work," he said, lifting up a heavy greatcoat. "We can chop off the bottom. And these quilts will work for padding."

"Where did those come from?" Gareth asked suspiciously.

"My room," Harry admitted.

"Your good bed quilts?" Susanna asked.

Reddening, he nodded. "Please? They're the only thing thick enough. I don't need all of them."

Susanna hated to disappoint him—but it was such a waste of good bedclothing.

Then she remembered that she could afford to buy new bedding for the entire castle and not even notice the expense.

"Go get my sewing basket," she said. "How many layers of padding do you think you will need?"

Chapter 16

"They're here! They're here!"

Even through the closed windows of the dining room, Susanna heard Harry's eager calls. She glanced outside and saw him running across the courtyard to the tower gate.

She refocused her attention on her sewing and continued to stitch the quilt padding to the back of Harry's jousting coat. Even if she wished to, she dare not go tearing out into the courtyard to greet the guests. Her position required a more mature response. The new arrivals would be presented to her in good time.

The thought made her smile. She acted as if she was already the lady of the house. Something that would not be final until she and Gareth made their trip to Scotland.

If only the tournament had not delayed their plans; if only they were already married. Each time Gareth touched her he created sensations that made her feel hot and cold at the same time. Even three days seemed a horribly long time to wait.

How marvelous it would be if one of Gawaine's friends would recognize her. There would be no need to fabricate a story for Gareth. Her memory could "gradually" return, and it would be too late for her uncle or Jonathan to stop the marriage. She hoped Gareth would be thrilled with the news of his good fortune.

She was proud of the work she'd done here in the last two days. Susanna felt confident that everything within the house was in order. Oh, there was bound to be some sort of crisis, but at least it would not be of monumental propor-

tions. If worse came to worst, she would turn the family—
including herself—out of their beds. Harry had already vol-
unteered to give up his room, proclaiming that he'd sleep in
the Great Hall as his ancestors had. Gawaine had snorted derisively and insisted he intended to enjoy the comfort of his
own bed.

It all depended on how many people arrived—and of which
sex. The ladies might have to share a bed, but Susanna was
determined that they would all have a bedroom to sleep in.

She looked forward to having some female companionship. Susanna had never been comfortable in the company of
other women—too often they resented her for the attention
her fortune attracted. These women would be ignorant of that,
and perhaps they would get along well.

Gareth stepped into the drawing room. He looked very
handsome in his dark green coat, top boots, and breeches.
Would that her wedding was today!

"Did you hear?" she asked. "Someone must be arriving.
Harry dashed out to greet them."

"I think the entire county heard." He sat down beside her
and slipped an arm around her shoulder, drawing her close
for a long, lingering kiss.

"Three more days," he whispered with a trace of longing
in his voice.

"I know," she replied.

He sat back and looked at the work in her lap. "Are you
still working on that coat?"

"It is nearly done," she said. "I can't guarantee that Harry
will not come to any harm while wearing it, but he should
be fairly well-protected."

Gareth pulled a long face. "That is what I fear most—
someone will be seriously injured during this playacting."

She patted his hand. "Do not worry. All will go well, they
will have the time of their lives, and Belden's fame will grow
far and wide."

"Why doesn't that make me feel better?" he grumbled.

"Every nincompoop in the kingdom will be coming here to play knight if we are not careful."

"I do not think you need to worry about that. I doubt the rage for jousting will last beyond the Season. Some new activity will catch their fancy next year."

"I hope so."

"Do you know any of the men coming with the marquis?"

"More by reputation than personal acquaintance," he said. "I don't exactly mingle with Eversdale's set. They're above my touch—in rank as well as finances."

"I can see why Gawaine has run into trouble in London if he is trying to keep up with them."

"At least he will come away from this circus with some money—enough to pay his pressing debts and then some. But I'm afraid he will be under the hatches soon enough once he heads back to town."

"We shall just have to find something else to capture his attention," Susanna declared.

Gareth shrugged. "I don't think there's much of a future in planning mock tournaments."

Susanna tapped him lightly on the nose. "I mean we need to find him an eligible female."

He laughed. "I don't think you will find the right sort among these guests, I fear. They are far out of reach for the second son of an impoverished baron."

"Even a duke has second and third daughters—or nieces." She flashed him a confident smile. "We shall find someone for him—if not among this group, in another."

"If he pulls this tournament off without a hitch, I will scour the country myself to find him a worthy bride," Gareth said.

Susanna jabbed him in the side. "I fear you will be too busy to do that."

He arched a brow. "Oh?"

"Once I am wed, I do not intend to let my husband out of my sight for more than a few hours. Gawaine will have to wait."

He grinned and brought her hand to his lips. "As you wish."

A light tap sounded on the door and Mrs. Jenkins stepped in.

"Master Gawaine announces that his guests are in the courtyard."

Gareth rose. "We must go greet them." He held out his hand to Susanna. "Come, my love. You are the mistress of the castle in all but name."

She took his hand and they walked down the hall and into the yard.

They were greeted by a scene of pure chaos as at least fifteen or twenty people, horses, grooms, and three pigs milled about. The noise was deafening. Susanna heard Gawaine yelling over the fray, giving directions to the stables, telling the lads where to put the pigs, and pointing to the door of the Great Hall.

"Perhaps we will wait inside." Gareth grabbed Susanna around the waist and pulled her back through the door. He hurried her through the passage to the Hall, and stood back as the wide doors were thrown open and the would-be knights flowed in. The rafters echoed with the noise of their booted feet scraping against the stone floor.

"They don't look much like knights right now," Susanna whispered in Gareth's ear. "It looks more like the hunt passing through."

"Gareth!" Gawaine hailed them from the door and pushed through the crowd toward them, dragging a round-faced, blond young man with him. "Stubby, here she is. The woman who broke my heart. The Fair Elaine."

Stubby bowed and Susanna, mindful that she was greeting a future duke, curtsied low. It was obvious where he'd gotten his appellation—the top of his head was level with her eyes.

"My brother, Baron Lindale." Gawaine continued the introductions. "The Marquis of Eversdale."

Stubby waved him off. "No need for titles here. Eversdale

will do." He glanced around the hall. "Wonderful place you have here, Lindale. Could have knocked me over with a feather when your brother offered it for our little tournament. Perfect site, perfect site. 'Preciate you taking us in on such short notice."

"It is my pleasure," Gareth said.

Susanna resisted the temptation to laugh at his little falsehood. She knew he wanted this to go smoothly, for Gawaine's sake, if not his own.

"I look forward to the arrival of your cousins," Susanna said.

Stubby nodded. "They should arrive sometime tomorrow."

"Traveling by coach is always slow," Gawaine explained.

"Ho! Stavely!" A dark-haired man came loping across the call. He came to a sudden halt in front of Susanna and executed a flourishing bow. "My lady, it is an honor."

"Leave off, Blevins; she's going to marry my brother," Gawaine said.

"The dull historian?" The man named Blevins regarded her doubtfully.

"The dashing baron," Susanna corrected him, casting Gareth a teasing smile.

Blevins slapped Gawaine on his back. "Alas, I share your pain at the loss. You even managed to understate her charms."

He held out his hand to Gareth. "Viscount Blevins. You're a lucky man, Lindale."

"I agree," Gareth replied, and squeezed Susanna's fingers.

Blevins turned to Susanna, and bowed again. "You, my lovely lady, may call me Percy. It would be an honor to serve such a beautiful damsel. I am at your service for the length of my stay."

"Why, thank you," Susanna said, taken aback by his courtly air.

"He's been dying to practice his version of chivalry on someone," Gawaine explained. He glanced back at the door. "Do you think we should see how St. Lowe is managing with his tent?"

Stubby nodded. "Probably has it wrapped around himself by now."

"I am looking forward to seeing this tent myself," Gareth said, and held out his arm to Susanna. "Shall we take in the sight, my lady?"

"With pleasure," she replied.

That night at dinner, Gareth presided over what he suspected was one of the most motley group of guests ever gathered under the roof at Belden.

Harry, in his enthusiasm, had unearthed some battered trestle tables in an abandoned corner of the castle and with the help of a hammer and nails had turned them into serviceable furniture. He had not been able to persuade Mrs. Jenkins to serve the meal on crusts of bread, however, and they were dining off a mismatched assortment of plates—albeit without their forks and spoons, which Harry had firmly banned.

And no one seemed to mind in the least. They were far too busy boasting of their prowess with the jousting pole, or placing bets on how tomorrow's practice would go, to pay much attention to what they ate or drank.

He glanced at Susanna who, according to Harry's instructions, sat beside him in the medieval custom. She was engaged in conversation with St. Lowe, whose tent was truly as ostentatious as Gawaine had described it. Gareth almost felt sorry for the others, whose staid pavilions paled by comparison with its tasseled splendor.

Watching her now, he was filled with pride. She had stepped effortlessly into her role as hostess and already had a coterie of loyal retainers who followed her about, eager to perform any chore she requested.

He'd been half afraid, half hoping that someone would recognize her, but no one had said a word. He still had to find a way to reveal the truth to her when they returned from Scotland. But for now, he pushed that worry aside and vowed to enjoy himself. The antics of Gawaine's friends would prove most amusing over the next few days, and as soon as they were finished, he and Susanna would be off to the border to start their married life together.

Susanna tossed him a swift glance and her eyes filled with joy as she caught his gaze. He smiled, delighted to see her enjoying herself like this. Life at Belden was rather tame on a day-to-day basis, and once they were wed, he would do more to provide entertainment for her. And to take her both to York and London, if she so desired.

Anything to keep her happy.

When the meal was over and the last plate cleared away, he took Susanna's hand and they slipped back into the main house.

"We'll leave them to their revels," he said as they hastened down the connecting corridor, leaving the Great Hall behind them.

"They will notice we have left," she said.

"I do not care." He pulled her into the darkened drawing room and drew her into his arms.

It was exquisite torture to hold her like this, imagining the delights that would soon be his, yet knowing he had to wait. Only three days until he could make her his, in name and in body.

"I wish the wedding was behind us," she whispered.

"Have you taken up divination?" he asked. He lifted her chin with his finger so he could look into her dark eyes. "I had the exact same thought."

"I never realized love would be like this," she said, her gaze never leaving his. "Wanting another person so deeply, hating every moment that you are out of my sight."

"I promise that you will be thoroughly sick of me within a week of our marriage," he said with a short laugh. "I do not intend to leave your side for a minute."

He kissed her sweet lips, knowing it would only add to his torment, but needing to touch her, to feel her, to assure himself that this was real.

"Gareth?"

"Hmm?"

"What is it like for you, when you kiss me?"

He closed his eyes. What could he say? That he was flooded with desire such as he'd never known, one that made him want to forget that he was a gentleman?

"I feel," he said at last, "that I am the luckiest man on earth."

"Only because I am the luckiest woman." She stood on tiptoe and gave him a long, intimate kiss that left him aching with frustration.

When she finally drew away, he put his hands on her shoulders. "If you kiss me like that again, I am not answerable for the consequences.

The look she gave him said she was well aware of that.

He took a step back. "Ah, do not tempt me, my love. We will be so busy the next two days, we will not have time to think of ourselves."

"Liar." She gave him a teasing grin.

Gareth laughed. "You are a minx. Now upstairs with you, before I forget all my resolve."

With a sigh, she drew her arms from his waist and started for the door. She halted in the doorway, and looked back at him.

"Three days," she said, and blew him a farewell kiss.

The moment she was gone, Gareth groaned aloud.

In the morning, following a hard practice, Gawaine and his "knights" sat in the shade of the viewing stand, clustered about Susanna, trying to impress her with their accomplishments.

It almost reminded her of being in London, when she'd been constantly surrounded by fortune-hunting fools. These men were only paying her tribute because she was the lone female at the castle. Susanna knew that once the other ladies arrived, she would be roundly ignored.

"Are you going to let me wear your token tomorrow?" Percy asked for the hundredth time.

She laughed. "Percy, I told you I promised it to Gawaine days ago."

"He could wear it while he's jousting and then give it to me when he's done."

"And what if you two meet each other in combat?" she asked.

Percy frowned. "Tear it in two parts?"

The loud "halloo" of a coachman's horn sounded and they all turned to look at the carriages coming up the lane.

Gawaine jumped to his feet and peered at the approaching vehicles. "Stubby, I think it's your cousins."

"And we were having such a good time," Stubby grumbled good-naturedly. "Now it will be 'Stubby, get me this' and 'Stubby, do that.' They treat me like a servant."

"You're a marquis," one of the others protested. "Assert your authority."

"Hah!" Stubby replied as he stood up. "You watch."

Two carriages pulled up and footmen jumped down from the perch and pulled down the steps. Gawaine was first to reach the door of the nearest one, extending his hand to the lady who stepped out and looked curiously about. To Susanna's amusement, he executed a low bow and the lady responded with a flirtatious giggle.

Susanna turned to Gareth, who was still at her side, and pointed to his brother. "I think Gawaine's broken heart is well on the way to being mended."

"Or dashed to pieces," he said. "That's St. Lowe's sister, if I'm not mistaken." He stood up and held out his hand to help her. "Let us find out."

They walked over to the carriages, which had disgorged their visitors. Stubby approached them with a woman even shorter than he on his arm.

"Lindale, my cousin Lady Emma Merritt. Lord Lindale, and his bride to be. Whose name we really don't know so we're calling her Lady Elaine."

Stubby's cousin regarded her with a curious air. "You really do not know who you are? How intriguing. I do love a good mystery!"

"Well, she won't be a mystery lady for very long," Gareth said, putting an arm around her waist. "She will be Lady Lindale come Sunday."

"Welcome to the castle," Susanna said. "I warn you, life here is a bit rustic."

"Stubby says we are going to have a jolly good time so I don't mind," Lady Emma said and turned to her cousins. "Stubby, would you get my reticule from the carriage? I seemed to have forgotten it."

With an "I told you so" look at Gareth and Susanna, he left to do Lady Emma's bidding.

"Is that handsome creature talking with Aurelia your brother?" she asked, glancing toward Gawaine.

"The very same," Gareth replied. "And Stubby left strict orders that you were not to go near him."

Lady Emma laughed. "Because he is improvident? Most of Stubby's friends are."

As if sensing he was under discussion, Gawaine broke away from the throng and came over.

"Did you see that? She talked with me! Matters are looking well."

"Dare I inquire the lady's name?" Susanna asked.

"Miss Aurelia Millbank. St. Lowe's cousin," he replied. "Isn't she the loveliest creature?"

"I thought I was," Susanna said, keeping a straight face.

Gawaine flushed. "Well, I mean . . ."

"At least he said that about you," Lady Emma said with a wry expression. "He's never once commented on my beauty."

"That's because you're Stubby's cousin and everyone knows you're going to marry him," Gawaine replied.

"Perhaps I shall change my mind."

Gawaine laughed loudly. "That's a hoot. Toss away all those millions? Not likely! No sense wasting compliments on you."

Susanna tapped him on the arm with her fan. "Behave yourself."

"I cannot help it." He grinned widely. "The prettiest lady is always the one I am courting at the moment."

"Well, there's no courting to be done here, so be off." Gareth put a possessive arm around Susanna's waist.

Lady Emma took her arm and drew her toward the carriages. "Come, you must be introduced, Lady Lindale. You don't mind if I call you that, do you? I mean, you are going to be Lady Lindale in a few days and it does seem better to call you by a name that will be yours rather than one that isn't yours at all."

Susanna nodded at the logic and allowed herself to be pulled forward.

"This is my sister, Beth, and cousin Helene. Aurelia, you should be careful with Gawaine! He is on the hunt after this lovely lady jilted him."

"I did not jilt—"

"Of course you didn't," Lady Emma said. "Miss Meadows, and Lady Sara, and here"—she paused before a tall brunette, dressed in an exquisite traveling gown with a bored expression on her face—"is Lady Katherine. Everyone, this is Lady Lindale-to-be."

"This is going to be so much fun." Beth squealed and clapped her hands. "Living in a real castle! And real knights, jousting for their lady's honor."

"It's all rather silly," Lady Katherine said. She glanced at Susanna. "I understand your brother-in-law is going to be my father's librarian."

"Librarian?" Susanna wrinkled her forehead as she tried to grasp the connection. "Oh, you mean Harry? You must be Lord Atherton's daughter, then."

Lady Katherine nodded and turned to Emma. "Emma, dear, cannot we go inside? I am dreadfully weary after all this traveling."

"Come, I shall show you all to your rooms," Susanna said,

suddenly filled with misgivings that the castle accommodations would be far beneath their expectations.

Yet there was nothing they could do about it now. If the ladies had a miserable time, they would only have their brothers and cousins and friends to blame for dragging them along.

Jonathan Wilding led his sweat-stained horse into the inn yard at the Seven Feathers in York. He'd been in the saddle since early light, and he was willing to swear on a stack of his unpaid bills that Susanna was not anywhere south of here.

What if they'd been wrong all along? He'd always assumed she would travel south, toward her home and friends, and had concentrated the search in that direction. Had she been one step ahead of them, realizing that's what they'd think, and fled north instead, hoping to fool them?

It made perfect sense. Damn that girl anyway! She'd probably been only a few hours north of York all this time, laughing at them.

Well, she would not be laughing much longer. He'd get a bite to eat and then continue his search—there were still a few hours of daylight left and he did not intend to waste them. Time was critical. He had to get her across the border before midnight on her birthday, only three days hence.

He found the inn surprisingly full for a midweek evening and was forced to sit in the taproom instead of gaining a private parlor.

"Why such a crowd?" he asked the barmaid as she brought him a tankard of ale.

"All sorts of travelers passing through," she said. "There's some big doings goin' on up at Belden Castle."

"Where is Belden Castle?" He'd never heard of the place. Probably some minor estate with a pretentious owner.

"'Tis to the north," she replied. "One of the oldest castles in England, or so it's said."

"Whose property is it?" he asked.

"The Baron Lindale," she said. "There's going to be an enormous gathering up there in two days. All York's abuzz with the news. They've been ordering food and supplies enough for an army."

"That should make the local merchants happy," he said. He glanced about the walls, noting that none of the posters advertising Susanna's disappearance were still here. He'd have to have a chat with that lawyer they'd hired.

"Tell me, do you recall the search for a missing young lady a few weeks back? There were handbills displayed all over York."

"I remember," she said.

"I don't suppose you've heard any rumors about her whereabouts. There's a hefty reward if she's found."

"I might have 'eard something."

"What do you know?" he demanded harshly.

She took a step back and he forced himself to smile. He did not want to frighten her. "She's my cousin and the whole family is worried sick." He set two shillings on the table. The girl grabbed the coins and slipped them into her pocket.

"Some says all these preparations are for a wedding up at the castle."

"So?"

"No one knows who the bride is"—she leaned forward and glanced about before continuing—"including the bride."

"What are you talking about?"

The girl tapped her head. "Forgotten who she is, or so they say."

"That's the most useless . . ." His voice trailed off. Could she be talking about Susanna? Was that why they hadn't found her, because she'd had an accident and could not remember her name? It would explain a great deal.

But it was only a rumor, after all. Why on earth would anyone want to marry a strange woman with no memory? The whole tale sounded suspicious.

His heart started pounding. Unless, of course, the story about losing her memory was a hum and Susanna had persuaded some gullible country yokel to marry her so she could keep the money. Now *that* made sense. He never really thought she'd be foolish enough to throw all that money away.

Jonathan jumped to his feet. "How do I get to this castle?" he demanded.

She shrugged. "I've never been there. To the north it is."

"How far? A few hours? A day? Farther?"

The girl shook her head.

Exasperated, Jonathan stomped out of the taproom and pushed open the door to the yard. The ostler would know.

After assuring himself of the directions, Jonathan returned to the taproom and called for his dinner. He had no intention of traveling farther on an empty stomach. And it might prove more valuable to linger in York tonight, to see if he could pick up any more news about this mysterious woman at the castle.

It was possible that this woman was not Susanna, or that the story wasn't even true. He had plenty of time to reach this castle tomorrow and see for himself. But he might also save himself some time—and a night spent in a backwater inn instead of the comfortable Feathers—if he asked more questions in town.

First, he'd go find that solicitor they'd hired and see if he had any more news. Then he'd start making inquiries in some of the taprooms in York. An inquisitive barkeep might know a great deal more than the most learned man of the law.

And if he discovered no new information, he'd ride on to the castle tomorrow. It was a slim lead, but the first one they'd had and worth investigating.

He fully intended to find that wretched female in time.

Chapter 17

The morning of the tournament dawned with bright sunshine. Susanna hoped it was a good omen.

From her window, she watched the bustling activity in the courtyard below. The competition was not set to begin for a while, but already the knights were strutting about in their colorful garb. She saw Harry darting through the throng, a broad grin on his face. He was certainly enjoying his visit with the past.

She wondered what he thought of Lord Atherton's daughter.

Dressing quickly, Susanna headed downstairs. While Harry, Gawaine, and the others were looking forward to today, she could not wait until tomorrow, and her marriage to Gareth.

The dining room was deserted, so after eating a quick breakfast, Susanna left the house and walked down to the tourney field.

It looked like the proper setting for a spectacle. The combat arena was marked off by ribbon-bedecked ropes. Flags fluttered from poles at each corner and at one end stood the viewing stand—transported from Stubby's estate. The ladies were to sit there and cheer on their champions.

"Doesn't it look wonderful?" Harry appeared at her elbow. "I can't wait for the jousting to start."

"Please be careful," she said. "Gareth would not forgive himself if you or Gawaine are hurt."

"I will be safe," he said, plucking at his sleeve. "Your handiwork will protect me."

"Susanna is right." Gareth stepped up beside them. "If you so much as damage a single hair on that head, you'll have to answer to me."

"Don't worry, I'm going to win," Harry said with a cocky grin, before he walked away.

"I am so glad you are not going to participate in this silliness," Susanna said. "I am worried enough about your brothers."

"If they survived their childhood here at the castle, they'll survive this," he said. He fished around in his pocket and drew out a gaily wrapped package. "I know the tradition is for the lady to give her token to the knight, but since I am not jousting . . ."

Susanna took the package and eagerly unwrapped it. Inside were hair ribbons of every shade of blue.

"It is not much," he said with a shy smile. "I shall buy you a proper wedding present. But for today . . ."

Susanna stood on tiptoe and kissed his cheek. "They are lovely, Gareth. I shall wear them in my hair and tie them to my sleeves. I will be the most decorated lady in the stand."

He gave her a swift hug. "One more day," he whispered in her ear.

Soon the signal came for the knights to ready themselves and Susanna made her way to the tourney field. She waved at Gareth, saluted Harry, and slowly made her way through the growing throng to the viewing stand. It looked as if half of Yorkshire had come to watch the spectacle.

She took her seat on the platform and leaned forward with a mixture of eagerness and apprehension to watch the first joust.

It was St. Lowe, resplendent in his shiny new armor, facing one of the unarmored knights. She prayed no one would be injured.

Eversdale, acting as jousting master, dropped the flag and the two men spurred their horses forward, lances lowered, thundering toward one another. Susanna sucked in her breath, cringing in anticipation of the collision.

The two men raced past each other without striking a blow.

They reined in the horses and turned about, ready to start a new charge. Eversdale again signaled and the horses rushed forward.

Susanna closed her eyes.

The loud thud of wood on metal told her something had been hit and she dared a glance. The one knight was on the ground, signaling he was all right, while St. Lowe circled the arena in triumph. The ladies beside her clapped.

Susanna knew by the time that Gawaine and Harry rode, she would be frantic with worry.

Jonathan, mingling with the crowd surrounding the jousting field, edged closer to the wooden platform where the ladies from the castle were seated. If the unknown woman was Susanna, no doubt that was where she would be.

He squinted hard, trying to make out their faces, but he was still too far away. He elbowed his way past a fat farmer and crept closer. Jonathan had no desire for Susanna to recognize him—if indeed, she was here at all.

A huge roar sounded from the crowd and he took advantage of the excitement to push toward his goal. From this point he should be able to—there. The dark-haired woman in the middle. She was staring intently at the jousting field, displaying only her profile.

Turn this way, he begged silently. *Just a slight turn of the head . . .*

It was her. His heart pounded. He'd found Susanna at last. He was not going to lose the money after all!

Jonathan quickly backed away, making certain he kept out of her sight. He could not confront her in front of all these people. No, he would have to find a way to approach her secretly. At least this mob would be a help—no one would mark his presence; strangers at the castle would not arouse any excitement.

He wondered anew if she was really suffering from a loss of memory. He needed to find out; if she was, it would make his task far easier. He could then come forward and claim her for his cousin, and she would not know to protest.

If she was shamming, however, his task was more complicated. But even that could work to his benefit. The threat of exposing her secret might give him the chance to talk with her privately.

Once he had her alone, he would grab her and be on his way before anyone noticed she was gone. That would take delicate planning.

First, he must determine her state of mind. But how? He considered for a moment. He'd have to test her, see if she reacted to the mention of her name. He'd send her a note, addressed to Susanna Chadwick. From concealment, he could watch and gauge her reaction. If she looked puzzled, he was in luck. He could come to the rescue of his poor, lost cousin.

And if she displayed the merest glimmer of recognition . . . well, he would then have to take the other approach.

If she was pretending not to know who she was, she might be very interested in keeping that information quiet. She'd agree to meet with him then.

And once he had her in his clutches, he'd gag her and bind her and toss her into the carriage and head for the border. No more kind treatment until they were safely wed.

He retreated to where he'd left the gig and rummaged through his luggage until he found his writing box and began penning his note.

Susanna fanned herself against the rising afternoon heat. She felt sorry for the jousters, who must be sweltering beneath their heavy clothes and armor. But they all gamely struggled on and looked to be enjoying themselves.

She glanced across the arena, searching for Gareth. He'd stuck to his decision not to joust, but had taken on the role of squire for both his brothers. Gawaine had ridden in one of the first rounds, and unseated his opponent, and Harry was due to meet his challenge soon.

She felt a tug at her skirt and looked down. One of the ladies' maids handed her a note. She unfolded it eagerly, expecting to see some words from Gareth.

The noise of the crowd masked her gasp as she read the words printed on the paper.

> Susanna Chadwick: I know who you are. Before I
> reveal this information to everyone, I think we should
> speak. I will write again soon, to arrange a meeting.

With trembling fingers, she folded the paper and hastily stuffed it into the pocket of her gown.

She had been wrong. One of the guests *had* recognized her.

Yet this was not a disaster. In fact, it would solve her worst problem. But something about the tone of the note made her uneasy. She sensed the hint of a threat—although what could anyone threaten her with? Her only crime had been pretending to lose her memory. Someone could make all the accusations that they wanted, but they could never prove that she'd been faking.

However, even the implication would be bad enough. Gareth would be shocked—and highly disappointed. He was such an honorable man. What would he think of her if he learned the truth?

A cold tendril of fear crept up her spine. Was it possible that she would lose him if he knew what she had done?

She shook her head, striving to quell her growing apprehension. She was reading far too much into this note. The person only wanted to spare her distress by speaking with her privately first.

But why wait? Why not meet with her now? What was the point in delay?

Unless this person did not want to be seen talking with her.

Dread welled up inside her. Had Jonathan managed to find her?

She glanced up in alarm, quickly scanning faces in the crowd, but it was a futile action. In this crush, she might never see him.

Calm yourself. Why would he be here? And even if he was, he certainly would not want her to know. His only advantage lay in surprise. He would not have sent her this note and put her on her guard. No, this note had to be from one of the guests, who'd chosen to remain silent until today, for whatever reason.

She glanced out onto the tourney field, but all the excitement had gone from the day. She would not feel easy again until she had met with this person, and learned what they wanted from her. For they wanted something, she was sure of it.

What if she destroyed the note and pretended she'd never received it? Even if the person later revealed her secret, she could express delight in knowing her name and eagerly ply them with questions about her life. Meeting with the sender would only confirm that she did know who she was. And that she could not do—she did not want Gareth to know she'd been lying to him.

Her mind made up, Susanna turned her attention back to the knights on the tourney field. From this moment on, she would pretend that the note never existed.

She had to ignore it. The risk was too great.

The moment Susanna opened the note, Jonathan knew. There'd been no look of puzzlement on her face; no, that expression had been pure shock, followed by a frantic visual search of the crowd. Susanna Chadwick was in full possession of all her mental faculties.

Now that he knew, he would plan accordingly.

It meant he could not confront her openly, for she'd throw

his earlier kidnapping attempt into his face and he'd never get her out of here. No, he would have to use his other plan, to lure her away from the castle and then overpower her.

He only needed to make certain that she would agree to meet him—alone.

But now that he knew she had been pretending all along . . . *Tsk tsk.* What a shameful way to start a marriage. What would the baron say when he discovered that his future bride had been lying to him? Surely, he'd be most displeased.

Displeased enough that Susanna would not want him to know? That's what he'd gamble on. It was the threat he needed to get her to meet with him. If she was playing the game he thought she was, she'd be more than eager to keep the news quiet. The truth would hurt her more than it would hurt him.

The more he thought on it, the more he realized that he should reveal himself to her. Once she knew from whence the threat came, she'd be even more eager to speak to him. If she was so dead set on marrying this baron, she might be willing to pay a pretty penny to keep her secret hidden. He could let her think that he was only interested in a bit of blackmail . . .

Jonathan had no intention of letting her marry the man, but he would allow her to think that.

He grinned to himself. His plan was getting better and better. He'd send her a new note, demanding a meeting. By the time nightfall arrived, she'd be frantic with worry over what he might do and would gladly talk with him.

Frantic enough that she would not be as cautious as she should. All it took was a few quick moves on his part and she'd be trussed up like a goose. And across the border by tomorrow afternoon, and he'd soon have every single penny of her fortune in his hands.

Despite her resolve to ignore the note, the remainder of the joust passed in a blur for Susanna. She could not think; she could not concentrate. She barely noticed when Harry took

his first ride, or when Gawaine vanquished his second foe.
All she could think about was the person who'd sent her the
note, what they wanted from her, why they'd chosen to approach her this way.

She didn't even start when a new note suddenly was
handed to her.

For a moment, she wanted to tear it into pieces. If she
did not intend to meet with this person, there was no need
to read any more of the messages. She would just have to
wait for the inevitable disclosure and try to brazen her way
out of it.

But curiosity got the best of her and she finally unfolded
the missive.

> I think the baron would be sadly disappointed to
> learn that his bride-to-be has been pulling the wool
> over his eyes. Don't you agree? I feel we should
> discuss the matter privately. I will let you know
> when the time is right.

A wave of dizziness passed over her. It was worse than she'd
even thought. This person wanted to cause trouble, wanted
to put up a barrier between her and Gareth.

But why?

She glanced about again and carefully scrutinized the gentlemen standing alongside the tourney field. As her gaze
moved from one face to another she suddenly locked eyes
with one of the bystanders.

Jonathan.

Her stomach lurched and Susanna feared she was going
to be ill. She staggered to her feet and, tripping over the
others, raced to the edge of the platform. She ignored the
helping hands extended to her, jumped to the ground, and
ran toward the castle. On reaching her room, she slammed
the door shut and twisted the key in the lock, then flung herself on the bed.

What was she going to do? Jonathan was here. Gareth

would keep her safe from him—but at what price? Jonathan's presence could only mean disaster. She did not need his threatening notes to tell her that.

He did not need to tell Gareth the truth to ruin everything. He could play along with her subterfuge, express delight at finding his missing cousin, and claim he wished to restore her to her "worried" family. She'd have to confess then, in order not to go with him. Jonathan wouldn't have to say a word—she'd be forced to make the explanations.

She would have to tell Gareth her tale—that she'd been lying to him and his brothers from the start. Because she had not trusted them, either with her safety or her fortune.

Susanna did not even want to contemplate how Gareth would react to the news.

She never should have lied to him. Or at least, once she realized he would keep her safe from Jonathan and her uncle, she should have told him the truth.

But she'd been selfish. Selfish, because she wanted the chance to attract a man without him knowing about her money. And she'd succeeded—he'd fallen in love with the poor, unfortunate girl he thought she was.

What could she say to him now? That it had all been a test? He'd be hurt, angry, and humiliated. And surely would not wish to marry her.

Except of course, for the matter of her money. Only a fool would throw that away, no matter how cruelly he'd been deceived.

She beat the pillow with her fists. She could still buy herself a husband. But with Gareth she'd wanted it to be different. She'd wanted him to want *her.*

Now, with her cousin here, she had no choice. She had to go to Gareth, and tell him the truth, before Jonathan interfered. He would twist everything and make it sound even worse.

What Gareth would say, she could only guess, but it was the only way. If there was a chance—any chance—that he would still want her, it would have to be because she was able to make him understand her motives. It would be a hard thing to explain, but she had to try. Her future happiness depended on it. She had to convince Gareth that she'd been terribly wrong to lie to him, but had felt at the time that she'd had no choice.

If only he would agree with her. But she did not want to hold out hope where there was little. He'd been slighted once by a woman and she did not think he would take kindly to knowing that he'd been wrongly treated by another.

Gareth rapped sharply on Susanna's door.

"Are you all right, my love?" He'd raced to the castle the moment he'd heard she had fled, fearing she was ill.

A muffled moan came from inside the room. He tried the door, but it was locked.

"What is wrong? Let me in!"

He heard light steps cross the floor, the key turned in the lock and the door opened. Susannah stood there, her face tearstained.

"Good God, what is wrong?" He rushed to her, holding out his arms. "What has happened?"

She turned away and stared out the window. "Everything," she said.

He looked at her, puzzled, confused by her despair.

"Was the jousting too much? Or the sun? I knew we should have provided shade for the ladies."

She turned around and looked at him, the expression on her face bleak.

"It was not any of those things, Gareth." She gestured toward the chair. "Please, sit down. There is something I must tell you."

Instead, he stepped toward her and took her hand. "You worry me, my love. I do not want to see you like this."

"Perhaps you will after you hear what I have to say." Her voice was filled with unexpected bitterness. "Please sit, so I may get through this."

Bewildered, he released her hand and sat down. What could she possibly say to him that would be so terrible?

Fear clutched at his heart. *She was not going to marry him after all.* This could not be happening to him a second time. Just this morning she'd been so happy, smiling and laughing with him as they'd shared a few private moments in the drawing room. What could have gone wrong?

He watched her as she paced the length of the room and then stopped before the windows.

"I have perpetrated a great sham on you and your family," she said in a quiet voice. "It is not true that I lost my memory. I have known who I was from the first moment I arrived." Her voice cracked. "My name is Susanna Chadwick."

Gareth stared at her, stunned beyond belief. He'd never suspected such a thing. She was not suffering from amnesia, had known who she was all along? She had been lying to them all this time?

He covered his face with his hand. Her news was a shock, but it did not compare with the lies he'd been telling her.

Gareth's hand dropped and he looked up at her. "I know."

Confusion crossed her face. "You knew I was pretending?"

He shook his head. "I know you are Susanna Chadwick. That time I went to York . . . There were handbills plastered all over the town, with your image on them."

"Then why did you not—oh!" She clapped a hand over her mouth.

"The money," he said, and it was his turn to sound bitter. "That damnable money. That was why your relatives were searching for you, wasn't it? They wanted it for themselves?"

She nodded.

He laughed at the sheer irony of it all. "And you lied to us—so we wouldn't take advantage of you as well."

Susanna sighed deeply. "My cousin Jonathan snatched me from London, intending to take me to Scotland and force me to marry him. I escaped and fled into the countryside, hoping to throw him off my trail . . . and found myself here." She turned her tearstained face toward him. "I did not dare trust anyone. You might have written him or my uncle—or forced me to Scotland yourself."

Gareth stood and took a step toward her. "It was about the money at first, I admit it. Can you blame me? You've seen what it is like here." He took a deep breath. "But that changed, I swear it. It was you I fell in love with. The girl who took me on a picnic, and told me to hold on to my dreams. The girl who kissed me in that magical circle."

"Do you know how many proposals of marriage I have received in my life?" she asked.

He did not want to glance at her, suspecting that the look in her eyes was as icy as her voice.

"Quite a few, I imagine."

"Hundreds."

He forced a sickly smile. "I wager we are the only set of three brothers who asked."

She whirled about to face him. "Do you know why I did not tell you the truth? Because I feared you would react like all the others. That I would not be able to believe a single word that came out of your mouth, for I wouldn't know if it was prompted by your feelings for me, or my money."

"Su-sanna, I am sorry. I did not realize . . . I know you have no reason to believe me when I tell you that the money does not matter."

"No, you certainly have no need of it."

He winced at the sarcasm in her voice. "That is not fair. I could be the richest man in the kingdom and my feelings for you would not change. I love you, Susanna."

She gave a short, sharp laugh. "And pray tell, what is love? The knowledge that you can buy anything that catches your fancy? Or spend months living in an elegant town house in London while sampling the delights of the city?"

"You know that I do not want that," he said.

"But money would allow you to have a fine estate to hand down to your descendants."

Her words tore at him; he knew how true they were. It was the one thing he wanted; the one thing her money would ensure. She knew that as well.

"I see you do not have a response for that."

"You know I do not. But it is still possible to have that without your fortune."

"Not easily."

"No, not easily," Gareth said. "But I have not worked this hard to see it all slip through my fingers. I intend to work to save Belden and all who belong to it. And I want you at my side while I do it."

"Or at least my bankbook."

Gareth ran a hand through his hair. He did not have a golden tongue. How was he going to convince her that he was sincere, that her money did not matter? That he loved and adored *her*.

"I suppose Harry and Gawaine know as well?" she asked.

He nodded.

"That explains a few things," she said. "I really was quite surprised when Harry proposed to me. Tell me, was it a contest? With the prize—me—going to the winner?"

He did not bother to reply, knowing that she already knew the answer. Why had he come up with that damnable scheme in the first place? He should have ridden back from York, marched up to her, given her the handbill, and let her decide her future for herself.

But he hadn't because he'd wanted to protect her from her relatives. And the jest was, she had been using him in a similar manner to hide from them. He felt a quick flash of anger.

"For someone who's been less than honest with me, I would think I could expect a little consideration and understanding."

"At least my subterfuge came from a sense of self-preservation," she said. "Yours stemmed from greed."

Gareth's anger flared. "I may have been wrong not to tell you, but your hands are not exactly clean either. You lied to me—to all of us—for far longer."

"To protect myself," she retorted.

"From what? A man who loves you?"

"A man who loves my money."

He turned away. She was not going to listen to him; she was hurt and angry and disappointed. He realized now that he'd gambled his entire future on his lie—and now he'd lost everything.

Chapter 18

After Gareth left, Susanna sank down on the bed again, too upset to even cry.

He was just like all the others. He only wanted her money.

She should have known better, known that no man would ever want her for herself.

Thank goodness she had learned the truth now, before it was too late. She might have married him, blithely thinking that he really loved her.

How she had wanted to surprise him when she revealed her story—that she had money enough to restore the castle, keep the farm going, and provide the family with a future that would endure for generations to come. She'd envisioned his shock, and then delight, at learning what she'd really brought to the marriage.

When all along, it was what he'd been expecting.

Susanna laughed bitterly. She had Jonathan, of all people, to thank for opening her eyes. At least there was nothing more he could do or say to harm her now—the damage had already been done.

And tomorrow, she would leave for home—for the short day that it remained hers. She did not think she would be thrown out of her grandfather's house immediately following her birthday, but she could not stay there long.

A great many things needed to be arranged in the next few days. She must firmly calculate how much money she had, and then find a place to live. She knew she would not starve, but beyond that, she faced a very modest future.

With a shock, Susanna suddenly realized she did not know how she was even going to get home. She did not have money for a seat on the Mail. And even if she did, how was she to get to York?

She refused to ask Gareth for help. Perhaps she could persuade one of the departing guests to provide her with transportation as far as York. Surely, someone would be leaving tomorrow and she would not have to remain here another day. Each minute she spent under Gareth's roof would be sheer torture.

There was no question of her attending the banquet tonight. Gareth could make what excuses he wished for her absence. She had no intention of leaving her room until it was time to depart. She had no desire to see Harry or Gawaine either—they had been in on the secret, after all. The *competition*. How naive of her to think that three men could really be so smitten with her. She had developed quite an inflated sense of her own worth.

When, actually, no one wanted *her* at all.

Gareth did not know where to go, what to do after he left Susanna's room. He stood in the main entry hall, bewildered, numb with shock from the day's revelations, and the crumbling of all his plans.

"Gareth! There you are. Where is your lady? We need her for the crowning."

He turned to see Gawaine striding down the hall, a big smile on his face.

"I fear she is indisposed," Gareth said. "You shall have to crown another queen of the tournament."

His brother's expression turned to one of concern. "Nothing serious, I hope?"

Gareth laughed bitterly. "Oh no, nothing serious, nothing serious at all. Only that she knows who she is and realizes we have been after her money all this time."

"What? You didn't tell her, did you?"

He rubbed a hand over his brow, still ashamed of the pain

and hurt he'd seen on her face when he'd told her the truth. "She never lost her memory," he said quietly. "She was afraid to trust us with the truth—rightly so, as it turns out."

Gawaine stared at him in amazement. "She was pretending all along?"

"When she arrived here, she'd just escaped from her cousin, who'd kidnapped her and was taking her to Scotland and a forced marriage. She feared we would try the same if we knew about her fortune."

"We wouldn't have done anything like that," Gawaine said indignantly.

"Oh?" Gareth made no attempt to hide the self-loathing he felt. "Did we behave any better? I kept the truth from her, and allowed her to fall in love with me, because I wanted the money."

"We gave her a choice," Gawaine said. "She could have picked me or Harry."

Gareth shook his head. "I—all three of us—deceived her, and she will never forgive us that."

Gawaine gave him a consoling pat on the shoulder. "Give her time—she'll come around. Women are always changing their mind. What am I going to do about a queen for the tournament?"

"I really do not care!" Gareth snapped, irritated by Gawaine's blithe acceptance of the situation. This was not a simple misunderstanding that could be remedied in a few days' time, or with glib words. The break between himself and Susanna was irreversible; she would never believe anything he said to her now.

"I think I'll pick Miss Millbank, then," Gawaine said and dashed toward the door. He stopped suddenly and called back over his shoulder, "I won the tournament, you know. Knocked St. Lowe flat on his back."

He saw the pride in Gawaine's face and for a brief instant, Gareth shoved his pain aside. "Congratulations."

Gawaine gave him a cheery wave and headed out the door. In any other circumstances, Gareth would be happy for his brother, but right now, he could not feel any emotion beyond despair. Susanna was forever lost to him. Nothing else mattered.

Jonathan anxiously paced the perimeter of the tournament field, impatient for the next act of his little play to begin. He'd been pleased when Susanna fled to the house—he wanted her upset and on edge. But when she had not returned after a time, he felt disappointed. It would be easy enough to torment her with his little notes inside the castle, but he would be deprived of the pleasure of seeing her reaction.

He glanced at the sun, which seemed to be taking an eternity to make its way across the sky. He could hardly wait for darkness, and his meeting with Susanna. He'd have her trussed up in the carriage on the way to Scotland in no time.

It was past time to remind her that he was not going to go away. She could try to hide inside the castle, but she could not escape him. Concealing himself in the shade of one of the pavilions, he penned her another note.

Do not think that hiding will protect you. Unless you consent to speak with me, I will reveal all to your precious baron.

Your loving cousin

That should increase her agitation. He sealed the note and went in search of a servant to deliver it.

That accomplished, he walked back toward the tourney field to watch the last of the day's events. The crowd, which had been swelled with onlookers from the neighborhood—and as far away as York—was thinning. All the better for his plan—fewer eyes to see.

Jonathan started toward his carriage. He needed to make certain that everything was ready when he confronted Susanna.

The first challenge was to silence her, so she did not raise the alarm. A simple gag would accomplish that. She might even realize the hopelessness of her situation and go along with him peacefully.

He unconsciously rubbed the back of his head. Then again, a woman who hadn't hesitated to smash a water jug over his head merited cautious handling. Better to bind her hands as well. Then he would overpower her by sheer strength and get her into the carriage. At that point, he'd tie her feet, too. He might even tie her to the carriage—he wouldn't put it past her to try to leap out, even at danger to herself.

Susanna Chadwick was a determined woman. But he was equally determined. Without her money, he was ruined. And he did not take lightly to the idea of ruin, or a life of exile on the Continent. Marriage to Susanna was the only thing that would save him from that fate.

Susanna eyed the note slipped under her door with annoyance rather than fear. Jonathan no longer held any power over her—her confession to Gareth had seen to that.

He probably intended to harass her with these missives until she met with him their meeting later. She was miserable enough without having to endure any more of his annoying letters. She vowed to put an end to it, and send him on his way.

She hated the thought of going back to the tourney field, where she might encounter Gareth, or his brothers, but it was the only way she could find Jonathan. She was determined to confront him now, so he would leave her in peace. Among the crowd outside, she would be safe. She still did not trust Jonathan in the least.

Susanna rinsed her face in the wash basin and checked her appearance in the glass. Her cheeks were pale and her eyes slightly reddened, but she looked presentable. She repinned her hair and then let herself out of her room and started downstairs.

When she emerged through the gate, she saw that everyone was still crowded around the tourney site, and for a fleeting moment, she wondered how Harry and Gawaine had fared at the joust. With a gulp of dismay she remembered Gawaine's intention to crown her queen of the tourney if he won. She did not wish him ill, but she prayed that he had not met with complete success; she did not relish disappointing him.

The large crowd meant it would be difficult for her to spot Jonathan quickly. She longed for the vantage point of the platform where she'd been sitting earlier, but she would attract less attention if she remained on the ground. She would just have to look all the harder.

It was difficult not to be caught staring by the onlookers, and more than one man eyed her with heightened interest when he caught her scrutiny. Susanna hurried past these men, even at the risk of missing a glimpse of Jonathan.

She skirted the edge of the throng and tried to remember what her cousin had been wearing. She'd felt such shock at seeing him that she had not paid much attention to his appearance. Surely he'd be wearing a coat, but what color? And was he in breeches and boots, or trousers?

He had not been wearing a hat, of that she was certain. But that only eliminated a small percentage of the men. She could rule out those without blond hair, or anyone tromping about in armor or mock-medieval garb.

That only left about a third of the crowd for her to inspect. She sighed and continued walking.

Jonathan could barely believe his eyes when he spotted Susanna on the edge of the crowd. What was she doing here? He thought she'd stay away until he sent for her. Why had she come back?

Then he understood. She was trying to pretend that all was well, in case her earlier disappearance created questions that she did not wish to answer. That told him his guess had been correct—that she did not wish her secret revealed to the baron. That last note must have thoroughly rattled her.

All to the good. It was time to unsettle her some more.

Keeping a careful eye on her progress, he moved toward her in the opposite direction. He saw no sign of the baron nearby; Jonathan did not want to confront her in front of him yet. He moved slowly, but deliberately, careful to stay out of her vision, until he was only a few paces away from her.

He stepped up behind her and bent his mouth to her ear. "How delightful to see you again, cousin."

She jumped and whirled to face him. But instead of panic on her face, he saw relief.

"I was hoping to find you here," she said.

"Oh?"

"We must talk."

He grinned. Was she really going to make it this easy? "Then let us go behind the tents, where we will not be overheard."

"I am quite content to speak with you here," she said. "Where others are watching."

"Afraid of me, cousin?"

Her expression hardened. "I know you."

He shrugged. "As you wish. I merely thought you'd rather be private."

"We can go over behind the viewing stand. It is private enough."

Disappointed by her caution, he followed her to the platform.

"I came to tell you, Jonathan," she said, "that your threats won't work."

"Threats?" He laughed. "Why would I wish to make threats against my darling cousin?"

"Don't lie to me." Her eyes flashed with anger. "It's too late now. You can't do anything to hurt me. I told Gareth everything."

He stared at her in disbelief. "You did what?"

"He knows I was only pretending to have amnesia," she said. "There is no need for you to speak to him now."

Jonathan struggled to salvage his bravado. There was still a way to make this work—there had to be. "And how did the baron take the news?"

One look at her face told him all he needed to know.

"A pity the baron was not more understanding. You should have told him of your fortune—he might have been willing to overlook your lie in that case."

"He already knew about the money," she said. "That's the reason he wished to marry me."

"From what I hear, he's in need of it."

"Well, he's not going to get a penny of it," she said, anger flaring in her eyes.

"He's willing to toss a fortune away because of a little tarradiddle?" Jonathan snorted his derision. "The man is a fool."

"I will not marry a man who only wants my money," she said.

Jonathan burst out laughing. "Susanna, you are the veriest ninny. I suppose you are going to carry on in this noble manner and whistle your grandfather's money away?"

She nodded.

"You *are* an even bigger fool," he said harshly.

"Some things are more important than money," she replied.

"Name one."

"Love."

"Oh, my poor deluded girl." He shook his head with mock pity. "You actually fell in love with the fellow, didn't you? And all along, he was only after your money. The news must have come as a shock."

She turned away but he grabbed her arm.

"Think on this," he said. "Your birthday is tomorrow. If you are not wed by midnight, the money is gone. Forever. You may think it romantic to live out your life in a tiny cottage in some quaint village, but I assure you, Susanna, you will soon regret your decision. And by then, it will be too late."

She lifted her chin defiantly. "It is my choice."

"Are you so certain that the baron will let you go? From what I hear, he has a desperate need for the funds."

"Gareth is an honorable man," she cried. "He would not force me into marriage against my will."

Jonathan felt a growing frustration. Matters were not going as planned. He was rapidly losing the advantage over her. *Think!* How could he persuade her to meet him later tonight, when he would be ready and waiting with his gag and rope?

"If you are so adamant about leaving, my carriage is at your disposal."

"I will walk all the way to Suffolk before I set foot in your carriage again," she said heatedly.

"Now, Susanna, do not be hasty. You may need my assistance in the near future. Your baron may not turn out to be the honorable man you claim if he learns you intend to leave. You might be glad to have a friend come to your aid."

"If you excuse me, I think our conversation is finished."

He lay a hand on her arm again. "I will remain here for a while, in case you change your mind."

"That I shall never do." She turned and stalked away.

Oh, yes you will, my dear. And I know just the way to make you swallow those words.

Chapter 19

Susanna returned to her room, relieved at having her confrontation with Jonathan over. She had no more reason to fear him.

Yet his words stuck in her mind. *"You are a fool."*

Was she? To insist on love as the basis for marriage? Neither Gareth nor Jonathan seemed to consider it important. Was it more important than having a home and a family?

All her life she'd wanted a family of her own and Gareth could give her that. In return, she could provide him with financial security. Was that such a devil's bargain? To trade what she wanted most for what he needed? With love the only thing lacking?

Jonathan might be right. There were worse things than a loveless marriage. Like living alone forever.

She knew that Gareth would be kind to her, would treat her well. He would not run through her fortune in an orgy of indiscriminate spending. No, he would carefully husband her resources. He, too, had a deep sense of family, and knew that it was his duty to provide for future generations. They could work together to achieve that.

Would it be enough for her?

It would all be so much simpler if she had not fallen in love with Gareth. That had not been part of her plan. She'd only intended to trade her money for the security marriage to one of the brothers would bring. Was it fair to demand that he love her as she loved him, when love had not been her original intention?

She should swallow her pride and tell Gareth that she would marry him after all. Perhaps, in time, he might even grow to love her.

Dare she harbor that hope?

She really had only two choices. Walk away from Belden and Gareth and resign herself to a life lived alone.

Or stay, and have almost everything she wanted.

But if this was not going to be a marriage of love, she had no intention of submitting her freedom—and her fortune—to his control. If they married, she would retain her independence. Susanna would do as she pleased, with or without him. If she wanted to spend the Season in London, she would do so. If she chose to travel, he could not object. Gareth would be her husband, but he would not be her master.

She knew he would agree to whatever terms she demanded. Because he needed her money. It would not be a negotiation, but an ultimatum.

Yet he only had himself to blame, for having deceived her. If he'd been honest with her from the start, this never would have happened. In fact, they could have laughed about how they'd both come up with the same solution to her dilemma. She never would have fallen in love with him, they would have married as friends, and she would not have felt she was missing something.

Sighing, Susanna walked toward the door. Now came the difficult part—finding Gareth and presenting her offer to him. She did not doubt that he would accept. She only feared that her own resolve would waver before she found him.

Gareth had retreated to his study, knowing it was the only place in the house where he wouldn't be disturbed by the revelers. Even though the banquet was hours away, the Great Hall was already a picture of merriment as the tired knights refreshed themselves after their hard-fought battles.

Merriment was the last thing he wanted right now.

He glanced up in irritation when he heard the door open,

thinking Gawaine was back to crow over his achievement, but to his surprise, it was Susanna. He jumped to his feet and started to rush toward her, then checked himself when he saw the grim expression on her face.

"I should like to talk with you," she said, her voice low and strained.

He gestured toward the chair by the window. "Please, sit."

Pain filled him as he watched her cross the room, her back rigid, her face pale and drawn. Was it only this morning that he had held her in his arms, kissing those rounded cheeks and wishing this was their wedding day? In the space of a few hours, they had become strangers to each other. He stood awkwardly beside the desk, not knowing if she wished him to remain at a distance, or come nearer.

She cleared her throat. "I have thought about our conversation earlier and—"

"Susanna, I swear that I never had any intention of hurting you. I—"

She held up her hand and he bit back his apology.

"There is no need for further explanations," she said. "I have come here to offer a solution to both our problems."

He gingerly perched on the edge of the chair facing her. "What do you propose?" he asked.

"As you know, if I am not wed before midnight on my birthday, I lose my inheritance. A considerable sum of money. I have decided that while it may be a noble gesture to give it away, it is also a foolish one."

Hope leaped in his heart.

"To put it bluntly, I need a husband and you need money. I propose we make a business arrangement that will satisfy both our needs."

He gulped. "Business arrangement" was not what he'd envisioned their marriage to be. "What type of arrangement?"

She regarded him with a steady gaze that told him how confident she was of her proposal.

"Simply this," she said. "We will go to Scotland as planned tomorrow and be married. Then I shall notify my man of business and arrange to have a sum of money transferred into your account. A sum that will be adequate to pay all the debts and mortgages on the estate."

Gareth swallowed hard, dismayed by her plan. "Susanna, you do not have to do that."

"I am not finished. Each month, an additional sum will be transferred to you, for the castle expenses. Should you ever need any additional moneys for the estate, they will be given, as long as they are within reason."

"I am to have an allowance, then," he said, the very words cutting him as he spoke. She was buying herself a husband.

"If you wish to call it that."

"And what of you?" he asked. "You are being most generous. What do you hope to gain from this 'arrangement'?"

"A home, and a family to call my own. The respectability that goes with being the wife of a baron. The freedom to live my life as I wish."

The more she described it, the worse it sounded.

"Do you intend to live here?" he asked at last.

"When it pleases me," she said. "I have a large estate in Hampshire that I must oversee, and I may choose to keep a house in London." She paused and looked down at her hands for a moment. "I also intend to settle money on your two brothers, so you will not have to support them out of your funds."

"Susanna, you cannot do this. *I love you.* This is not what I want. I want you, marriage. A family, if we are blessed. This is a cold-hearted business arrangement."

Her gaze as it met his was as chilling as her proposal.

"Do not talk to me of love," she said. "Will the arrangement meet your needs?"

He turned away, unable to look at her. She was offering him everything—everything but herself. The one thing he wanted most.

And it was entirely his own fault. He had been trying to get his hands on her fortune. That he had fallen in love with her in the process did not matter. His first motive had been the money, and that was the one thing she understood.

Could he live with this arrangement—tied to his wife's purse strings, generous though they were? It was not what he wanted from her, from marriage.

But if he said no, she would leave him, forever. He knew she could walk into the Great Hall right now, make the same offer, and any number of men would agree to marry her in an instant. She might even choose to marry her blasted cousin—at least there would be no illusions between them.

Gareth had no choice. Either he accepted her proposal, unpalatable as it was, or allow her to walk out of his life forever.

And that he could not do. She was hurt, angry, upset right now. But he had one thing in his favor—time. His wooing of her had been clumsy—and hasty, by necessity. But once they were married, he would have all the time in the world to convince her that he truly did love her—and to rekindle her love for him as well.

It was a gamble, one that he could not be sure of winning. But he had no chance at all if he let her go.

"I accept," he said quietly.

Her expression did not change at his answer. She calmly nodded and rose. "Very well, then. We shall leave for Scotland in the morning, as planned?"

The finality of her words hit him and he held out a pleading hand to her but she neatly side stepped away and avoided any contact.

"Tomorrow," he agreed, bowing his head.

"I do not wish to attend the banquet tonight," she said. "I ask that you make my excuses to the guests."

"I will." Gareth watched with a growing despair as she let herself out of the room.

Was their any chance for him, or was he clinging to a hopeless dream?

He had to think there was hope. Just as he'd hoped to find

some way to save Belden, to save the estate, he had to hope that he could one day convince Susanna of his love.

He ran a hand through his hair and glanced at the clock on the mantel. The banquet was slated to begin in a little over an hour. He needed to find Harry and Gawaine, and tell them of the latest turn of events. He would ring for Mrs. Jenkins, and be certain that Susanna was treated to the choicest tidbits from the banquet.

And he should stop feeling like he had just sold his soul.

Jonathan stood in the shadows of St. Lowe's gaudy pavilion, staring up at the castle. Susanna was inside those walls, somewhere. And unless he found a way to lure her outside again, it would be nearly impossible to get his hands on her.

He had few alternatives. It would be much harder to waylay her on the road once she left; no doubt she would be traveling with one of these playacting knights, and would be well-protected. No, his best chance was to grab her tonight.

He could only hope that when the evening's festivities were over, the entire castle would sleep soundly and he could drag her from her bed without attracting attention. If she raised the alarm before he could silence her, all was lost.

But far more would be lost if he did not get her to Scotland by tomorrow. The reward was worth the danger he'd be putting himself in.

Now all he had to do was discover which room was hers, and plan his moves for later tonight.

Back in her room, after leaving Gareth, Susanna sat down on the bed, staring blankly into space.

She had thought she would feel better after speaking with Gareth. But instead, she felt even worse than before.

Trying to retain her composure while talking so matter-of-factly with the man she loved had been sheer torture. It had taken all her willpower not to show her distress. And when he'd finally agreed to her proposal, even though she'd been expecting that answer, she'd almost burst into tears.

What had she expected him to say? No?

Deep inside, she realized that she'd wanted him to. Wanted him to find the thought of living with her in such an arrangement so repugnant that he would refuse. At least then she would know that he cared for her.

But instead, he'd accepted her offer. Their marriage would be a financial arrangement, with no promise that it would ever be anything more.

Remember that humble cottage in the country, she told herself. *The clothing mended and patched, the seams turned. The endless days and nights of being alone.* The future she'd just arranged for herself was better than that—wasn't it?

Regretfully, Susanna realized it was not.

Living with Gareth, without his love, would be the worst thing she could imagine. Anything was better than that. *Anything.* Despite his protestations of love, she knew better. It was her money he loved so dearly. He'd just proven it.

She laughed bitterly. It had taken all her courage to confront him in the study and make her offer; now she was backing away from it.

Susanna realized that she'd been fooling herself to think that she could endure the arrangement she'd proposed to Gareth. It had sounded tolerable when she'd first thought of it—Belden would be saved and she would be able to live her own life, free from want.

But it was as she'd said to Jonathan earlier—there were some things in life more important than money. And love was one of them.

A loveless marriage would be a prison for both her and Gareth. She would resent him for not loving her; he would resent her for the money she provided. It would be a miracle if they were still speaking to one another within the year.

And that she could not endure. She would rather remember the possibility of what might have been, rather than suffer a miserable existence. This way, if she left, she could still hold on to her dreams. Staying here would only shatter them completely.

She dared not face Gareth again, to tell him she had changed her mind one more time. It would be more than she could endure. It was a cowardly act, but she would have to tell him in a note.

More important, she had to find a way to leave the castle as soon as possible. The moon was full tonight, and it would be easy to travel. She wanted to get as far away from Belden as possible before morning. But how?

Percy Blevins. Had he not pledged his undying support for her? She could assure him that he was doing her an enormous favor if he drove her to York during the night. The moon was full; they could easily travel. Would he be willing to help?

He had to. It was the only way she could get away from here quickly. Now that she had decided on her course of action, she wanted to leave immediately.

She sat down at the desk and penned a hasty note to Percy, asking him to meet her in the courtyard in one half hour. She rang for a maid to deliver the note, then sat back down again to pen the much more difficult letter to Gareth.

She was still struggling with that letter when a message arrived from Percy, saying he would be delighted to undertake any commission she had for him. It gave her the impetus to finish saying what she needed to Gareth. She folded the paper, sealed it, and wrote his name across it in bold letters. If she left it here, he would find it eventually.

Percy agreed to meet her in the courtyard so she hurried down the back stairs, hoping not to meet anyone on the way. She made it outside unnoticed and quickly walked over to the waiting man.

She slipped her arm in his and led him to the tower. Not until they climbed past the first turning of the stairs did she stop. She intended to be neither seen nor overheard.

"I need you to perform an enormous favor for me," she began.

"Anything for you, my lady."

"I need to go to York. Tonight."

"Tonight?" He looked at her doubtfully.

She nodded. "I need to . . . get away from Lindale. I cannot spend one more night under his roof."

"What has he done?" Percy roared in anger.

Susanna hung her head. "I cannot say. But I must leave."

Percy clenched his fists. "I will see Lindale now."

"No, no." Susanna grabbed his arm. "All I wish is to get away from here—as quickly as possible."

He bowed. "My carriage is at your disposal. I can have the horses hitched in ten minutes."

She shook her head. "We cannot leave before the banquet starts—someone might notice."

"You cannot expect me to sit in the same hall with Lindale, my lady. That I will not do."

"No, no. Just wait until everyone gets inside and begins eating. Say, in another hour? About nine?"

"Nine it is. I shall meet you in front of St Lowe's tent. Do you have luggage? Do you need help with it?"

"No, I can carry all that I have." She leaned over and kissed Percy on the cheek. "Thank you. You are a true knight to help a damsel in distress."

Even in the dim light, she saw him blush.

"I will do anything for you, my lady." Percy took her hand and brought it to his lips. "It is an honor to serve you."

She beamed at him. "I thank you for your devotion."

Voices sounded from the courtyard below. Harry—and another she did not recognize. Susanna gave Percy a gentle push down the stairs. "Go," she said.

Gareth would be furious when he found out that Percy had been part of this harebrained scheme. But by the time he discovered that, she would be safely heading south on the Mail.

No doubt Percy would be angry with her, as well, for she was deceiving him as to her real reason for going to York. But the situation was desperate, and she feared if she told him she was merely running away from Belden, he would raise all kinds of objections.

This way was safer.

She moved farther up the darkened steps, wanting to wait until Harry had left the courtyard before she went back down. Everything was set; by early tomorrow she would be heading south on the Mail for a last visit to what had once been her home. A wave of sadness swept over her at the thought of all she was losing, but she firmly pushed it away.

Nothing was worse than a loveless marriage.

"Such a touching story," a voice whispered in her ear and before she could cry out, a foul-tasting cloth was stuffed in her mouth and her arms were yanked hard behind her.

Chapter 20

Susanna struggled to free herself, but her arms were held in an iron grip.

"Struggle all you want," growled a low voice. "You're not going to get away from me this time."

Jonathan!

He quickly bound her hands, then reached around her head and tied another cloth over her mouth.

Susanna berated herself for being caught like this. She should have stayed with Percy, gone back to the house with him. In trying to avoid Harry, she'd been caught in her cousin's trap. She should have known he was not going to give up the money without a fight.

"We'll wait a bit, until I am certain that the way is clear," Jonathan said. "The banquet is just starting and everyone will soon be inside; no one will see us."

She had to get away now. She tried to spit invective at him, but it only came out as faintly garbled sounds through the gag. Not nearly loud enough for anyone to hear.

"I think the way is clear," Jonathan observed and he pulled her to her feet.

She knew that her best chance to escape was here at the castle, where people were nearby. When they reached the bottom of the steps, she would make her move.

He pushed her ahead of him, keeping a tight grip on her arm while staying a few steps behind her as they descended the winding stairs. When she reached the final step, Susanna halted suddenly, hoping he would bump into her and lose his footing. But he stopped and prodded her to continue.

She took a few faltering steps across the courtyard, then lashed back at him with her foot. He gasped as she caught him squarely on the shin and she jerked her arm free from his grasp. Susanna started to run toward the house, but a sudden jerk of her bound hands stopped her and she fell backward on the cobbles.

Jonathan viciously wound a hand through her hair and hauled her to her feet. Susanna's eyes stung with pain.

"Don't try that again," he hissed, and shoved her toward the castle gate.

If she could get free of his punishing hold, she might be able to knock him off the bridge. His booted feet thudded heavily on the wood. She pulled her arm, wincing as his grip tightened, but knowing she must distract him. Tugging again, she succeeded in drawing him off balance. Once again, she swept out with her foot and knocked him to his knees.

Run, run, run her brain screamed. But he was between her and the gate and struggling to his feet. She ran straight toward him, hoping to knock him down again but her foot caught in her skirts, and she tripped, crashing atop him. Before she knew what happened, he'd rolled over on top of her, crushing her bound arms beneath her.

"I told you not to try anything again," he said in a menacing tone and Susanna braced herself for a blow. Yet he only scrambled to his feet and again jerked her up.

This time, he took no chances, holding her firmly by both arms and pushing her in front of him.

They skirted the edge of the deserted pavilions and Susanna knew that even if he had not gagged her, there was no one around to hear her calls for help. Everyone was inside at the banquet.

Yet he still had to get her to Scotland and a great deal could happen on such a long journey.

They reached his carriage and she balked, refusing to climb inside.

"Why do you have to make this so difficult?" he grumbled, and before she knew what was happening, she found herself on her backside again. He grabbed her ankles but she kicked out at him. She knew one of her blows must have hit their mark for he swore loudly and then wrenched her ankle to the point of pain. Susanna bit down on the gag.

She continued to struggle, but finally he succeeded in lashing both her feet together and she knew she had lost this round. He hauled her upright, bent and slung her over his shoulder, then unceremoniously dumped her on the floor of the open carriage. To add insult, he then grabbed her hands and tied them firmly to the seat rail. She had no means of escape now.

He jumped into the driver's seat and the carriage rocked down the long, rutted drive that led to the road.

Of course he intended to haul her to Scotland again, probably tied hand and foot the entire way. She knew that Scottish marriage rules were lax, but she did not think even they would allow the bride to be held under restraint during the ceremony. She certainly was not going to state her willingness to go along with this travesty. Jonathan was going to have an ugly surprise when they reached the border.

Of course, he had probably already reasoned that out. He'd seek out the most unscrupulous marriage maker he could find, one who would willingly ignore the bride's objections if enough money crossed his palm. She could complain all she wanted, but once Jonathan had the marriage papers in his hand, her objections would hold little weight.

Susanna lay on her back, and glanced balefully at the moon shining down on them. It was supposed to have guided her and Percy to York tonight. Instead, it was going to guide Jonathan to Scotland.

She could not even count on Percy raising the alarm when she failed to meet him. No one would think to look for her until . . . it might even be as late as tomorrow. Eventually someone would go to her room, find her note to Gareth, and see that all her possessions were still there, and realize she had not left willingly.

By then, it would be far too late.

No one was going to rescue her.

Jonathan drove in silence. Each rut and hole in the road caused her to sway back and forth, bumping painfully against either the seat or the front panel. She had no way to brace herself and was at the mercy of the road, which twisted and turned its way through the rough Yorkshire countryside.

She prayed that Jonathan might get as confused as she had during her mad flight, and lose his way. He might be driving in circles at this very moment!

But then she remembered that it mattered little. No one would be flying to her rescue. They could wander Yorkshire for weeks without anyone the wiser.

Except that he had to reach Scotland before midnight tomorrow. And she realized that the moon was providing him with a perfect compass. Jonathan only needed to follow it west and he would be traveling in the right direction.

Despite her discomfort, Susanna finally slept, for when she opened her eyes again there was the faintest glimmer of light in the sky. A new day was dawning. What fate did it bring her?

Despite his protests, Gawaine and Harry both insisted that Gareth preside over the banquet—at least for the first hour. Reluctantly he agreed, counting off the minutes until he could leave.

He'd told them of his arrangement with Susanna, which they'd greeted with approval. He explained it dispassionately, not telling them of the pain he felt inside. They were merely delighted to learn that Susanna was staying and that there would be money for the castle.

And while several guests expressed disappointment that Susanna was not able to join them, her absence did not dampen the festivities for anyone but himself. He wanted her here by his side, as she had been the previous two nights.

Despite the crowd, in her absence, the Great Hall seemed empty and cold.

When Gareth finally judged he could make his escape without attracting too much notice, he got up from his chair. Gawaine gave him a bleary-eyed look.

"Going so soon?" he asked.

Gareth nodded. "I pass the banquet crown on to the tournament champion."

Gawaine grinned at him.

Gareth retreated to the main house, and the blissful quiet of his study.

He wondered what Susanna was doing now. Sleeping, if she had any sense. He could step out into the courtyard and see if there was a light still on in her room, but he resisted the temptation. There was nothing to be gained from that knowledge. She would not wish to see him if she was awake.

He sat in his worn armchair and poured himself a brandy. He did not want to think about the conversation he'd had with her earlier this evening, or the bargain they had struck, but he could not keep it out of his mind. Tomorrow they would be wed, but not at all in the manner he wanted. Belden would be saved, but the method of it left a bad taste in his mouth.

How long would she stay here after the wedding? Long enough, he hoped, to keep tongues from wagging—for her sake, not his. A month, at least, if he was lucky. A month in which he could do his utmost to persuade her that he truly loved her.

Would she ever believe him? He would have to show her every day, in words and deeds, what she meant to him. And even then, he could not be certain that she would see the truth.

There was really only one way he could persuade her. One simple act that would tell her once and for all how much he cared for her.

His heart pounded at the thought. Harry and Gawaine would no doubt tell him he was insane, but Gareth knew it was his only chance for happiness. Even if it ultimately cost him Belden, it was the only thing he could do.

The *right* thing.

He set down his glass and strode toward the door. He did not care if Susanna was asleep or awake. He was going to go to her now, and tell her what he'd decided.

Tell her that he would not marry her until the day following her birthday. Tell her that he was willing to give up the money, and all that it meant for the future of Belden. It was the only way he could prove that he loved her.

He mounted the steps two at a time, eager to see the look on her face when he spoke to her. She'd be wary, and skeptical, but when she finally realized what he meant, what he was saying, she would look at him with new eyes.

Eyes that would again filled with love, instead of with disappointment.

Gareth knocked on her door but received no answer. Impatient, he knocked again, then tried the lock. The door swung open and all was dark inside.

"Susanna?" he whispered.

He stepped into the room, holding his candle aloft.

The bed was empty, the room deserted.

He glanced frantically around the room, saw the letter with his name upon it lying on the dressing table, and his stomach lurched. He snatched up the paper, tearing it open and reading first with disbelief and then dismay the words she had written. The paper slipped from his fingers and fluttered to the floor.

She intended to leave Belden. Leave, because she did not want to live in a loveless marriage.

Then a surge of elation swept through him. She *did* love him! There was hope—more than hope—that he could convince her that he felt the same.

Yet he felt a growing unease at her absence. Where was she now? Had she gone down to the banquet?

A chilling thought stopped him. She'd written that she intended to leave, but surely she did not mean tonight? No one would embark on a journey at this late hour.

He quickly glanced about the room. Her cloak was draped across the chair; her comb and brush sat on the dressing table. Gareth heaved a sigh of relief. She had not left yet. Now he merely had to find her.

Gareth whirled about and ran into the hall, vowing to find her before she had a chance to set her plans in motion. Taking the stairs at a breakneck pace, he dashed through the connecting corridor and into the Great Hall, where he'd find help.

The din was so loud he knew he would not be heard over it, so he pushed his way through the throng, looking for his brothers. Gawaine was nowhere to be seen. Gareth looked for Harry and found him at last, over by the fireplace.

"Susanna is planning to leave," he yelled when he drew close.

"What?" Harry cupped his ear.

Gareth leaned closer. "Susanna is leaving!"

Harry looked confused. "When?"

"Tonight." He motioned Harry to follow him and they hurried out into the courtyard.

Harry regarded him with bemusement. "I thought you said she was going to stay."

"She changed her mind and is planning to travel south, but I aim to stop her before she leaves. Help me find her."

"When is she planning on leaving?"

Gareth shook his head. "I don't know. Her things are still in her room so she still might be making the arrangements. She can't be doing this without someone's help."

"I'll help you look for her."

"I'll check the house," Gareth said. "You look in the cellars and the passageways."

Gareth raced through the house, looking in each and every room, but it did not take long to confirm that Susanna was not there. With each empty room, his apprehension grew.

Where was she? She could not have left already.

He met Harry in the courtyard, and from his glum expression realized his brother had not found her either.

"Perhaps she has gone out by the tents," Harry suggested.

Gareth pushed past him and hurried through the gate and across the drawbridge, startling a man leading a horse and gig toward them. Gareth held up his lamp and saw it was Percival Blevins.

Who only yesterday had pledged his undying devotion to Susanna. Gareth's pulse quickened. Had he caught them in time?

"Where are you going?" he demanded

"Uh, n-nowhere," Percy stammered. "Just came out to get some fresh air. And—uh—exercise the horses."

"Nothing like a moonlight gallop to get their blood up," Gareth agreed sarcastically. "What are you really up to, Blevins?"

Harry stepped forward and grabbed the lead horse's bridle. "You look like you're planning on going somewhere."

Even in the dim light, Gareth saw Percy redden.

"I might be," he replied.

"Well, then, don't let us stop you. Be on your way."

Percy looked at him for a moment, glanced up at the castle, and then back at the tents behind him.

"If you must know," he said in a low whisper, "I am giving aid to a lady in distress."

Gareth's heart leaped at his words. No doubt Blevins meant Susanna, and he was in time to forestall her flight.

"I think the lady has changed her mind and no longer wishes to leave," Gareth said.

"I would prefer to hear that from the lady's lips herself," Percy replied stubbornly. "Since it is from you that she flees."

"What?" Gareth stared at him.

"That's what she said."

Gareth shook his head. "Then the sooner we find her and get this mess straightened out, the better. Where were you going to meet her?"

Percy looked highly uncomfortable. "Well, that's just the thing. She wasn't there."

Relief washed over Gareth. "How long ago?"

"Past fifteen minutes," he said. "I sent her a note telling her to be ready, but when I got there, she wasn't waiting."

"Good, that means she is still here." Gareth looked at his brother. "Harry, you stay here with Blevins. If Susanna appears, do not let her out of your sight. I'll check her room again."

He raced back into the house and up the stairs. Yet no one answered his knock and when he pushed open the door, one glance told him that the room had not been touched.

Damn!

He looked about one more, searching for some clue to tell him where she was. A crumpled wad of paper caught his eye. He picked it up and smoothed it out, his horror growing as he read the words:

Do not think that hiding will protect you. Unless you consent to speak with me, I will reveal all to your precious baron.

Your loving cousin

The cousin who'd kidnapped her in London!

Cold fear cramped his stomach. He knew now why she hadn't appeared at her rendezvous with Blevins, why her clothes were still here.

He dashed for the door.

Harry and Blevins were where he'd left them.

"Did you see anyone talking today with Susan—Elaine? Anyone showing her particular interest?"

Blevins nodded. "I saw her talking with some fellow."

Gareth grabbed him by the lapels. "Where? When? What did he look like?"

"Just an ordinary fellow," Blevins stammered.

"How did she look? Nervous? Afraid?"

Blevins pulled out of his grasp. "Angry, I'd say."

"Spread out!" Gareth ordered. "Look between the tents. Look in them, for God's sake. But find her!"

Fearing he'd miss something in the dark, he tried not to hurry as he scanned the ground, looking for any sign of a carriage or a horse or anything that showed someone had been here earlier—and gone.

Gareth lifted the lamp and peered more closely at the ground. The grass was crushed and bent, from footprints and . . . he saw the distinctive track of two carriage wheels pointing toward the lane. Someone had driven through here not too long ago.

There. On his left. Something light against the ground. He bent closer. It was a hair ribbon, trampled into the dirt. Gareth bent down, picked it up, and held it closer to the light.

It was the very one he'd presented to Susanna earlier today.

He pressed a hand to his temple. *Think.* Had she been wearing it when he last spoke to her, in the study? *Yes.*

A new wave of fear swept over him. A missed rendezvous, a crumpled ribbon, a departing carriage. The bastard had kidnapped her again.

They could already be several hours ahead of him. But Gareth had the advantage of knowing exactly where they were going—and the fastest way to get there. With luck, he might be able to catch them in time.

But did Susanna want him to?

He had to believe that she did. Had to believe that when she said she loved him in her note, that she meant it. Had to believe that when he told her that he was willing to give up the money, that he loved her more than all else, that she would finally realize that he was telling the truth.

If he got to her in time.

"I need a horse," he said to Harry.

"You know where she's gone?"

"Gretna," Gareth said, his voice hard. "And not willingly, I wager. But I intend to make sure that she does not get that far."

"Her cousin again?"

Gareth nodded. "I fear so."

"Take St. Lowe's horse," Percy said. "He's the fastest thing here."

"I rather think St. Lowe might object," Gareth said dryly.

"In the cause of rescuing a damsel in distress?" Blevins grinned. "It's his knightly duty."

"I'll arrange matters," Harry said and dashed back to the castle.

"I'm sorry that I believed her story," Percy said to Gareth. "But she seemed so upset—"

"The lady is an accomplished storyteller," Gareth said. "I hope that this last episode will cure her of that forever."

In fewer minutes than he had expected, Harry returned, Gawaine at his side, leading St. Lowe's prancing horse.

"I had the devil of a time convincing St. Lowe that he didn't need to go with you," Gawaine said, handing Gareth a small bag. "Money, in case you need to grease any palms for information."

Harry held up a bulging saddlebag. "I tossed in some food."

Gareth leaped into the saddle. Gawaine handed him one last parting gift—a pistol.

"Wish me luck," Gareth said and urged his horse down the lane at a brisk trot.

He had to get to her in time.

Chapter 21

Gareth rode as hard as he dared through the moonlit night, slowing only occasionally to rest his horse before moving on again. His greatest advantage lay here in the dales, where he knew the paths and trails that a carriage could not follow. Every mile he cut from his route, the more time he gained.

Only when the moon set, in the last hours before dawn, was he finally forced to halt. Breaking his horse's leg on a rock was not going to further his aim.

While the horse grazed nearby, Gareth sat and ate one of the meat pies Harry'd packed for him and anxiously watched the eastern sky for the first hint of the coming morning. Once he was able to discern shapes in the predawn light, he was back in the saddle.

It was nearly mid-morning when he reached Brough. He knew there was an inn here; if he was lucky, Susanna and her captor had changed horses and he'd get word of them. But the man who ran the stable said no one had stopped that morning. Gareth spent precious time questioning townspeople about whether they'd seen a man and woman in a carriage pass through, but his efforts were hampered by the fact that he had no idea what kind of vehicle they were in, or what Susanna's cousin even looked like.

He felt a nagging doubt as he remounted his horse and set off down the road. What if he was wrong? What if they were not going to Scotland? The right piece of paper would permit them to be wed anywhere.

But Scotland had been the plan before; surely, it would remain the plan now. They had to change horses at the next town. He'd get news of them there.

Riding hard, he reached Appleby in good time. Gareth stopped at the first inn and made inquiries, but no one had changed horses there. He rode on to the next hostelry, a much larger establishment. Its size encouraged him. It looked to be exactly the sort of place a traveler would stop for refreshments and a change of horses.

No carriage had stopped there today.

Gareth's spirits plummeted. There was only one more inn with horses in town, and from what he gathered, it was not a prime spot.

He rode into the deserted yard, dismounted, and looked about for someone to question. Finally he found a stablehand mucking out a stall.

"Have any travelers stopped here today?" he demanded.

The man continued working. "Changed horses for a fellow this morning."

"Was there a woman with him? Dark haired?"

The man nodded slowly.

Gareth nearly shouted with excitement. "How long ago?"

The man shrugged. "Don't know for sure. Maybe an hour or two."

An hour! If he rode like the devil, he could catch them before they reached Carlisle. Gareth dashed out the stable door and raced for his horse.

Susanna was tired, hungry, sore, and thoroughly out of sorts. The only bright spot to her day was that Jonathan had at last removed her gag and allowed her to sit on the carriage seat— even though he still tied her to it.

He'd remained at her side when they'd stopped at that tiny inn to change horses, keeping a warning grip on her arm. But she'd never uttered a word. Her goal was to lull him into complacency until she could get away.

Carlisle offered her best chance of escape. It was pointless to try to flee in one of these small towns; there was no place to hide and no way to get back to Belden.

Belden. Susanna thought longingly of the castle, and Gareth, and how foolish she'd been to think of leaving him. She'd never be in this fix now if she hadn't.

And even if she did manage to escape from Jonathan, and found a way back to the castle, it would be too late. There wasn't enough time to get back to Scotland before her birthday. She would have nothing to offer him but herself.

And she feared that was not enough.

With a sickening feeling, Susanna suddenly realized that if she did consent to this farce of a marriage with Jonathan, she would still have her money—at least until he managed to squander it all. If she acted quickly, she could give some to Gareth. It would be a fitting slap at Jonathan.

But would Gareth accept her help? She knew how proud he was and feared he'd refuse. Could she persuade him that it was what she wanted, that she meant it as gift and a thank-you for giving her shelter at the castle?

If he did refuse, she'd find a way to force it on him. She knew the name of his solicitor; she'd give him the money and have him hold it for Gareth.

She so wanted to help him—but could she actually marry Jonathan in order to do so?

If only she had more time. Time to get away from her cousin, return to Belden, and convince Gareth to marry her as they'd once planned. But time was running out. It was past midday already, and even if she wrested the reins from Jonathan and turned the carriage around, it would be impossible to drive back to Belden, and then reach the border by midnight.

Marry Jonathan and guarantee Belden's future? Or give up the money and pray that Gareth would still want her?

If she only had to think of herself, there would be no question—genteel poverty was far better than marriage to her cousin. But she loved Gareth; wanted to do whatever she could for him. Money was the thing he needed most, and it was the only thing she could give him. And in order to do so, she had to marry her cousin.

She turned to Jonathan. "I am willing to marry you, you know."

He laughed. "Think I'm going to untie you? Think again. You're not going to fool me twice."

"Keep me tied if you wish," she said. "I assure you, though, I will not try to escape."

"And pigs fly," he said.

"Did I not behave perfectly when we stopped? What do I have to do to prove myself?"

"No," he said curtly.

Sighing, she turned away and stared blindly out at the passing landscape. She could not blame him for being distrustful. Perhaps, as they neared the border, she could convince him that she was in earnest. It was humiliating to be trussed to her seat like a convict. She'd made her decision and she intended to stick to it, whether he believed her or not.

For if she could not have Gareth, she could at least save Belden for him.

Gareth's spirits rose each time he neared a carriage on the road to Carlisle. *Would this be the right one?* And each time, his hopes were dashed. He could not believe that he was so far behind them, not when he'd cut across the dales.

He passed an open carriage filled with giggling young ladies and their escorts, and felt envious of their carefree day.

Suddenly his horse stumbled and sank down on one knee. Gareth jumped from the saddle and groaned as he saw the animal favoring one forefoot. He'd never catch them now!

The carriage drove past, the young ladies waving to him, but they did not stop and it would not matter if they did. There was no room for him. Despairing, he took the limping horse's reins and started walking down the road.

*   *   *

Susanna looked up eagerly as the signposts indicated only two miles to Carlisle. She ached for a chance to stop and stretch her legs and get something to eat.

"I swear to you, Jonathan, I will not try to escape. Can we please stop in Carlisle? I would like to have one decent meal today."

"While you run to the authorities?"

"I will not run." Her exasperation grew. Why wouldn't he believe her? "Do you think I want to give up all that money? You may not be my first choice of husband, but short of grabbing some stranger off the street, you are the only option I have."

"Perhaps you have decided to see reason," he mused, then shook his head. "But I dare not take the risk. If I lose you now, I'll never find you again in time."

"Fine," she snapped. "But if I am too weak to utter my vows once we are over the border, you only have yourself to blame."

"Have another plum." He handed her one from the sack he'd purchased at a farm they'd passed.

Susanna turned away, pointedly ignoring him. If he was not going to see to her needs, she was not going to give him the least bit of encouragement.

She wondered if Jonathan would be agreeable to maintaining separate households. She could live in the country, he in London. But no, he probably would object—it would cost more money. And once he discovered that she'd given funds to Gareth, he would be more than furious. He'd demand that they live under the same roof just for spite.

She prayed that Gareth would one day appreciate her sacrifice.

Gareth guessed he'd been walking for nearly an hour when he heard the sound of an approaching carriage. He turned, hoping against hope that by some freak chance he'd pulled ahead of them. But it was only a light gig with a man at the reins. He pulled up alongside Gareth.

"Horse lame?" the man asked. "Can I give you a ride?"

"Gladly," Gareth said.

"There's a farm around the next bend. You can leave your animal there." He struggled to hold his restive team. "These fellows won't like moving at a slow pace for long."

Gareth tied his horse to the rear of the gig and climbed into his benefactor's carriage.

"Hazelton," the man said, holding out his hand.

"Lindale," Gareth replied.

"Business in Carlisle?" Hazelton asked.

Gareth quickly glanced at him and decided he could use a little extra help.

"It's my sister," he lied. "I'm trying to catch her. She's off for Gretna with a worthless fellow."

Hazelton reined in the horses. "Why didn't you say so?" He shoved the reins into Gareth's hands, jumped down, and began untying the horse. "I'll see to this fellow. Just leave the team at the Green Man—ask anyone, they'll point you the way. They can set you up with a new mount in no time."

Gareth had barely mumbled his thanks when Hazelton slapped the near horse on the rump and they took off at a gallop.

His hopes soared again. Would he make it in time?

Susanna squirmed on the carriage seat. She had finally persuaded Jonathan to stop briefly in Carlisle, and she'd welcomed the chance to get out of the carriage and stretch her legs. But he'd kept a sharp eye on her the entire time, and once they were on the edge of town, he'd retied her to the seat.

Now they were nearing the border, and she wished there was a way to delay the inevitable end to their journey. She'd gone over and over again in her mind her reasons for agreeing to marry Jonathan, and knew that it was the only way she could help Gareth, but still, it did not mean she was eager for the ceremony to take place.

"I hope there is a decent inn at Gretna," she snapped to Jonathan. "I would like to sleep in a real bed tonight."

"I fully intend to see that you do," he said with a snicker.

She gave him a withering look. "Don't you dare think that I will be sharing a bed with you."

"But, cousin dear, we will be man and wife. It is traditional."

"If you want to see a penny of my money, you must promise me here and now that you will not lay a finger on me," she retorted heatedly.

Jonathan reined in the horses and looked at her, an incredulous expression on his face. "Cousin, you cannot mean such a thing."

"I most certainly do," she said.

He shrugged and snapped the reins, urging the horses on. "We'll see what you have to say after you are married—and under my dominion."

"If you want my consent to this marriage, I must have your agreement first," she said.

"Fine," he grumbled. "You can sleep in another county for all I care. Just so long as we are wed."

She sat back in the seat, a smug smile on her face. He'd soon learn that he was not going to have his way in this marriage. Perhaps she would insist that she stay in the country after all. It would not be so bad being married to him if she never had to see him.

Except that she would think every day of Gareth, and of what they could have had together. And realize the emptiness of the life she had chosen.

But it was for Gareth that she was doing this. She had to remember that, even though she knew it would not bring her much cheer in the years to come. It was her decision and she intended to stick to it. Something good had must come from her grandfather's money.

Gareth easily found the Green Man in Carlisle and arranged for the stabling of Hazelton's team and another mount for himself. The smell of the roasted mutton wafting from the taproom was tempting, but he thrust his hunger aside and pulled an apple out of his pocket. Finding Susanna was more important than appeasing his stomach.

Within minutes, he was back in the saddle and racing toward the edge of town.

The sun was sinking lower in the sky as he rode west, warning of the passage of time. If he did not reach Gretna soon, he could despair of ever catching them.

The new horse galloped swiftly down the road, his long stride eating up the miles. He had to be near the border now.

Ahead, in the distance, Gareth saw a carriage driving in the same direction he traveled. As he drew closer, he saw a man and a woman seated in the open vehicle.

A woman with dark hair.

He kicked his mount into a gallop to close the space between then. Was it Susanna?

As if hearing his thought, the woman turned, and he saw her clearly.

"Gareth!" she cried.

The driver glanced over his shoulder, then applied the whip to his team. Gareth ground his heels into his mount and it sprinted forward. Slowly, inch by inch, he started to gain on the speeding carriage. His horse's nose was nearly even with the wheels now, pulling ahead.

Susanna turned toward him again, shouting something but he could not hear over the noise. He had to get to the horses' heads, and grab the reins to slow them. He didn't even glance at the cousin as he pulled past. *Only another foot and he could—*

A sharp pain slashed across his back. *The bastard had struck him with the whip.* Gareth grabbed for the near rein, jerking it hard. A burning pain stung his hand and he nearly lost his grip.

Gritting his teeth, Gareth jerked the rein with all his strength. The near horse swerved toward the right, pulling the other with him, and the carriage lunged toward the edge of the road and the ditch beyond.

Gareth hauled the reins to the left, using his own mount to force the racing horses back, trying to slow their pell-mell progress before they all crashed.

Another lash from the whip struck him and he lost his grip on the reins. He heard Susanna's screams, and suddenly the carriage veered to the left and careened toward the other side of the road. He tried to grab the rein again but his left arm was numb and everything seemed to move at a snail's pace. He watched in horror as one horse stumbled, pulling down its mate. The carriage wobbled first to one side and then the other before flipping on its side and sliding along the road with a tremendous screech. The man flew from the wreck and rolled across the road.

Gareth leaped from his horse and ran to the overturned carriage.

"Susanna!" he cried hoarsely.

"I am all right," he heard her call and he skidded to a stop beside the crashed carriage. She looked down at him, her legs dangling, but she was still in her seat, where he saw she'd been securely tied.

"Put your arms around my neck," he commanded her and he supported her while he loosened her bonds. When she was finally free, he gently set her feet on the ground.

"You are all right?"

She nodded and then gasped.

Gareth whirled around to see her cousin racing straight toward him.

"I'll get you for this, Lindale!" he screamed. "You'll not cheat me of my due!"

Gareth balled up his fist and hit him square in the nose. Blood spurted from the cousin's nostrils as he stared in disbelief, then his eyes rolled up and he slumped to the ground.

Susanna sank in a heap on the road and burst into tears.

Gareth knelt beside her, cradling her in his arms, running

a hand over her hair. "There, there," he said. "It is all over now."

"I did not think you would come after me," she sobbed. "My note said I was going home."

"We found Percy and pieced together part of the tale. But I was not certain until I found this." He pulled the crumpled hair ribbon from his pocket. "I realized then you had not gone willingly."

"Oh, Gareth!" Her eyes were filled with a mixture of despair and hope. "Can you ever forgive me?"

"For what?"

"For . . . for," she whispered and started crying anew.

"Do not cry," he said, holding her close. "Come, I want to get you back to Carlisle. You can eat and have a hot bath and get a good night's sleep."

She ran a hand over his stubbled cheek. "You look as if you have not slept at all."

"I haven't," he said. "I could not, worrying about you." He took her hand and brought it to his lips. "And tomorrow, when you are feeling better, I should like to marry you."

"But my birthday is today," she protested.

"I know." Gareth took a deep breath, praying he would find the right words. "And that is why I do not wish to marry you until tomorrow. It is the only way I know to show you that it is you I love, my dear, sweet Susanna. I do not want your money. I want *you.*"

She closed her eyes and he feared what she would say— that she no longer cared for him, that she planned to spend her life alone—or worse, that she intended to marry her cousin. How could he ever live without her? But to her surprise, she laughed and then turned her gaze on him.

"Do you really love me?" she asked, her voice husky.

He leaned over and kissed her. "I may not be a knight in shining armor, but I came to save my damsel in distress. I love you with all my heart."

She hugged him. "Then it is rather silly to let all that

money go to waste. We can ride to Gretna from here and be married within the hour."

He stared at her. "What?"

She smiled. "I believe you, Gareth. You *do* love me. And I adore you."

Her soft whisper was the sweetest sound he'd ever heard. The woman of his heart loved him! He thought he would explode with happiness. Instead, Gareth kissed her again.

When he finally released her, he glanced at her cousin's inert form. "What are we going to do with him?"

Susanna laughed. "We can collect him on the way back from Scotland. I don't think he is going to go very far."

He hugged her close. "I cannot wait to marry you."

"Even if I am a rich heiress?" she asked, her voice teasing, her eyes brimming with laughter.

"Even so."

She leaned close and kissed him gently. "You truly are my knight in shining armor."